The Laura Black Scottsdale Mysteries

The Laura Black
Scottsdale Mysteries
by B A Trimmer

~~~~

Scottsdale Heat

Scottsdale Squeeze

Scottsdale Sizzle

Scottsdale Scorcher

Scottsdale Sting

Scottsdale Shuffle

Scottsdale Shadow

Scottsdale Secret

Scottsdale Silence
~~~~

Scottsdale Silence

Scottsdale Silence

B A TRIMMER

SCOTTSDALE SILENCE
Copyright © 2021 by B A Trimmer
All Rights Reserved

Without limiting the rights under copyright reserved above, no part of this publication may be reproduced, stored in, or introduced into a retrieval system, or transmitted in any form, or by any means (electronic, mechanical, photocopying, recording, or otherwise) without prior written permission, except in the case of brief quotations embodied in critical articles or reviews.

This is a work of fiction. Names, characters, places, brands, media, incidents, and dialogues are products of the author's imagination or are used fictitiously. Locales and public names are sometimes used for atmosphere purposes. Any resemblance to actual events, companies, locales, or persons living or dead is entirely coincidental.

Editors: 'Andi' Anderson and Kimberly Mathews

Composite cover art and cover design by Janet Holmes using images under license from Shutterstock.com and Depositphotos.com.

ISBN: 978-1-951052-30-0
Saguaro Sky Media Co.
060121pb

E-mail the author at LauraBlackScottsdale@gmail.com
Follow at www.facebook.com/ScottsdaleSeries/
Twitter: @BATrimmerAuthor

Thanks to
Katie Hilbert for
her wonderful ideas

*Thanks also to Bonnie Costilow,
Jeanette Ellmer, Barbara Hackel,
Diana Hepner, Millie Knight,
Judith Rogow, Gail Shillito, and
Tony Tumminello*

Scottsdale Silence

Author's Note

Dearest reader, this book contains a fair amount of drinking,
some cussing, talking about sex, and plenty of suspenseful action.
Bullets fly, stun-guns zap, and we always have a happy ending.
If these sorts of things aren't your cup of tea, it's best that you know…

Introduction

If you've never read a Laura Black Scottsdale mystery, you may want to start with *Scottsdale Heat*, the first book in the series. If you'd instead like to begin with this book, here are a few of the key people in the story:

Laura Black – A Scottsdale native who has a degree in philosophy from Arizona State University. After working for a few years as a bartender, she now works as an investigator in a Scottsdale law firm. She wants to make the world a better place, but she also has bills to pay.

Sophia Rodriguez – Laura's best friend, who also works in the law office as the receptionist and paralegal. Sophie's a former California surfer chick and a free spirit. Although she's always enjoyed dating multiple men at the same time, she's currently exploring the concept of only having one boyfriend.

Gina Rondinelli – Laura's other best friend. She's a former Scottsdale police detective and the law firm's senior investigator. She has a strict moral code and likes playing by the rules. She's recently begun dating a former Navy SEAL named Jet.

Leonard Shapiro – Head of the law firm and Laura's boss. He's miserly and always pads his bills. He has few morals, loose ethics, and no people skills, but with the help of Laura, Sophie, and Gina, he usually wins his cases. After several years of halfhearted dating attempts, Lenny is now dating a cougar named Elle.

Maximilian Bettencourt – Laura's boyfriend and number two man in the local crime family. Before coming to Scottsdale, he was a secret operative for the U.S. government, mainly in Eastern Europe. For Laura's safety, they need to keep their relationship a secret.

Anthony "Tough Tony" DiCenzo – Head of the local crime family. He likes Laura and almost thinks of her as a daughter. Through various adventures over the past year, he owes Laura several favors.

Gabriella – A former government operative from somewhere in Eastern Europe. She currently works as a bodyguard for Tony and Max. She takes pleasure in hurting and killing men. She's being hunted by Viktor, the head of an international crime organization.

Danielle Ortega – Laura's friend and the head of a rival crime organization. Her father is Escobar Salazar, the ruthless leader of an international drug cartel called the Black Death.

Johnny Scarpazzi – A top lieutenant in Tony DiCenzo's organization.

Milo – Sophie's boyfriend. Milo works as a mid-level minion for Tough Tony DiCenzo.

Grandma Peckham – Laura's longtime neighbor, Mary Peckham. She's about to marry a retired dentist named Bob Henderson.

Andrew "Jet" Kramer – Gina's current boyfriend. They met at the law office when Jet was a client. He got his nickname back when he was a Navy SEAL.

Suzi Lu – A professor of computer science at Arizona State University who is also the professional dominatrix "Mistress McNasty." One of her clients is Johnny Scarpazzi.

The Cougars – A group of wealthy, sexy, and fashionable women who like to troll Scottsdale nightclubs looking for athletic younger men for hook-up type relationships. Through a series of adventures, Laura, Sophie, and Gina have become junior members of their group known as "pumas" or cougars in training.

Elle – One of the cougars. She lives in a beautiful house in North Scottsdale and has been dating Lenny for almost two months.

Jackie Wade – Another one of the cougars. She owns and runs the Scottsdale Saguaro Sky golf resort.

Danica Taylor-Sternwood – Danica is a friend of Laura's and works as a featured stripper at a Scottsdale gentlemen's club called Jeannie's Cabaret. She's married to resort manager Alex Sternwood.

Tio Francisco – Brother of Escobar Salazar and the real power behind the Black Death.

Señor Largo – The brutal and sadistic enforcer for the Black Death cartel. He's worked with Laura before and once saved her life.

Roberto López – Danielle's boyfriend and personal bodyguard.

Prologue

"What do you know about Scottsdale General Hospital?" asked the man with the pink stun-gun.

I had awakened to find myself firmly tied to a metal chair in a small cinderblock room with an oil-stained concrete floor. The place had a musty chemical smell.

The face of the man asking the question completely filled my field of view. He was close enough for me to count the pores on his nasty thin face and smell the tuna fish he'd had for lunch.

His long dark hair was slicked back, and his eyes bugged out of his face, giving him an almost cartoon-like appearance. Another man was behind me, holding my head so I couldn't turn it away.

"I don't know anything about Scottsdale General," I said, slurring my words like a drunk. "Other than the guys there have a weakness for skinny blondes."

My stomach still ached and twitched from the first time he had shocked me. It was making it hard to think clearly.

The man held up the stun-gun for me to look at as he again activated the switch. The smiling cartoon kitty on the front of the bright pink device seemed to be at odds with the pain and torment the weapon was designed to cause.

I watched as an intense white spark popped and flashed between the two electrodes. The man slowly brought the stun-gun to within an inch or two of my face, just below my left eye.

The snapping noise the thick spark produced was deafening and brought a fresh wave of fear. My cheek soon grew uncomfortably warm as I waited for him to shove the device against me.

"Now then," he calmly said. "Let me ask you again. What do you know about Scottsdale General Hospital?"

At times like this, I wonder why I've decided to stay with the law office. Before this, I'd been a bartender at Greasewood Flat. It was a fun place to work and the worst thing that ever happened was a drunk guy would sometimes throw up on me.

Since I started working as an investigator, I'd been harassed, kidnapped, and tortured. I've been knocked unconscious and threatened with harm more times than I could count.

How did this escalate so quickly? I thought. *I was only taking pictures of naked people having sex.*

Chapter One

I woke up to the sound of a text notification on my phone. I opened one eye, fumbled the phone off my nightstand, and saw a text from Sophie, my best friend, and coworker. She pretty much demanded that I come in right away; Lenny, my boss, wanted to see me.

Crap.

I put the phone down and glanced around. The room was in full daylight, but I had no idea what time it was. Honestly, I really didn't care. It had been a long couple of weeks since I'd been able to sleep in.

Marlowe, my overly pampered cat, lifted his head and looked at me, annoyed I'd disturbed him. I put my head back on the pillow and was asleep within seconds.

~~~~

Sometime around ten, I went in through the back security door of the law offices of Halftown, Oeding, Shapiro, and Hopkins, my place of employment. I walked past my cubicle in the back and up to the front reception area.

Sophie was working at her desk. She looked up from her tablet as I came in. Her eyes were bright as she smiled at me.

"You sure took your time getting in here today," she lightly scolded, her smile at odds with her words.
~~~~

Sophie's parents came up from Mexico about a year before she was born. Although Spanish is her second language, she only has an accent when she thinks it will get her something.

"You're lucky I came in at all," I grumbled. "What are you so happy about?"

"Take a look," she said as she flipped open a newspaper to the society page and pointed.

About halfway down the page was a picture of a beautiful blonde woman with long curly hair, a light tan, and a huge smile. It had likely been taken as a publicity photo since she was wearing a Cardinals cheerleading outfit.

"Isn't this the cheerleader who was out with Snake?"

"Yeah, it is," Sophie said, still smiling. "Would you read the article out loud? I want to hear it one more time."

"Okay," I said as I started reading the copy.

"Cardinals release cheerleader Hayley Reynolds for violating the team's non-fraternization policy.

As we reported last month, Miss Reynolds was seen after the San Francisco game in the VIP room at Nexxus, the popular nightclub in Old Town Scottsdale. She was in the company of several Cardinals players and was seen getting chummy with backup quarterback, Snake McCoy. Sources within the team report this wasn't the first instance of her violating the policy. Reynolds had been with the team for the last four seasons. In addition to cheerleading, she's been featured in several local television commercials with Honest George Anson promoting his Phoenix area auto dealerships."

Sophie started laughing. "I love hearing you read that. It makes me feel warm and happy all over."

"Wow, I'd always heard cheerleaders were discouraged from dating the players, but I didn't think you could get fired over that."

"I wish I could have been there when they told her the news. I would have loved to see her reaction. I wonder if she only sniffled a little, with maybe a single tear?"

Sophie stuck out her lower lip and pretended to wipe her eye.

"You know," she continued, "I bet she completely lost it and started wailing like a five-year-old. I'm thinking the full waterworks, with big wet sobs, wailing, and lots of snot. It would have been hilarious to watch security escort her from the building." Clearly, she'd been giving this some thought.

"I wonder how Snake feels about his part in getting her fired?" I asked. "I bet he feels pretty bad about it."

"It's his own fault for going out with that nasty bimbo when he could have been with me," Sophie grumbled.

"Have you talked with him since you found out about the cheerleader?"

"Nope, and I'm not going to. He's roadkill and can have that skanky-ass ho all to himself. Although, he might not want her anymore, now that she's back to being an aspiring actress or whatever she was before she became a cheerleader."

I plopped down on one of the red-leather wing chairs next to her desk.

Sophie looked at me, concerned. "You look beat. You've got the dark-circles-under-your-eyes thing going on."

"I am beat, and I could use a day or two off. Yesterday was the first day I didn't work since Thanksgiving break. That was like three weeks ago."

"But you got to spend pretty much that entire weekend with Max."

"I know. Thanksgiving was great. Max told his housekeeper to take the day off and he cooked me a delicious turkey dinner."

"I'm still surprised Max can cook."

"So was I. There's a lot I don't know about him, at least not yet."

"I'm still a little mad at you since you didn't take any pictures of his house. All you've told me is how beautiful it is, but I already guessed that."

"There isn't a lot to say about it. It's not gigantic like Muffy's. It only has four bedrooms and an office, but everything's so beautiful. He has a great kitchen that looks out over the living room and the big picture windows."

"And you said Max has a huge deck?"

"I think I love his deck best of all. It runs the entire length of the house and overlooks the pool, Paradise Valley, and Camelback Mountain. The weekend was warm enough for us to sit on it every night with a couple of drinks and watch the sun go down. It was wonderful."

"How'd you get along with his housekeeper? Beatrice?"

"She's nice. There's a separate apartment in the back where she lives. She came back the day after Thanksgiving and was with us the rest of the weekend. I guess she's been with Max ever since he bought the house. She told me he never has visitors and it was good to be able to cook for more than him."

"I'm glad to hear he doesn't have a lot of women over. It's always a creepy feeling when you go to some guy's house and there's a closet half-full of miscellaneous women's clothes. It makes you wonder."

"Does that happen to you a lot?"

"Sometimes," she said with a shrug. "Hey, when are you getting your new car? I thought it was supposed to be in by now."

"I'm waiting for the dealer to call. It's still listed as 'In Transit' on the website."

"It'll be great for you to ditch your old one. It's halfway fallen apart. Are you going to sell it to a junkyard, or should we ditch it somewhere?"

"I'm thinking about keeping it."

"Seriously? Why would you keep that POS?"

"In case I have to do something that could damage my new car. You know, stakeouts and stuff. I don't want the new one to end up looking like the old one. Or ending up like Tony's car."

"Well, good luck with that. I know how you treat your vehicles."

"How's Lenny?" I asked as I nodded my head in the direction of his closed office door. "Did he go out with Elle again?"

"Jeez, it's all I've been hearing about," Sophie said as she rolled her eyes and shook her head. "Yeah, they went out Friday night. Elle went out with the girls on Saturday, but then she and Lenny went out again last night."

"They've been seeing each other for almost two months. Do you think it's turning into a real thing?"

"That's a good question. I wouldn't think anyone could have a relationship with Lenny. I mean, yuck."

"I know. The thought grosses me out as well. I guess we'll find out if it's an actual relationship as time goes on."

"I hope it lasts a while longer. He's been in a relatively good mood since he started dating her."

"You said Lenny wanted to see me? It's not another assignment, I hope. I just finished the last one yesterday morning. I was hoping for at least two or three days off before the next one."

"Sorry. You know how crazy busy it gets this time of year."

"Fine, but please tell me it's not another cheating spouse."

"Well, I can tell you it's not, but it is."

"Jeez, I need to find another job."

"I heard the Cardinals have an opening for a new cheerleader."

"Shut up. Do you have a file for the new one yet?"

"Nope, other than her husband's a doctor over at Scottsdale General, I don't know a lot about it. But the wife will be here in about half an hour, so you can hear everything for yourself."

I sighed and gave Sophie a look.

"Sorry," she said. "Not all of your assignments are going to let you find a lost gold mine or a treasure chest full of antique jewelry. But look at it this way, a doctor will mean a nice house. You'll have lots of big closets to hide in."

"You think you're being funny. But if I have to hide in one more closet, I really might quit."

~~~~

My name is Laura Black. I've been the junior investigator at the law office for a little over three years.

The firm was started back in the eighties with four partners. Since then, the three senior partners have all left the group. One moved to Pensacola and two of them died.

One met his end in a skiing accident in Colorado. The other one had a heart attack while doing the nasty with a law student intern named Jeanette.

She ended up becoming the publicist for several A-list Hollywood actors, including Stig Stevens. I've actually worked with the woman on an assignment. She seems nice.

The remaining partner, Leonard Shapiro, my boss, has remade the firm into one of the most successful boutique law offices in Scottsdale. To maximize his profits, Lenny prefers keeping to high-profile
~~~~

criminal, civil, and family law cases.

The more desperate and hopeless the case looks, the more he likes it. Anxious clients don't ask up front how much everything will cost.

~~~~

The door to the street opened and the client came in. She was a pleasant-looking woman, somewhere in her mid-forties, with short brunette hair and subtle makeup.

She was dressed in designer labels and had a high-end bag but otherwise didn't go out of her way to display her wealth. The only jewelry she wore was a wedding set, but the center stone must have been close to three carats.

"I'm Jessica Palmer," she said as she walked up to Sophie's desk. "I have an appointment with Leonard Shapiro."

We made introductions, then Sophie went into Lenny's office to let him know the client had arrived. She came out a few seconds later. "Mr. Shapiro can see you now."

The three of us went into the office. The client took the chair directly in front of Lenny's oversized desk while I sat to the side. Sophie took the chair near the door, in case she had to answer the phone or greet someone coming in off the street.

We really need to get someone in to help Sophie run the office.

"Mrs. Palmer," Lenny said. "Thank you for coming in. How can I help you?"

"It's like I explained to you on the phone," she said, her voice was a little shaky. "I believe my husband, Michael, is having an affair. If it's true, I'd like to divorce him."

Lenny looked her over and turned to Sophie. "Would you make me a Beam on the rocks? Mrs. Palmer, would you like a cocktail or perhaps a glass of wine?"
~~~~

The client blew out a breath. "It's early, but thank you. A glass of wine might help."

Sophie got up and poured the drinks. By now, I was used to not being offered one. In fact, if Lenny did give us a drink at one of these client meetings, I'd be a little worried.

Sophie placed Lenny's Jim Beam on his desk and handed Mrs. Palmer a glass of chilled pinot grigio. Our client took a couple of sips and it seemed to relax her.

"Mrs. Palmer," Lenny said. "Go ahead and tell us what's going on and what you'd like us to do." He was using his concerned lawyer's voice. I'm sure he practices it in front of a mirror.

Our client took a deep breath and started speaking. "My husband, Michael, is head of surgery for Scottsdale General Hospital."

"Would that be the main hospital campus on North Hayden Road?" Lenny asked, making notes on a yellow legal pad with his black Montblanc pen.

"That's right. Three or four times a month, when my husband comes home from work, he seems distant, almost angry. When I ask him about it, he always says it's nothing. If I press him, he'll say he had a hard case in surgery, that sort of thing. But this has been going on for several months and I'm starting to become concerned."

"When did you start to suspect he was having an affair?"

"It was a couple of weeks ago, right after Thanksgiving. He came home in a foul mood. When I asked him about it, he snapped at me. He said everything was fine, but he'd had a long and crappy day at work."

"What did you do then?" Lenny asked.

"All of the surgeons are scheduled through a central office. I happen to know someone who works there. I called her the next day to find out if he'd had a tough case or if he'd maybe worked on something unusual the day before."

"What did she tell you?"

Our client's voice became quiet and she looked down at her hands in her lap. "She said he hadn't been scheduled for anything past noon. In fact, he'd listed himself as unavailable every Tuesday and Thursday afternoon for the entire month of December."

"Did your friend see that as unusual?" Lenny asked.

"Not really," she said with a laugh. "Several of the surgeons there have standing times off during the week. Most of them use the time to play golf."

"Did she say how long he's been taking Tuesday and Thursday afternoons off?"

"He's been doing it since early in the summer. That makes it almost six months."

"I take it he told you he'd been working on all of these days?"

"Yes, like I said, whenever I'd ask him what was wrong, he'd blame some difficult case that day. He'd then sit in his den and watch television until he decided to come to bed."

"What would you like us to do?" Lenny asked.

"I'd like to find out for sure. If he's started seeing someone new, I'd like to start divorce proceedings, right away. We have two boys in their early teens and I'd like custody."

"Is there a prenup involved?" he asked.

"No, back when he proposed to me, he said he wanted one. But I refused."

It's always at this point I hope Lenny will suggest marriage counseling. Whatever problems couples are having in their marriage, there might still be a chance they could work things out if they could openly talk to each other about it.

Instead, Lenny's lips curled up in a smile. Looking at him, I could almost hear the sound of an old-fashioned cash register bell ringing.

"Very well," he said, again using his lawyer's voice. "Not having a prenup will simplify things and help us out considerably."

Our client visibly relaxed and took a big sip of her wine.

"Sophie will have some paperwork for you to complete," Lenny continued. "We'll also need a twenty-thousand-dollar retainer to get started. After that's squared away, we'll get right on it."

Jessica seemed a little put out by the retainer's high-dollar amount. She raised an eyebrow, sucked in a breath, and was about to say something, but instead, she let out a deep sigh and took another long sip of her wine.

Our new client stood and Sophie walked to the wet bar to refill her glass. They both then went out to work on the paperwork while Lenny asked me to stay behind.

As they left, I marveled at how, once again, Lenny had judged precisely how much the client would be willing to pay. He'd then pushed it to the limit.

"Twenty thousand seems a little high for a couple of days of surveillance," I said, not being able to help myself.

"Really?" he asked, surprised. "I had been about to ask for twenty-five. But I decided to pull myself back a bit. It's pretty obvious what's going on with the husband. Plus, I had Sophie check out her finances."

"And?"

"She comes from a wealthy family and her husband pulls down almost a million a year as head of surgery at the hospital. They have two kids in their early teens, so the divorce will drag out for at least a year. Maybe more, depending on how hard he wants to fight it. I can easily see pulling another twenty-five or thirty thousand from her before this is over."

Hearing this was disheartening. Sometimes I really do hate my job.

"Look," Lenny said, speaking slowly as if to a child. "This one should be simple. Tomorrow's Tuesday. The guy's going to be in the hospital all morning. Sometime around noon, he's going to take off. He's a doctor, so he'll likely be driving something flashy. Even I could tail someone like that. Follow him around, figure out if he's nailing some broad. If he is, take some pictures."

"Yeah," I grumbled. "More pictures of naked people having sex."

"Why are you complaining?" he asked, genuinely confused. "It's like I keep telling you. You've got the eye for it. Some of your pictures lately have been quality work. As good as anything you can find on the internet."

"Eeeewww."

"Hey, if you don't like your job, you could always go back to bartending. You said you enjoyed doing that."

"Fine, I didn't say I wouldn't do it."

I went out to reception in time to see Sophie run the client's credit card. The signed paperwork was already sitting on her desk.

"Jessica," I said. "Do you have a few minutes? I'd like to get some basic information from you."

She said she did and we went into the conference room. After about thirty minutes, I had everything I needed for my day of surveillance.

~~~~

Gina, Sophie, and I walked down the street for tacos and a Corona. The weather was a little cool, but several heaters were scattered in the seating area to keep the chill off. After my last assignment kept me busy for so long, it was great to catch up with them.

"What's going on with you and Jet?" I asked Gina. "You've been dating him for over a month already."
~~~~

"It's been almost two months," she said, smiling. "We get along so well. As soon as I get a few days off, we're planning on going up to Page. I want to take him hiking up Antelope Canyon. He's also never seen Horseshoe Bend. I thought we'd get there for the sunrise."

"I went up there with my family when I was a kid," Sophie said. "It was a freaking long drive from California, but my parents let me spit into the Grand Canyon, so that was pretty cool."

"In the movies, John Wayne threw a beer bottle into the canyon from there," I said.

"They'd probably arrest you if you tried to do something like that now," Sophie said.

"What about you?" I asked Sophie. "How is it having only one boyfriend at a time?"

"It's harder than I thought it would be," she said. "Don't get me wrong, Milo's a great guy and everything. But when I go out with the cougars, and all of those hot guys start buying me drinks? It's been a challenge not to go home with at least one or two of them."

"Here's to taking home hot guys from the bar," Gina said as she held up her beer.

"Hot guys from the bar," we both said as we lifted our beers and clinked our glasses together.

~~~~

We went back to the office, and I was thinking about going home, when Lenny popped his head out and walked to reception.

"I'm glad you're all here," he said. "There's something I want to ask you about."

From his tone, we knew what he wanted to talk about. I heard Sophie moan and I looked at Gina. I knew they both felt as uncomfortable as I did.
~~~~

Ever since Lenny started dating Elle, he's been asking embarrassing personal questions about dating and relationships. The only reason we kept humoring him is that we were the ones who had nudged him into dating Elle in the first place.

As usual, Lenny ignored our moans and sideways glances. "I've been dating Elle for almost two months, and it's been great," he said. "But all we ever seem to do is go out to dinner and then head to her place. I want to ask her to go with me somewhere, like maybe for the entire weekend. I was thinking Vegas."

"That seems reasonable," Gina said, clearly relieved the question wasn't about a disgusting personal hygiene issue. "How can we help?"

"Every time I bring up the idea of doing something more involved than a dinner date, she shuts me down. I don't know if I'm being too subtle or somehow asking wrong."

"I don't know if there's a wrong way to ask someone out," I said. "Tell her you think it would be fun if you spent the weekend together and offer to take her to Las Vegas."

"I could do that," Lenny said. "But I've been thinking…"

Sophie barked out a short laugh. She then quickly tried to hide it by pretending to cough.

"Anyway," Lenny continued as he looked down at Sophie. "I was thinking maybe the reason she doesn't want to do anything more than an evening at a time with me is that she doesn't know how I really feel about her."

I started to get a bad feeling about where this was going. "And how do you feel about her?" I asked.

"I'm in love," he said, a big stupid smile on his face. "I'm thinking about asking her to marry me."

"No!" we all shouted at once.

Sophie started to laugh nervously and I could tell Gina was getting annoyed, so I stepped in.

"Um," I said. "You've only been going out for seven or eight weeks. Perhaps you should give it some time, like maybe six months or even a year, before you tell Elle you love her. It's the sort of thing that can spook a woman if you hit her with it too soon."

"Really?" Lenny asked. He seemed genuinely perplexed. "I thought all you gals liked it when men fell in love with you?"

"We do," Gina said in her motherly tone. "But it's best if it's felt on both sides before you start voicing it. Otherwise, it can quickly sour the relationship."

"You're serious?" Lenny asked. "That seems to fly in the face of what I see whenever I watch a movie on the Hallmark channel. The women there seem to fall in love after three or four dates. But, hey, I'll take your word on it."

~~~~

I stayed in the office long enough to finish catching up with both Gina and Sophie. I then drove back to my place to enjoy my last few hours of freedom before things started getting busy again.

As I walked down the hallway to my apartment, I heard the TV playing in Grandma Peckham's apartment. I hadn't talked to her for a few days, so I knocked.

I had to knock a couple of times, but I eventually heard the TV volume go down. A moment later, Grandma opened the door. Today, she was wearing her pink jogging suit.

"Why, Laura," she said in her always cheerful voice. "Come in, dear. How have you been? We haven't had a chance to do more than say hello in the hallway since you spent the weekend at your new boyfriend's house."

"I know. It's been busy at the office."

"It's the Snowbirds," Grandma said as she shook her head. "Every
~~~~

year, there seems to be more of them. It's getting to the point where I'm nervous even driving down to the store. Having one old lady driving down the street doesn't seem to be a problem. Young people have such good reflexes. But when everyone on the street is a senior, it can make driving a challenge."

"How's the wedding going? It's in a little under two weeks."

"Well, it's mostly going okay."

"What part's not going well?"

"Honestly, I'm starting to worry something's going to go wrong with the ceremony."

"I suppose all brides get nervous before the wedding. I'm sure things will go smoothly."

"Oh, I'm not worried about getting married," Grandma said. "It's my wedding planner."

"I didn't know you had a wedding planner. I thought your granddaughter Megan was doing all of that."

"She's been helpful, but if you remember, we took over a wedding they were going to have at the Scottsdale Barrington for New Year's Eve. I also inherited their wedding planner."

"You said the other couple canceled and you were able to use their caterer, their flowers, and their photographer. I know it saved you a lot since you could use the deposits they'd already paid."

"Yes, I'm saving a great deal, but I've been hearing nothing but horror stories about the wedding planner. She seems nice, but when I talked to the people at the Barrington, they said her weddings over the past few months have mostly been disasters."

"That doesn't sound good. What kinds of things have happened?"

"Photographers not being on time, limos not showing up, and one where the minister was over an hour late. The worst one I heard was when the caterer tried to serve prime rib at a vegetarian wedding."

"Wow. Any of those would be enough to ruin the day."

"Honestly, I think that's why the other couple canceled. They didn't want to risk their wedding."

"Most of those issues seem like bad luck as much as anything else. Have you talked with your wedding planner about it?"

"I did. She's not sure why the problems keep happening. She seems as angry and bewildered as anyone about the whole thing."

"How can I help?"

"Well," she said. "I was thinking. You're a detective, would you talk with her? Maybe you could find out what's wrong."

"You know I'm not a detective. I'm only an investigator at a law firm."

"Oh, I know, but it's pretty much the same thing."

I let out a sigh to show Grandma how I felt about getting put in the middle of something like this. She only looked at me with her little old lady smile.

"Okay, fine," I said. "I guess you can consider this part of your wedding present."

"Thank you, dear. I knew you'd want to help."

"Have you and Grandpa Bob decided where you're going to live? I know you'd considered moving over to his place."

"We'd talked about me going over there. We even talked about getting a place in Sun City. But I think he's moving over here. My place is a little bigger, plus my furniture is so much nicer. And honestly, I don't want to pack everything up."

"That's great news," I said. "I was really hating the idea of you moving away."

Chapter Two

"You're going to investigate a wedding planner?" Sophie asked when I walked into the office the following day.

"She's doing Grandma Peckham's wedding and something always seems to go wrong."

"What kinds of things?"

"According to Grandma, it's something different each time. Last weekend, a hip-hop DJ showed up for a wedding between two seniors. They wanted waltzes and slow dancing and instead got Snoop Dogg and Grandmaster Flash."

"What do you think? Is the wedding planner a ditz?"

"I don't know yet. Grandma says she appears to be okay, but her weddings seem to go to hell. She thinks that's why the other couple canceled. They didn't want to risk it."

"I remember my wedding," Sophie said. "I was pretty much mental that day. If something crazy like that had happened, I might have lost it in front of everybody."

"What did you end up doing last night?"

"I went out with the girls. We spent most of the night in the Living Room Lounge. Elle was there and she asked me about Lenny."

"Oh no. What happened?"

"Lenny said he wanted to ask her about something the next time they went out. According to Elle, Lenny was acting a little squirrely when he told her."

"What did you say?"

"I said I thought Lenny was going to ask her out for a weekend in Vegas."

"Okay, how did she react?"

"She didn't look happy. When I asked her about it, she said she wasn't sure if having an actual boyfriend was working out or not. She said this right before she started chatting up this football player from ASU."

~~~~

I went back to my cubicle and pulled out my phone. Grandma had given me the contact information for her wedding planner, a woman named Kristine Darby.

When I called her, she said she'd be happy to meet with me and could do so right away. I didn't need to be up at Scottsdale General Hospital to start following Michael Palmer until about eleven-thirty, so I said I'd be right over.

~~~~

Kristine Darby worked out of her home, which turned out to be a little south of Gainey Ranch, about two blocks from where Danica and Alex Sternwood lived.

When I drove into the neighborhood, I realized I hadn't been here since I'd gone over to Danica's house to look for Alex when he'd turned up missing. It startled me a little to think that had been almost a year ago.

I quickly found Kristine's house. It was a lovely ranch with white stucco and a red tile roof. Like all the houses in the neighborhood, the tropical oasis landscaping in the front was beautiful.

I parked in front of the house and knocked on the door. The woman who met me seemed pleasant enough.

She was about my age, a little taller, and dressed a lot nicer. Slender but not athletic. She had styled blonde hair that hung a little past her shoulders and subtle makeup. She wore several gold jewelry pieces, including a wedding band and an engagement ring with a center diamond that must have been over two carats.

"You must be Laura Black," she said as we shook hands. "Call me Kristy. Please come in. I have a room in the back I use as my office."

She led me to a bright den in the back of the house. I could see out a picture window to a sparkly-blue lagoon-style pool with a big splashy waterfall. Her backyard was landscaped with a dozen orange and palm trees, along with one of the most beautiful arrangements of flowering plants I've seen.

"I love your house," I said. "Your backyard is gorgeous."

"Thanks," Kristy said with a laugh. "I grew up in Denver and really hated the snow. I always wanted to live in the tropics on a white sand beach next to a blue ocean. Scottsdale is as close as I've come so far."

The room had a small round conference table and several comfortable chairs. As we sat, I looked around the office.

Kristy certainly seemed like she knew what she was doing. On a bookshelf on the back wall were several large catalogs and notebooks for everything you could think of associated with a wedding.

"You said you're with the Henderson-Peckham wedding at the end of the month?" she asked.

"Mary Peckham's my next-door neighbor. She wanted me to come over to make sure things are still going alright with the preparations."

Kristy's face fell a little. She also became somewhat quieter.

“Oh, sure,” she said. “Let’s take a look.”

A laptop computer sat on the desk and she opened it up. On the wall, a large TV mirrored what was showing on her computer screen.

She quickly brought up the details of Grandma’s wedding. There was information on the venue, the flowers, the catering, the DJ, the photographer, and a dozen other things that happen at a wedding.

“Um, yes,” she said as she went down the list. “Everything’s still on track. The venue at the Barrington is beautiful. We’ll have the Victorian Chapel and the Classic reception hall. We were able to get a last-minute change on the table stationary. And since it’s on New Year’s Eve, the Barrington has thrown in a midnight champagne toast, on the house.”

“You’re very organized, “I said. “It looks like you’ve been doing this a long time.”

“It’s been almost nine years. It started as a hobby back in college. But even as a kid, I liked throwing parties.”

“Is it a successful business?”

“Very much so. I know my husband, Andrew, thinks I work too much. And honestly, it’s not like we need an extra income. But we don’t have kids, and I’ve always enjoyed doing it. With our circle of friends, there’s always somebody ready to get married.”

“I’ve heard you’ve been having a string of bad luck lately.”

She let out a sigh. “I thought that might be why you came here. But I can assure you, before the wedding happens on New Year’s Eve, I’m going to reconfirm everything with each vendor, multiple times. I’ll do everything I can to make sure they have the perfect wedding.”

“Don’t get me wrong,” I said. “I’m not here to give you a hard time. I’m here to help.”

At this, she visibly relaxed. “Thank goodness,” she said. “I thought you came over here to let me know they’d canceled.”

"Has that been happening a lot?"

"Twice, so far. In addition to this wedding, there's been one in March. Fortunately, I've found other couples who've been able to take advantage of the arrangements. Still, my reputation has taken a serious hit."

"I know you've had a rough patch lately. Any idea what's happening?"

"The last several months have been a nightmare. I could see one or two things going wrong, but lately, every single wedding seems to have some sort of disaster."

"And you don't see any kind of pattern to it?"

She barked out a laugh. "I wish I did. But every time, it's something out of left field. I'm not sure if it's simply bad luck or if someone's actively behind it."

"Do you really think someone could be deliberately doing this?"

"I'm starting to suspect that may be the case. The odds of so many crazy things happening on their own seem pretty low. Honestly, I've been thinking about hiring someone to look into it."

"I'd only planned on looking into this informally, but if you're serious about getting to the bottom of it, I work at a law office here in Scottsdale. It's a little outside of what we normally do, but if there's the possibility you'll need to take legal action against someone, you could hire our firm. I'd be the investigator."

"Thanks, maybe you coming here today is a sign. I've wanted to clear this up and maybe I needed a push. If you give me the number, I'll give your office a call."

"Perfect," I said, handing her my card. "Call the office and Sophie will set up an appointment."

~~~~
~~~~

From Kristy's, I drove up Hayden Road and arrived at Scottsdale General Hospital around eleven-thirty. I then spent several minutes driving around the campus until I found the doctor's parking lot.

According to Jessica, her husband, Michael, drove a red Porsche Boxster. I quickly found it among the other high-end cars. I parked in a spot that let me keep an eye on the Boxster, but would also allow me to easily tail him when he left.

At about twelve-twenty, I saw a man get into the Porsche and drive away. He closely matched the picture Jessica had shown me of her husband. He was tall and good-looking, somewhere in his late forties.

I followed the Boxster south on Hayden until we had almost reached Indian Bend Road. He then turned west and pulled into a group of attractive townhouses on Via Camello Del Norte.

He drove past a dozen homes and pulled his car into the driveway of one of the nicer townhouses towards the rear of the group. He got out of the Porsche and used a key to go inside.

Since it looked like he'd be there for a while, I parked across the street and three houses down. I had a good view of the road, and from what I could tell, there hadn't been anyone else in the townhouse when he arrived.

Less than ten minutes later, a white BMW Z4 roadster pulled into the driveway next to Michael's Boxster. A pretty woman, about my age, got out and walked to the townhouse.

She was tall and thin, almost to the point of being skinny. She had long blonde hair that was styled so it bounced when she walked.

She was in a short strawberry-colored dress with a small matching cross-body bag and medium-heeled shoes. The outfit looked expensive, but was low-cut and revealing enough that it fell more on the slutty side of the fashion line.

Without knocking, she let herself into the house. From the way she seemed to know her way around, this wasn't her first time here.

I called Sophie and asked her to run a check on the townhouse and the blonde's license plate. Once we learned her name and where she lived, it might make surveillance simpler in the future.

~~~~

As I waited for them to come out, my phone started playing Rihanna's song *S&M*, Sophie's ringtone.

"Hey," she said when I answered. "How's it going?"

"They're still in there. But I'd say this is the right place for me to get the pictures. What did you find out about the townhouse?"

"The owner's listed as our client's husband, Michael Palmer."

"Okay, that makes sense. He has money. It wouldn't surprise me if he bought it as a stand-alone love-nest. What about the blonde?"

"The car's registered to a company called Progressive Possibilities."

"I've never heard of them."

"Me either. The business' address is only listed as a post office box in Paradise Valley. They don't have a website, so I imagine they're pretty small. I'm running a search now. I'll let you know if I find out anything."

~~~~

I'd been waiting in the car for about an hour when my phone started playing the theme to *The Love Boat*. Sophie had programmed this as Max's ringtone several months before. She laughs whenever she hears it, and I've never changed it.

"Hey," he said when I answered. "How's your afternoon? Does your new assignment look like it will be anything worthwhile?"

"Not really," I said with a laugh. "I'm doing a stakeout. Same as always."

"Will you be busy tonight, or will you still be involved?"

"So far, I think I'm free. Did you want to get together? It might be the last time for a few days."

"I have meetings later on tonight," he said. "But I'll have time for a quick early dinner. Swing by my office a little before five? You can see the changes we made. Then we can head down to the bistro."

"That sounds wonderful. I can't wait to see what you've done. Hopefully, I'll be on time."

~~~~

I ended up waiting almost three hours for them to leave the townhouse. When the door finally opened, the blonde came out first while Michael trailed behind her.

As she got into her car, I couldn't help but notice her hair was again perfect. I wasn't close enough to tell for sure, but I suspected her makeup was as well. I could only guess at how long she must have stood in front of the mirror to put herself back together after the afternoon's events.

As she walked to her convertible, my eyes focused on her cross-body bag. It wasn't nearly big enough to hold everything she would have needed to redo her hair and make-up.

Even though the townhouse was owned by Michael, the blonde must have loaded up the bathroom with her things. I was starting to agree with our client. This had probably been going on for quite some time.

I waited in my car for another five minutes to make sure neither Michael nor the blonde would return. Putting on a baseball cap to partially obscure my features, I reached over and grabbed my clipboard. It held a dozen pieces of paper crammed under the clasp.

One of the best pieces of advice I'd ever gotten from Gina was the use of the clipboard. As long as you're holding one, people will assume you're somehow on official business. They'll usually leave you alone, even if you're doing some otherwise suspicious activities.
~~~~

Holding my clipboard, I walked up to the townhouse and rang the doorbell. I didn't think anyone was still inside, but I've been fooled before. It's always embarrassing when someone looks back at you while you're peeping into their window.

When no one answered after two rings, I walked around the unit to see what I could learn. A large window in the living room was uncovered and I was able to peer inside.

From what I could tell, the place had the sterile look of a home with furniture but no personality. It reminded me of a furnished apartment I'd once rented, soon after I'd graduated from college.

There were no pictures on the walls, no books in the bookcase, and no television anywhere. The entire living room consisted of a couch and two chairs.

Next, I found a window that looked inside the kitchen. Like the living room, it appeared to be unused. There were no appliances on the counters and nothing on the walls.

After walking around the townhouse, I determined the bedrooms were all on the second floor. Looking up from the outside, the windows appeared to all have closed shutters or miniblinds.

I sighed. If this was where Michael Palmer and his paramour would be meeting, I'd need to find some way to get in the townhouse and plant cameras. Hopefully, some way that wouldn't get me arrested.

~~~~

"How'd your meeting with the wedding planner go?" Sophie asked as I walked up to reception. "Is she a scatterbrain Jane?"

"No, she seems alright. Her name's Kristine Darby and she's as concerned as anyone. She wants to hire us to look into it."

"That makes sense, she called a little earlier, and I set her up with an appointment. At least you won't have to sneak around and do it behind Lenny's back this time. You know how much that annoys
~~~~

him."

"That's assuming he'll take her on as a client. We're pretty busy."

"Why would he care? You're the one who'll be doing all the work. Wave some money in front of Lenny's face and he'll let you do it."

"You're probably right. Were you able to find out anything about Progressive Possibilities?" I asked.

"Not a lot. The only thing I've been able to find out so far is they're listed as a company that provides personal services."

"What? Like an escort service?"

"Maybe. Or maybe she does in-home massages or reads his palm and tells his fortune. Who knows? I'll let you know more as it comes in."

"Thanks, something about this seems off."

"What did you decide to get Max for Christmas?" Sophie asked. "It must be hard to get something for a guy who could buy his own department store."

"You're not kidding. I've been searching the internet and found half a dozen high-end French roast coffees. I hope he likes them. Some of them were like thirty dollars a pound."

"I know what you mean. I asked Milo what he wanted, and all I could get out of him was he was thinking about getting a Kill-A-Bear knife."

"What kind of knife is that?"

"It's the military fighting knife they issued to the marines in World War II. I guess the marines shortened the name to KA-BAR. Fortunately, the same company still makes them and sells them over the internet."

"It sounds like a good knife."

"According to the company, the knife got its name when a guy was in the woods and actually killed a bear with it."

"Damn."

"I know, right?"

Lenny opened his door and walked over to us. "What have you got so far on the Palmer investigation? Did he have an appointment with a woman today?"

"Yes, they met at a townhouse off of Hayden. She's a pretty woman with long blonde hair. From the way they acted, it wasn't their first time together."

"A townhouse?" Lenny asked. "Who owns it? The blonde?"

"No, Sophie ran a check on it. It turns out our client's husband owns the property."

"Wait a minute," Lenny said. "How did he buy real estate without his wife's signature?"

"It looks like he used the name of his surgical group, but he paid in cash, and it's his name on the deed," Sophie said.

"Nice work," Lenny said. "Hiding assets is always a good sign. See what else you can dig up. He may have assets stashed all over the place."

"No problem," she said. "I've already started a search."

"At least it'll make it easier to run surveillance on him," Lenny said as he looked at me. "Go ahead and load up the place with video cameras."

"Breaking and entering?" I asked.

Lenny shook his head. "Sophie, call our client. Have her sign a blanket authorization for video surveillance on all of her properties. Don't list any specific location."

"Will that fly if her name's not on the deed to the townhouse?" I asked.

"It's still marital property. By the time they untangle the actual ownership, the issue of surveillance will be moot."

"By the way," I said as casually as I could. "I found us a new client. She should be calling to set up an appointment."

"Oh really?" Lenny asked. He was looking at me like I was trying to pull something on him. "This doesn't have anything to do with Tony DiCenzo, does it? After dealing with him the last time, I don't ever want to hear that name again."

"No, nothing to do with him."

"Is it a criminal or family law case?"

I shook my head. "She's a wedding planner and she's concerned because something always goes wrong with her weddings."

Lenny looked at me like I was an idiot. "A wedding planner? That's it? You do realize I can't take someone to trial over a bad wedding."

"I know, it's probably only billable hours. But she's the wedding planner for my next-door neighbor. I'll need to look into it, one way or the other. We might as well get paid for it."

"Well, I do like your way of thinking, but this isn't the time of year to take on charity cases."

"It shouldn't take too long and I don't think it'll interfere with anything else. Weddings are usually at night or on the weekend."

Lenny thought about it for a moment, then looked at Sophie. "Okay, when she calls, give her an appointment. It sounds like this will be a quick one."

"She already called," Sophie said. "She'll be here first thing tomorrow morning. How do you want to set her up?"

Lenny eyed me as if he'd known I'd planned it this way all along.

"Fine. Give her a fifteen-thousand-dollar retainer and forty percent off the full hourly rate."

"Fifteen thousand?" I asked.

"Okay," Lenny said as he rolled his eyes. "I know. She's a friend of a friend. I'll tell you what I'll do. Sophie, go ahead and make it ten thousand."

He then looked back at me. "Just make sure to use up the whole thing. In fact, it would make me happy if you went a few thousand over. She's a wedding planner. I used one back when I got married. Trust me, they know all about things going over budget."

~~~~

I drove up Scottsdale Road and pulled into the wide drive next to the enormous floral and fountain display that marks the entrance to the Scottsdale Tropical Paradise. It's one of the golf resorts Tony DiCenzo built back in the eighties and is where he located the corporation's business offices.

After parking in the visitors' lot, I made my way through the main entrance and up the curving stairs to the mezzanine level. From there, I headed to the offices of Scottsdale Land and Resort Management, Inc.

When I reached the big double glass doors, the security stations were gone. The two beefy guys in black polos who were usually there were also missing.

I opened the doors and entered the lobby. In all the times I'd been here before, this had been an open space. Now there was a desk and several comfortable chairs.

Behind the desk was a nicely dressed woman who was about my age. I'd seen her before but had no idea what her name was. She smiled at me as I walked in.

"Wow," I said. "I see they made some changes."
~~~~

"They fixed up the lobby about a week ago," she said. "It looks nice, don't you think?"

"It looks great. I'm Laura Black. I'm here to see Maximilian Bettencourt."

"Let me see if he's free," she said as she picked up the phone and made a call, presumably to an admin.

"You can go back," she said as she hung up. "Let me make a badge for you."

She took my picture and typed some information into her computer. A few seconds later, a plastic card came out of a machine. She then attached it to a colorful Scottsdale Tropical Paradise lanyard.

"This is a permanent badge," she said as she handed it to me. "You can keep it and use it whenever you visit."

She then showed me how to use the access gate built across the hallway that led to the rest of the offices. When I held my badge against the reader, a big piece of glass slid out of the way, letting me pass through.

I walked down to the executive offices. The admin desk I'd long associated with Gabriella was now occupied by Cheryl, a woman I'd met a few weeks before.

I walked to Max's office, but stopped short when I saw the nameplate on it. It said Tony DiCenzo. When I stuck my head in, Tony wasn't there.

"He's down here," Cheryl called out.

I walked down the hallway to her desk, where she was smiling at me. "We switched over the offices about a week ago."

"This all seems a little strange," I mused.

Cheryl glanced down at her phone. "Mr. Bettencourt is finished with his call," she said. "I'll buzz you in."

She reached under her desk and pressed a button. The door lock released and I went in.

Max was behind his desk. As I'd seen so many times with Tony, Max was reading through a stack of papers.

"Nice office," I said as I walked in. "You're moving up in the world."

"It still feels a bit strange to have Tony's office, but he insisted. Truthfully, I think giving me his office was his way of truly retiring."

"How's he doing? I haven't talked with him in weeks."

"He hasn't been this relaxed in years. I think he realizes the retirement was a good move. I know he wants to get together with you and go over the things he's been doing the last several months. Don't be surprised if he gives you a call sometime soon."

"That'll be great. I see you've started to make changes around here."

"Yes, if we're going to be known as a legitimate business, we might as well start to look and act like one. How did you like the new lobby?"

"It's nice. The card reader and security gate are a little different."

"I put the lobby back to where it was when I first got here. The access gate doesn't provide any active security. People can still jump over it. But it does give us a record of who goes in and out."

"I like the changes. I think they're an improvement. It really looks like you're starting to get out of the other side of the business."

"Yes, and you'll see a lot of other changes happening over here. I think it's one of the things Tony wants to tell you about.

"Are you ready for dinner?"

"I'm starving."

Chapter Three

I woke up early the following day. Dinner with Max had been delicious and relaxing. He had meetings to get to, so we couldn't stay too long. Still, it was wonderful to be with him.

I drove to the office and went in through the back-security door. Gina had beaten me in and was working on her computer.

"Good morning," I said.

"Hi, Laura. How does your new assignment look?"

"So far, so good. I've found where our client's husband and his mistress meet. It's a townhouse near Haden and Indian Bend. According to Sophie, the husband owns it. Lenny says it's marital property and is having me set up cameras."

"Hopefully, everything goes smoothly. Let me know if you need help with anything."

The door to the back opened and Lenny came in. He looked terrible. His eyes were puffy, and his clothes were a mess. My first thought was maybe he'd been mugged.

"Are you alright?" I asked as he walked towards us.

"What happened?" Gina asked.

"Elle and I were at dinner at Mastro's Steakhouse last night," Lenny said. His voice was quiet and distant. "We were sharing a warm butter cake for dessert, and things were going well, so I told her I'd like to plan a weekend vacation for the two of us at the Bellagio in Vegas."

"Okay," I said. "That sounds reasonable. What did she say?"

"She turned me down flat. So, I made the mistake of asking her why."

"What did she say?" Gina asked.

"She said she didn't know if it was a good idea if we do anything more than our dinners, at least not for a while. I could tell she was starting to get distant, and I was getting a little desperate, so, um, I told her I loved her."

"Seriously?" Gina asked, sounding a little pissed.

"I don't know how it happened," Lenny moaned. "It just came out."

"What happened then?" I asked.

"It really seemed to shake her. Like it took her a moment to come to grips with it."

"What did she say?"

"All she said was no."

"No?"

"That's it. She shook her head and said no. She then told me not to say anything else or follow her. Then she got up and took an Uber home."

"I'm sorry," I said. "It seemed like things had been going pretty well."

"Yeah, I know. The three of you tried to warn me about telling her how I really felt. But I could feel the whole thing slipping away and I panicked."

"What are you planning on doing now?" Gina asked.

"I don't know," he quietly said, his eyes to the floor. "I'd take some advice, if you have any. But honestly, I think it's over."

"I'd wait until later this afternoon, then call her to apologize," I said. "Tell her you let your emotions get the better of you and you agree it's too soon to have feelings like that."

"Yeah," he said, still sounding dejected. "That actually sounds reasonable. Thanks."

Lenny walked to the front offices. "Jeez," Gina moaned. "Lenny's going to be a hot mess for weeks."

"You've known him longer than I have. Is there anything we can do for him? I really don't want to deal with him as he figures out how to live with this. You know how pissy he's going to get."

"I don't know, but we'll need to come up with something. I seriously don't want to deal with his emotions any more than you do."

~~~~

Gina started working on a report, and I went up to the front. When I got to Sophie's desk, she looked concerned.

"What's up with Lenny?" she asked. "He looks like someone told him his baby was ugly. He didn't even say hello. He went into his office and closed the door."

"He went out with Elle last night. While they were at dinner, he told her he loved her."

"Oh, my God. He's such an idiot. What did she do?"

"She dumped him. She took off and left him sitting at the table."

"You know," Sophie quickly said. "This isn't our fault. We did try to warn him."

"Yeah, but you know Lenny."
~~~~

"Damn," she said. "Now we're going to have to deal with the fallout."

"I guess we didn't think it through when we set them up in the first place."

"Jeez, I don't want to deal with Lenny dragging his sorry ass around the office for the next month. What are we going to do?"

"I don't know yet. But we'll need to come up with something. You know how cranky he's going to get."

"Maybe we can find him somebody else?" Sophie asked. "Then he can have someone new for a rebound relationship. That would at least get him off our backs for a while."

"But what happens when that one doesn't work out? We'd be right back where we started."

"Hey," she said. "I can only work one problem at a time."

"When's Kristy coming in? You said first thing today."

"She'll be here at nine. We'll have to let her know Lenny's going through a break-up and not to take his moodiness personally."

~~~~

At five minutes to nine, the door to the street opened and Kristy walked in. I introduced her to Sophie and Gina. We told her about Lenny, his break-up the night before, and how he might be in a weird mood because of it. She sympathized and said she completely understood.

I'd already talked with her and knew what she needed. Still, Lenny needed to meet with her to go over his rates and the costs associated with the investigation. This introductory meeting also became the first billable hour in the log.

Sophie buzzed Lenny to let him know the client had arrived. He said to show her in.
~~~~

"She seems nice," Gina said when the door to Lenny's office closed.

"Yeah," Sophie echoed. "She doesn't seem like an airhead. Do you have any idea who's messing up the weddings?"

"Not a clue so far."

"How are you going to handle this?" Gina asked.

"I figured I'd go to a couple of her weddings and see if I can find out what the problem is. According to Kristy, it's something different every time, but there must be something common between them."

"Don't forget to check in with the husband," Gina said. "It doesn't sound like he has anything to do with this, but it might be helpful to get his perspective."

"Going to weddings sounds like fun," Sophie said.

"Come along then," I said. "I could always use an extra pair of eyes. Gina, do you want to come too?"

"Not unless you think you'll need some backup. We're already going to your neighbor's wedding next week. That's enough weddings for one month."

"Are you bringing Jet?" Sophie asked.

"I've let him know I'm going to a wedding on New Year's Eve and he's welcome to come along. But I'm leaving the decision completely up to him. I think it's a little too soon for me to start dragging him to weddings. What about Milo?"

"I'm still debating. Now that I'm dating him exclusively, I suppose it would make sense. But I'd probably have more fun if I didn't have him along. It's always entertaining being in a room with a lot of drunk single guys."

Gina shook her head and I rolled my eyes.

~~~~
~~~~

After about forty-five minutes, Kristy came out of Lenny's office. She held a glass of pinot noir and had the slightly dazed look many clients get after the first meeting with Lenny.

This is the point when what they are doing suddenly becomes real to them. It's also the time when they start to comprehend how expensive everything is going to be.

Sophie had the new client paperwork in a folder on her desk. She ushered Kristy into the main conference room to get her signature and collect her credit card information.

Once it looked like they were almost done, I joined them in the conference room and sat next to Kristy. After Sophie had gathered up the paperwork and took off, we both sat in silence for a moment.

"How are you doing?" I asked.

"It all seems a little unreal. But I'm glad we're starting. Hopefully, you can come up with something."

"I was thinking, the best way to get started would be to go to a couple of your weddings. I could see for myself what sorts of things are happening. If anything does go wrong, I'll be able to start looking into it right away."

"That's a great idea. When I'm working on an event, everything is going on at once. I don't have a lot of free time to look into whatever problem just occurred."

"When's your next wedding?"

She let out a breath. "It's tonight. The ceremony will be at Our Lady of Peace at McDowell Mountain Ranch. The reception is at the Scottsdale Barrington. I'll have one on Saturday night at the Tropical Paradise. Christmas is Sunday, so I'll have the day off. Then it all starts up again. I have one on Tuesday at the Saguaro Sky, then the Peckham wedding is back at the Barrington on New Year's Eve, which is on Saturday."

"Wow," I said. "I didn't know you were so busy."

"This time of year, I average two weddings a week. Next to Las Vegas, Scottsdale's about the most practical place for a destination wedding in the winter. Our weather is perfect and all the resorts have beautiful ceremony and reception facilities."

"Would you mind if I bring Sophie with me?" I asked. "She sometimes spots things I miss."

"No problem, bring whoever you'd like. Keep in mind, as wedding planners, we don't eat unless it's a buffet and then only after everyone else goes through. We also don't drink unless we pay. Brides tend to get fussy if they see strangers at their open bar."

~~~~

I arrived back at the townhouse on Via Camello Del Norte a few minutes after eleven. I figured this would be early enough for me to finish installing the video cameras, in case Michael and the blonde decided to return for a Wednesday afternoon romp.

When I reached the townhouse, I was surprised to see the blonde's white BMW in the driveway. Instead of Michael Palmer's red Boxster, a black Mercedes was parked next to the BMW.

I parked where I had the day before and called Sophie. "Hey, chica, could you run a plate for me? The blonde's back at the townhouse, but there's a different car parked next to her."

"Okay. Do you think Michael's using two cars, or is this someone new?"

"I don't know. Jessica only told us about the red Boxster, but he seems good at hiding things from her. Call me when you find out anything."

I sat on the street and kept an eye on the townhouse. Ten minutes later, Sophie called back.

"The Mercedes is registered to Manuel Montoya. He's an M.D.
~~~~

and is listed as the Chief Strategy Officer of Scottsdale General."

"Seriously? Chief Strategy Officer? Where do they come up with these titles? It sounds like he sits in his office and plays games all day. Do you have a picture of him? I'd like to compare it with whoever comes out."

"Not a problem. This guy has his picture all over the internet. He seems to be on the board of every medical charity in the Valley. Here, this is a good one."

My phone dinged as Sophie sent me a picture of Doctor Montoya. He was a serious-looking man, somewhere in his mid-forties, with dark hair and a full mustache.

I'd just finished studying the photo when I looked up to see the blonde coming out of the house. She wore a grape-colored dress that was even more revealing than the one she had on the day before.

She was leading a man who was clearly Doctor Montoya. He walked directly to his car while she turned and used a key to lock the door.

They each got into their cars and took off. Like the day before, I waited a few minutes to make sure neither of them was going to double back. I grabbed my trusty clipboard, a bag full of spy cameras, and my set of lockpicks, then walked to the rear door of the townhouse.

From my snooping the previous day, I knew this back entrance was out of view from the street. I could work on picking the lock with less chance of getting caught.

One of Gina's skills was the ability to open the types of locks commonly found in houses. Thanks to many training sessions with her, I was starting to get a knack for it. I wasn't nearly as skilled as she was, but after ten minutes of trial and error, I was able to open the door.

When I got inside, my suspicions that nobody actually lived in the house were confirmed. Except for some wine glasses and an ashtray, the kitchen had nothing in any of the cabinets. The refrigerator was also empty, except for some bottles of wine.

There wasn't anything on the shelves in the kitchen or living room, so I couldn't put cameras in either place. It would have looked pretty weird if something new had simply popped up.

When I walked up the stairs to the master bedroom, I was relieved to see the space was well used. Besides being cluttered, the room smelled like some high-end perfume mixed in with several salon beauty products.

Walking into the bathroom, I saw the assortment of hair tools and makeup the blonde kept at the townhouse. These were openly displayed on the vanity, a clear indication she had claimed this as her territory. She had evidently been doing this for weeks, if not months.

Fortunately, the bedroom had built-in bookshelves, which were stuffed with the blonde's things. I quickly set up three cameras facing the bed, all from different angles. I also set up one so it faced toward the door of the bathroom.

For the cameras, I'd chosen some of my favorites. The first was a small kitty-kat figurine with the eye of the cat as the camera lens. For the second, I used a box of tissues with a cheap-looking cover. In this one, the camera lens was disguised as the center of a painted flower.

I also used a small brown stuffed bear with the camera lens hidden as a button on his coat. These objects were the kinds of things someone might notice, but they'd almost always assume the other person had brought them in.

For the last camera, I used one that looked exactly like a standard cell phone charger. It even worked as a charger in case someone needed to power up their mobile.

I plugged it directly into a wall socket, so this one had the advantage of not requiring a battery. The only downside was I couldn't point it directly at the bed.

As I was installing the cameras, I noticed someone else had already placed spy cameras throughout the room. I searched in the obvious places and found a total of four other cameras.

Surprisingly, they hadn't worked all that hard to disguise them. I wasn't sure what to do with them, so I left them alone. I mentally crossed my fingers that no one had been watching while I was in the room.

I made a few final adjustments, then went outside to the back of the unit to set up a signal-repeater. This would allow the cameras to send the images to the office over the internet.

I'd just finished installing and setting up the equipment when I heard a car pull into the driveway.

Damn.

I stood at the back of the townhouse, away from the windows, until I heard the sound of the front door open, then close again. I waited for a couple of minutes, then confidently walked back out to the street, my clipboard still in my hand.

I made it back to my car and had just closed the door when a maroon Jaguar convertible came down the street and slid into the driveway next to the blonde's white BMW. A man, about fifty-five years of age, got out and walked to the front door. Without knocking, he went inside.

I wasn't sure what to make of it, so I called Sophie.

"Hey," I said. "You're not going to believe it. But the blonde came back to the townhouse. She's with another man."

"Seriously? That's her second one today. That woman has some kind of stamina. One good session with a guy is enough to tire me out for hours."

"Would you be able to run his plate? I'm curious to know who he is?"

"Sure, give me the numbers. I'll see what I can dig up."

~~~~

If the blonde followed her usual pattern, she'd be entertaining the man for the next three hours. I used the time to drive over to the Filiberto's at the Pavilions at Talking Stick. I was getting hungry and I needed to use the bathroom.

While I was at lunch, enjoying chips and a carne asada burrito, Sophie called to let me know the car was registered to Isaac Elmaghrabi, MD. After she mangled the name a couple of times, I had her spell it out for me. According to the website for Scottsdale General, Doctor Elmaghrabi was the Chief Medical Operations Officer.

Sophie also sent me a couple of internet pictures of the doctor. He was a slightly overweight guy who matched the man who had gotten out of the Jaguar.

When I arrived back at the townhouse, it was a little after two o'clock. I breathed a sigh of relief when I saw both cars were still in the driveway.

~~~~

A little after three, the front door of the townhouse opened and the blonde stepped out again. I cringed a little when I saw she had on the same purple outfit as she'd been wearing earlier in the day when meeting with the first man.

Close on her heels was Doctor Elmaghrabi. He walked directly to his car, without giving the blonde a hug or a final kiss. While she was still locking the front door, he fired up his car and took off.

Maybe it was only me, but I could see he didn't look happy, even from where I was. This was certainly not the look I would have expected from a man who had spent an afternoon of passion with a beautiful woman.

~~~~
~~~~

I drove back to the office. When I got there, Sophie was at her desk, talking with Gina.

"Hey, Laura," Gina said. "How'd it go today? Did you get the cameras installed?"

"Yeah, that part went okay. But the weird thing is we're not the only ones taking videos in the bedroom."

"Oh, really?" she asked.

"I found four other cameras in the room."

"Well..." Gina pondered, "it could be law enforcement with some serious warrants. But I'd guess it's simply somebody else making recordings for their own purposes. Hopefully, they weren't watching while you were over there."

"The townhouse is owned by our client's husband," I said. "He might suspect his mistress is using his house to entertain other guys. Maybe he put the cameras there to confirm his suspicions?"

"Or maybe he already knows she's there with other men and he wants to watch?" Gina asked.

"Yeah," Sophie said with a wicked smile. "A lot of guys think that's hot."

"Sophie told me about the two other men she had over there today," Gina said. "Both of them were doctors?"

"They were," I said. "She seems to go after men with money."

"Well," Gina said, "if she's charging all of them, she'll be making an excellent income."

"Still," Sophie said, "using your sugar daddy's crib to host other guys? That's pretty bold of her."

"Yup," I said. "It's messed up, no matter how you look at it."

"You're telling me," Sophie said. "If Michael doesn't already know about it, I bet he'll be totally pissed when he finds out. I would imagine he bought the townhouse thinking it would be his private hideaway."

"I wonder if she changes the sheets between men?" Gina pondered.

"Oh, that's nasty," Sophie said, wrinkling her nose. "I don't think I'd like to be rolling around on someone else's love stains."

"I wouldn't worry so much about the sheets," I said. "I hope she at least takes a shower between the men. Being number two for the day and getting sloppy seconds would be disgusting."

"Eeeewww," Gina said, puckering her lips.

"Jeez, why'd you have to say that?" Sophie groaned. "That's so gross. Now I'll have that image stuck in my head all day."

The door to Lenny's office opened, and a cloud of cigarette smoke rolled out. Lenny came out of his office with two fingers of Beam on the rocks. He walked over to Sophie's desk and collapsed into one of the red-leather wing chairs. He looked tired and deflated.

"Did you call Elle?" I asked.

"Yeah," he said with a snort of laughter, shaking his head. "I called her."

"What happened?"

"I did like you advised. I told her I'd let my emotions get the best of me and I knew it was too soon to talk about things like that."

"What did she say?"

Lenny sighed and took a sip of his Beam. "She said she really likes me, but dating me more than a few times had been a mistake. She feels bad that she let it go so far and it was all her fault."

"So, is it over?" I asked.

Lenny nodded. "Yeah, I think so."

The three of us looked at each other, but no one seemed to know what to say.

"I need a cigarette," he said as he looked at the floor.

Gina glared at him, and Lenny seemed to sense it without looking up. "I know," he said. "I'll open my window, so you three don't need to deal with the smoke."

He got up, walked back into his office, and slowly closed the door.

"Wow," Sophie said. "Being told it's not your fault is always the worst way to get dumped. That means she didn't think you were even worth the effort. If some guy's going to leave me, I want it to be because I did something to piss him off and he hates me."

"It's a weird feeling," I said. "But I feel terrible for Lenny and what he's going through."

"Yeah," Sophie said. "But you know what this is going to mean. For the next couple of weeks, he's going to alternate between being pissy and looking like he's about to cry. I don't think I can handle that."

"Do you have any suggestions?" Gina asked. "I have excuses to be out of the office, but you'll be stuck here."

"I know," Sophie said with a moan. "I don't know what we can do, other than to try to hook him up with someone else."

I shook my head. "I don't know either, but we've got to come up with something."

~~~~

I went to the back offices and logged into my computer. I wanted to make sure the camera feeds were all working correctly.

When I opened my video folder, there were already several files from the Palmer townhouse. I had one file, per camera, for each hour they'd been in operation.

These files would keep coming in until the batteries in the cameras
~~~~

wore out. I knew, from experience, it would take five or six days for that to happen. If I hadn't gotten the evidence I needed by then, I'd have to go back and install new batteries in all of them.

I did a quick review of what I'd gathered so far. As expected, the videos featured the blonde with Doctor Elmaghrabi.

It didn't take me long to get the gist of what they did together. The blonde seemed to be very skilled at her job. Mostly, what the doctor had to do was lay back and enjoy himself.

I fast-forwarded a few times to make sure nothing of note happened. Most of the session seemed to be the blonde entertaining the man in all sorts of creative ways.

Flipping open my logbook, I made a notation that the video files weren't relevant to the investigation and deleted them. This was a standing rule at the law firm, since we often ended up with compromising videos of unrelated people.

One bit of satisfaction I gleaned from looking at the videos was the great locations I'd chosen to hide the cameras. I was getting high-definition shots that clearly showed both who was in the room and what activities they were involved in. This was precisely what Lenny needed for him to score the high-dollar settlements his clients looked for.

I was also able to confirm my suspicions about the blonde. After she was through with Doctor Elmaghrabi, she spent over half an hour in front of the mirror, fixing her hair and completely redoing her make-up.

I also noted that she didn't change the sheets. When they were done, she simply flipped the covers and bedspread back into place and smoothed everything out.

That's so gross.

My phone rang, showing a local number I couldn't place. When I answered, it was Cheryl, the new executive admin at the Tropical

Paradise.

"Miss Black," she said in an efficient voice, "Mr. DiCenzo would like to meet with you for three holes of golf. He's available tomorrow morning, if that's convenient for you."

I thought about it for a second and couldn't come up with anything I'd need to do in the morning. "Um, sure. When and where?"

"It will be the tenth, eleventh, and twelfth holes of the Kokopelli course at the Blue Palms. He'll meet you at Mulligan's Grille. Mr. DiCenzo thought you might be familiar with it."

"Yes, I know where it is. What time?"

"He's expecting to arrive at approximately ten o'clock. He also wanted you to know he'll have a set of clubs for you at the valet."

"Great. Tell him I look forward to it."

I disconnected and sat back in my chair. I was a little surprised but pleased to hear Tony was golfing again. My only worry was I hadn't picked up a club since the last time I'd golfed with him, and that was back in the spring.

Chapter Four

Kristy's first wedding was at Our Lady of Peace at McDowell Mountain Ranch. Sophie and I drove separately, but we both made it to the church about two hours before the ceremony.

I'd never been here before, but the venue was beautiful. The front of the church had big picture windows that looked out over the northern parts of Scottsdale. Mummy Mountain and Piestewa Peak were prominent in the distance.

Kristy had apparently already been here for some time and was quietly checking everything. Sophie said she'd look around, so I decided to follow our client.

Watching the wedding from Kristy's perspective was a rather strange feeling. She was carrying a tablet with a schedule of everything that would happen and who would be involved with each step.

As we walked around the building, she did a final check with the officiant, the photographer, the videographer, and the limo driver. She was very friendly with everyone and never seemed to be in a rush, but she also didn't waste any time.

"Is everything going okay?" I asked.

"So far, everything's going smoothly. Keep your fingers crossed."

Next, we stepped into a dressing area in the back, where the bride and bridesmaids were in the final stages of getting ready. Everyone was smiling and laughing. One of the bridesmaids had her camera out and was taking pictures of everyone.

"I'll tell you a wedding planner's secret," Kristy said quietly to me as we walked back into the sanctuary. "You can always judge how well things are going by listening. If things are going okay, you hear what we just heard, excited talking and laughing. When there's a problem, all you hear is silence."

Sophie was still looking around the alter and gave us a thumbs-up as we got closer. "Everything looks good out here," she reported.

We then watched as Kristy inspected the flowers, the programs, the sign-in book, the birdseed bundles, and the candles. I was impressed by her focus as she scrutinized each item.

She also checked what she called the path-of-white. This turned out to be a wide roll of white paper. There was a blue velvet cord threaded through the core and tied in a loose loop.

"I've never seen a roll of paper called the path-of-white before," I said. "What's it for?"

"It's so the bride can walk on it," Christy said in a matter-of-fact voice.

Sophie and I both gave her a look.

"The idea is that the bride is very pure on her wedding day, so she needs an equally pure path to walk on as she makes her way to the alter. Before the bride walks down the aisle, the ushers grab the cord and unroll the paper, from the alter to the back of the church."

"What happens to the path-of-white once the bride walks on it?" I asked.

"Some brides roll it back up and keep it, but most of the time, it gets thrown away."

"How much does that cost?" Sophie asked.

"The path-of-white is sixty-five dollars," Kristy said.

Sophie rolled her eyes and I knew I was doing the same thing.

"Is there anything else to do before the ceremony?" I asked.

"No, that's it. I think we're set. We've scheduled forty-five minutes for pictures, then there's a break of half an hour for the guests to arrive."

~~~~

The pictures went off without a hitch. Everyone but the ushers then went back to their rooms and waited to be called.

The ceremony was sweet and moving. Both the bride and groom cried the entire time, which I always see as a good sign.

After the ceremony, we waited for the ten minutes it took for everyone to sign the marriage certificate. Then the happy couple left the church under a shower of birdseed.

As the bride and groom climbed into the waiting limo, Sophie and I drove over to the Barrington. It was a lovely tennis club combined with a wedding and reception center on Scottsdale Road, about half a mile south of Kierland Commons.

We parked and made our way into the venue. The main reception hall was a gorgeous space.

Massive crystal chandeliers provided warm amber lighting. Marble columns lined the room with thick red velvet drapes hanging against the walls. There was ample room for the two hundred or so guests, along with an oversized dance floor and a stage for the band.

A bar was set up against one of the walls with a discrete sign noting it was operating on a cash basis. Sophie looked at me, then scampered over to get a drink.

Kristy walked up, the tablet in her hand again.

"Well?" I asked.
~~~~

"Everything looks perfect," she said. The relief in her voice was unmistakable. "The only thing not out yet is the cake. They should also be circulating with the appetizers in a few minutes. I'll need to go back and check on it."

I followed Kristy into the kitchen, where a staff of about ten people were bustling about. I saw three people making salads, three working on appetizers, and a chef finishing up a potato and cheese dish. I had to admit, I was impressed at how busy everyone looked.

Since everything looked great to me, I was surprised by Kristy's reaction.

"Crap!" she called out as her head darted from one side of the kitchen to the other. "No, no, no."

"What is it?"

"Nothing's ready, nothing. They're only now starting. The desserts should already be done as well as the salads. They should be serving the appetizers now, and they're still making them."

She hurried to a row of ovens and looked in the window at several racks of cooking meat. "The entrees should be out of the oven in twenty minutes, but it looks like they've only just put them in."

"Somebody must be in charge back here," I said.

"Yes, and I need to find him."

Kristy went out the back of the kitchen to a loading dock. Three people were easing a stunning multi-level cake from a van onto a stainless-steel cart.

"Francisco?" Kristy called out, a touch of panic in her voice.

A tall, good-looking man in a white linen coat and a chef's hat seemed to be in charge. As we approached, he turned to us and smiled.

"Kristy," he said in a deep voice. "I'm glad you're here. You can help us with the cake arrangement."

"Forget the cake for a moment," Kristy said, a touch of desperation in her voice. "Francisco, why is nothing ready?"

"What do you mean?" he asked, clearly puzzled.

"The appetizers should be out already. You need to be serving salad at seven forty-five. You're nowhere close to that in there."

"Seven forty-five?" he asked as he shook his head. "No, I have eight forty-five."

He saw the look she was giving him. "It's easy enough to clear this up," he said. "Let me get the work order."

We followed him into the kitchen and over to a desk in a corner. He picked up a metal clipboard with several papers on it and flipped through to the third or fourth page back.

"No, here it is. I'm not sure where the disconnect is, but the work order lists the first course at eight forty-five. Take a look," he said as he handed her the clipboard. "See for yourself."

Kristy looked at the paperwork and sighed. "I'm not sure how the time was changed, but I had it in at seven forty-five. I reconfirmed everything with Maggie two weeks ago."

"I don't know what I can tell you," Francisco said, also frustrated. "I can only go by what's on the order. I can speed things up by maybe ten minutes. Fifteen if you don't mind if the beef is a little rare."

The look on Kristy's face was horrible. It was like she was watching her house burn down. "Francisco," she quietly said. "I know it's not your fault. Do what you can. I'll go out and open up the bar. Maybe we'll get lucky and the bride will be late."

Unfortunately, as we walked back into the reception space, there was a round of clapping and several yells of delight as the bride and groom entered. Kristy walked up to her, with me trailing behind.

"Everything looks so beautiful," the bride said as she took in her reception space. She was beaming with happiness at how perfect her special night was turning out. "You outdid yourself."

"Thank you," Kristy said. "All I did was to help make your vision a reality."

"I think everyone's about here," the bride said as she looked around. "When should we start directing them to the tables?"

"Everything tonight is going well, exactly as we planned. But I did want to let you know, the caterer is running a little behind."

The look on the bride's face went from blissful to bridezilla in an instant.

"What?" she demanded to know. "Dinner's going to be late? Are you F-ing serious? How late?"

"Forty-five minutes, um, maybe an hour."

"An hour?" the bride fumed. "Are we supposed to have everyone standing around for an hour, doing nothing while they wait for dinner?"

"Let me make a proposal," Kristy said, using a tone I could only classify as her official wedding-planner voice. "Let's switch the bar from cash to open. An hour is about the time it takes for everyone to have two to three drinks."

The bride's eyes flared. Clearly, this was an expense she had not anticipated.

"No, no," Kristy said as she held up her hand. "The cost of the open bar is on me. We'll keep it open until the first course is served. That way, the guests won't even know we were running behind."

The bride shook her head, clearly upset. "Kristy, you promised that tonight was going to be perfect. This isn't perfect."

Without saying another word to us, the bride grabbed a couple of bridesmaids and loudly complained that the dinner would be late. They all patted her shoulder and told her it would be okay. Then everyone drifted to the bar and started ordering drinks.

Kristy also went to the bar and had a quick discussion with the staff about opening the service for the next hour. As she was walking back, she was met by the mother of the bride. After a brief discussion about the delay, we could see the bride's mother wasn't any happier than the bride.

When Kristy came back, she looked tired and discouraged.

"You wanted to know what sorts of things have been happening?" she asked. "Well, this is it. I know, without a doubt, the dining schedule was correctly set up. I called the business office here two weeks ago to double-check and everything was perfect. Somebody purposefully went in and changed things around."

"How much will you lose because of this?" I asked.

"At eight dollars a drink, this will run me around twenty-five hundred, maybe three thousand dollars."

"Ouch."

"At this point, it's not the money. It's my reputation. The bride is the daughter of one of the leading money managers here in town. Once they find out I've had another problem, word will spread."

"You said you worked with a woman named Maggie on the catering?" I asked.

"That's right, Maggie Simms. She's the scheduler here at the Barrington."

"Could she have something to do with the switch?"

"I don't think so. I've worked with her for years and we get along great. She's organized and efficient."

"Well, first thing tomorrow, I'll talk with her. Hopefully, this will open up an avenue for the investigation."

Kristy took off to make sure nothing else was going wrong. A few minutes later, Sophie came over to stand next to me. She'd been at the bar, having a conversation with a good-looking guy.

"What happened with the dinner?" she asked. "Both the bride and her mother are at the bar saying some nasty things about our client."

"The dinner was supposed to start at seven forty-five, but now it won't begin for another hour."

"Jeez, no wonder they're so pissed. What happened?"

"It looks like someone switched the times. I only hope nothing else goes wrong."

~~~~

The following day, I got up early, dressed in an outfit that would work for golf, and headed into the office. Knowing things would still be awkward with Lenny, I stopped along the way and got a box of doughnuts.

I'd made sure to get the cinnamon swirls Lenny liked and the chocolate creams with sprinkles for Sophie. Gina seldom ate doughnuts, but I'd gotten an assortment in case she was in the mood.

No one was in the back, so I took the box up to reception. As I suspected, Gina was sitting in one of the red leather chairs. Sophie was at her desk, sipping on a gas station coffee.

They were talking about the problems at the wedding. At the same time, Sophie absent-mindedly flipped through the Southern California Surfline reports on her tablet.

Sophie looked up and saw what I had in my hands. This brought a broad smile to her face.

"Oh my God," she said as she snatched the box of doughnuts and tried to make up her mind which one to have first. "I so need these today."

I looked over to see that the door to Lenny's office was shut. "Have
~~~~

either of you talked to him yet?" I asked. "How bad is he?"

Sophie shook her head. "He showed up about ten minutes ago. He's a mess. Fortunately, he's still in his sad phase. I don't even want to think about how bad it will be when Lenny starts to get pissy."

"We've got to do something," Gina said. "Have either of you come up with an idea?"

"Well, I was thinking," Sophie said. "Remember last spring when we worked on that assignment for Mistress McNasty? Remember how Lenny drooled all over her boots when she came in? Maybe he could date her for a while?"

"Um, I'm not sure he could afford her," I said. "Even for Lenny, that might be a stretch."

Not to mention, he'd be dating Johnny Scarpazzi's girlfriend.

"Still, that's not a bad idea," Gina said. "Even if Suzi's out of his league, there must be some sort of budget dominatrix out there. I bet Lenny won't be too particular about who he's with for the next couple of weeks. We just need someone to take his mind off Elle."

"I could ask Suzi if she has any friends who are looking for new clients," I said. "You never know."

"At this point, it's worth a shot," Gina said. "To be completely honest, Lenny is starting to get on my nerves."

~~~~

We chatted for the next twenty minutes about Lenny, Suzi Lu, and the wedding. Sophie ended up eating three doughnuts before she'd had enough.

Gina got up, saying she needed to take off and be productive. As soon as she went through the door to the back offices, Sophie stood up.

She walked over to the front window that looked onto the street.
~~~~

When she found what she was looking for, she motioned for me to come and join her.

"Take a look at this," Sophie said in a hushed voice.

"What is it?" I asked.

"See that white cargo van parked in front of Gilbert Ortega's gift shop?" she said as she pointed down the street.

"Yeah, what about it?"

"I've been seeing it on our block all week. They move it every couple of hours, but it's always the same van."

"How do you know it's the same van? All white vans pretty much look alike."

"This one has three little antennas sticking up on the roof near the front. Can you see them?"

"Sort of. It's a long way away. Do you think it has something to do with one of Lenny's cases?"

"Lenny? No, I'm thinking it's more like the Men in Black."

"Seriously? Are you starting to worry about using the secret software again?"

"Maybe. After all the crazy searches I've done for you over the past couple of months, I think I've ended up on their radar. I think they're monitoring me to see what else I've been up to."

"But you've been using the secret software for a year and a half. You've run all sorts of searches. Don't you think if they didn't like what you were doing, they'd just revoke your access?"

"I don't know how they'd react. I only hope they don't want to disappear me into one of their secret underground interrogation facilities."

"Why would they do that?"

"Who knows why? As far as I know, it could be illegal for me to even know the secret database exists."

"Wait a minute, the government installed the software on your computer so we could search out the bad guys. How could it be illegal for you to have it?"

"I just have a feeling," she said.

~~~~

I glanced at the clock and figured the Barrington would be open by now. I looked up the number and called Maggie Simms, the woman Kristy said was the event scheduler.

Maggie answered right away, and I let her know who I was and why I wanted to meet with her. She said she'd be in all day, and I could stop by anytime.

~~~~

I had some time before I needed to meet with Tony, so I drove up Scottsdale Road to the Barrington. I parked next to the business offices and went in.

A woman who I took to be Maggie Simms was on the phone. She was an efficient-looking woman, about sixty years old, with short dark hair and reading glasses hanging against her chest with a cord.

She was seated behind a desk that was covered with colorful folders. She held up a finger to let me know she'd be with me in a minute.

As I waited, I looked around her office. It was an ample space that had scheduling boards on three sides. On the wall closest to her desk was a panel that apparently represented the current month. Each day had a long, slotted tray with several colored three-by-five cards in it.

As Maggie talked, she typed information into a computer, then wrote on one of the colored three-by-five cards. A printer next to her desk started printing out what turned out to be five or six pages.

Maggie hung up, grabbed the papers from the printer, stapled them together, and placed them in a colored folder on her desk.

"Sorry about that," she said. "How can I help you?"

"I'm Laura Black," I said. "I'm working with Kristine Darby. We had a reception here last night and there was a mix-up on the time the caterer was supposed to serve dinner. I'm here to help find out how it happened."

"Sure," she said. "Kristy called and said you'd stop by. I already pulled the file and it's there on the desk."

I picked up the thick file folder that must have contained thirty or forty pages.

"Wow, I didn't know so much went into a reception. What's in here?"

"These are the work orders for the layout of the Classic reception hall. We break up each function into its own work order. It makes it easier to keep everything straight."

As she was talking, I flipped through the file. There was a work order for the table service. There was also one for the plate and silverware layout, one for the bar, and one for the cake table. As I glanced at the file, there were another ten or so bundles of paper in it.

"What about the caterers?" I asked.

"It's all in there," Maggie said. "Kristy used our house caterer. We don't allow outside services."

Maggie asked for the folder. When I gave it to her, she pulled out a bundle of ten pages, held together with a metal clip.

"Here's the paperwork for the catering," she said. "You were looking for the serving time?"

"That's right."

Maggie flipped a couple of pages back. "It's listed here at eight forty-five. From what Kristy told me this morning, it should have been an hour earlier."

"Do you remember anything about this?"

"Not this specific change, but it would have had to come directly from her. I keep an email folder for each wedding. I didn't see it in there, so I'm thinking she probably called."

"It seems for something major, like a change to the serving time, someone would remember."

Maggie shook her head. "I either talk with Kristy directly or get an email from her three or four times a week. She probably has a dozen weddings scheduled here over the next eighteen months."

"Would it seem unusual for her to make a change like that?"

Maggie started laughing. "I wish it was. But truthfully, most of what I do here are last-minute changes. The brides will reserve the venue two years in advance. Still, they wait until two weeks before the wedding to completely change their minds about everything. It's unusual if I don't have at least two or three changes for an event."

"When you talked to Kristy this morning, did she recall making the change?"

Maggie smiled and shook her head. "No, she didn't remember this specific change. It's a shame. Kristy was always one of the better planners we dealt with. But lately, her events always seem to go wrong."

"Do you have any idea why this is happening?"

"Maybe she's trying to do too many weddings. It's easy to mess things up when you're juggling a dozen events at once. Trust me, I know."

"As long as I'm here. Could I get a copy of the Henderson-Peckham wedding on New Year's Eve? Grandma Peckham's my next-door neighbor and she asked me to help her out with it."

"Sure," Maggie said. "I understand. I've been getting a lot of people asking about Kristy's events."

~~~~

I got in my car and drove the short distance to the Blue Palms. As I pulled into the resort's entrance, I realized it was the first time I'd been here since everything had happened with Major Malakov. It was hard to believe it had already been three weeks ago.

I usually wouldn't use valet, but in this case, I drove right to it. I was running a little behind and didn't want to make Tony wait. Besides, I knew they'd have my clubs and be able to get me squared away.

I waited in a line of cars for about a minute, then a man in a Blue Palms uniform opened my door. As I climbed out, he handed me a claim ticket.

Another uniformed man took my name, then walked with me to a waiting golf cart. I saw it held a bag of new Lady Pings in the back. Without a word, we headed out.

As we drove to Mulligan's Grille, I looked to see if I could spot any residual damage to the Kokopelli course from the thousands of people who'd been walking on it, only three weeks before.

But it looked as pristine as ever. As always, I was impressed with the level of care and maintenance that went into these courses.

As we pulled up to the front of the restaurant, the man removed the clubs from the cart and set them in a stand near the entrance. He told me to have a good round, then got in his cart and took off.

I walked into Mulligan's and looked around. There were about thirty-five people in the place, all drinking, eating, and talking loudly. Fortunately, Tony hadn't arrived yet.

I took one of the stools at the counter in front of the open-air grill. I then watched as a man in a white apron and chef's hat cooked
~~~~

burgers, chicken, and steaks. The meat was sizzling on a thick metal grate, inches above a smoking bed of red-hot coals. The grilling meat smelled scrumptious.

A waitress stopped by and I ordered a Diet Pepsi. Next to the bar in the back, a woman played an acoustic guitar on a small stage.

Sitting in the grille, listening to music, and waiting for Tony, brought back some memories. Almost a year ago, I'd waited here for a meeting with him. At the time, I was terrified. Since then, I've come to know him as a friend.

I'd been there about fifteen minutes when the chef's eyes opened wide and he suddenly became very busy. I didn't need to look. I knew Tony had come into the grille.

I walked over and gave him a hug. "Laura Black," he said in his low, gruff voice. "It's good to see you again."

"I didn't know you were back to golfing," I said. "How long have you been going out?"

"I've been to the driving range several times, but this is the first time I've attempted to play a course. To be completely honest, the results have been mixed. Are you ready to head out?"

Chapter Five

We walked out to where the carts were waiting. One of the guys had already placed the set of Lady Pings in the back of Tony's red six-person cart.

Today, it was driven by Carson, a man I'd worked with when I'd recently stayed at the resort. He looked my way and acknowledged me with a nod.

"Hey, Carson," I said as I waved. "It's good to see you again. Thanks again for all the help you gave me a few weeks ago. I really do appreciate it."

His face turned a little pink when I praised him in front of Tony. "No problem, ma'am," he said in a flat voice. "Just doing my job."

Instead of the usual big green cart with the rest of the security detail, only a standard two-person cart was waiting behind us. There was only one man in it.

I'd seen him around before but had no idea what his name was. The lack of a proper security force around Tony struck me as a bit odd.

"How are you doing?" I asked as we took our seats in the back of the big red cart. "Every time I see you, it seems like you're walking better."

"That I am. The effects of the shooting are slowly dissipating. Of course, something like this will always leave a permanent scar. I fear I'll never be completely back to my old self, physically, that is."

"You've come a long way from where you started."

"That's true. However, as you'll soon see, I'm forced to rely on a cart for golfing, at least for the time being. I may have told you this before, but I believe the proper way to experience a golf course is to walk it."

"You did. You've said it's the only way to get a feel for whether or not they're keeping up with the maintenance."

"That, and you're able to get the overall impression of the hole. You can discover little features you'd likely miss if you drove by in a cart. Walking down a long fairway after a great shot can be an emotional experience."

"I'm glad you're able to get out again. Has it affected your game?"

Tony laughed. "As a matter of fact, it's thrown it all to hell. It's difficult to make a proper swing with a stiff back. But I'm gradually adjusting to the realities of my physical condition."

"At least you're golfing again. It's better than what could have happened. When Carlos shot you, I'd pretty much assumed you were dead."

"I won't say those fears were unjustified. As I've told you, at the time, I also feared the worst."

We reached the tenth hole on the Kokopelli course, a long par five with a slight dogleg left, hiding the pin from us. We each pulled out a driver and walked to the tee boxes.

"Why don't you choose a box and have honors," Tony said.

"Are you still hitting from the third one back?" I asked.

"Perhaps I'm a little optimistic, but it's the same tee box I've played ever since I built the course. I'm comfortable with it, even though my drives are now considerably shorter.

"Then it's okay. The third box will work for me as well."

I placed a ball on a tee and got ready to hit. I remembered when I'd hit my first shot here in front of Tony, Max, and Gabriella. At the time, I'd been more worried about them looking at my ass than about hitting the ball.

Somehow, playing with Tony today wasn't making me nervous at all. My bigger worry was simply trying not to embarrass myself with my rusty golf skills.

I hit the ball and my swing felt okay. The ball flew straight, but the distance was disappointing. For a moment, I felt a pang of guilt for not keeping up with my game.

Tony then set up his ball and hit a shot that was also straight but only went about seventy yards farther than mine. This was close to fifty yards shorter than what he'd hit earlier in the year.

Tony shook his head. "As I told you, my drives have gone to hell."

We climbed into the cart and took off. One feature that seems a little unusual about the courses at Tony's resorts is that carts aren't allowed on the grass of the fairway. The cart paths have raised concrete shoulders to remind golfers of that fact.

Carson stopped even with my ball. I grabbed a three wood and was able to hit a decent shot off the fairway. It landed short, but got a good bounce and rolled to within a hundred yards of the green.

Tony's shot again flew straight, but it was easy to tell his swing speed was way down. His ball stopped a good fifty yards from the pin.

As we got in the cart and started cruising toward our balls, I saw the spot where I'd almost been hit when I'd foolishly run across the fairway. This had happened during the pro tournament, three weeks earlier.

Unfortunately, I'd tried to cross just as one of the golfers had hit a solid drive. Luckily, the ball missed me, but I could still hear the *whizzing* sound the ball made as it sped by, inches from my head.

Tony chipped up to the near-side fringe of the green and two-putted for a par. I hit a poor shot into the sand trap, chipped out, then three-putted for a double bogey.

The eleventh hole was a straight par four with the pin in the back of the green. People were still putting, so we stood at the tee box and waited for them to finish.

"From what I understand," Tony said, "you and Max are still getting along well."

"So far, so good."

"I don't know how much he's explained about what's going on with the business. But in case you haven't gathered in the full picture yet, I'll fill in some of the details."

"That would be great. Max has only given me the abridged version so far."

"One of the reasons I delayed the handover to Max was my injury, of course. I needed to show the change of leadership was not made from a position of weakness, but as part of a well thought out succession plan."

"That makes sense. Max did explain that part to me."

"I know the delay might have seemed to be indecision on my part. Unfortunately, that couldn't be helped. The more important reason for the delay was to begin preparations for the split."

"What split?"

"Ah, I see Max hasn't completely filled you in yet." Tony let out a small chuckle. "One of the things I appreciate most about Max is his ability not to leak information."

"You were talking about the split?"

"Yes, and we talked a little about this last month. When I first came out to Arizona, I had our lawyers set up the company to separate the two sides of the business. By doing so, it became much harder for the authorities to prosecute the resort side of the company."

"Right. You said your goal was to eventually sever the connections between the two sides completely."

"And that's exactly what I've been doing. Now, with Max taking over as head of the resorts, the separation process has started."

"Are you getting rid of the other side? Like selling it or something?"

"No, it's still a strong business. But it's time to let it go its own way without being tied down to the resorts."

"Are you still going to lead that part of it?"

"What I told you about retiring is completely true. I'll be out of things, other than as an informal advisor."

"Then who'll take that part over? Are you bringing in someone new?"

"Not at all. Once the split finalizes, Johnny will lead that side."

"I thought he didn't want the position?"

"What he didn't want was to run the resort side of things. Johnny always thought the resorts needed to be led by someone who had a better public presence than he thinks he has."

"I never thought Johnny would be bad at running the resorts," I said. "Everybody respects him and he knows what he's doing."

"Johnny's told me more than once that the resorts need a marketing promotor to run them. His choice for that has always been Max."

"Tony, why are you telling me this? I know you've kept me at arm's length about that side of the business, and honestly, I'm grateful. The less I know, the better off I'll be."

"It's because this will start to affect your relationship with Max. As word gets around that the resorts are no longer part of the other side of what we do, it will give Max a certain amount of freedom to act more openly in public."

"I've already noticed that. We went out to dinner in the open this week. Do you think the police will stop looking into him?"

"Over time, I believe so. Once it's clear the resorts are no longer involved, the police will start to look elsewhere. They'll always find more glory in trying to stop something ongoing, rather than something that happened in the past."

"That would be wonderful."

"What you always have to keep in mind is Scottsdale's economy and real estate markets are built around the golf resorts. Look at a map of the city sometime and you'll see what I mean. It wouldn't be in the city's interests to have any of them tainted or shut down."

As I listened to Tony, what he was saying started to sink in. With Max gradually giving up control of the criminal enterprise, the pressure should start to ease up. It might never completely go away, but perhaps this would give us a chance to act like regular people for a change.

"Tony, that's great news. It's probably the best news I've had all year."

The foursome ahead of us finished putting and walked off the green. Tony had honors and again shot straight but ended up about a hundred and fifty yards short of the green. He seemed to accept his new swing with a shake of his head.

I stepped up and tried to add some power to my swing. The ball went further than on my first drive, but I ended up hooking it and the ball rolled into the rough.

We got into the cart and Carson took off. I looked behind us to see the man in the second cart following us.

"It seems a little strange to see you golfing without Gabriella watching over you," I said.

"These men are mainly here to prevent me from being harassed by people who may wish to confront me. I will admit, it does feel a little strange not having Gabriella, or at least Johnny, as my bodyguard, but it's not entirely unpleasant."

"How so?"

"Now that I've retired, my need for security has gone down a notch. It's given me a certain freedom of movement I previously did not have."

My shot from the rough was only okay and my ball rolled to the fringe of the green. Tony's shot looked beautiful, but the ball fell straight down and landed without rolling, five yards short of the green.

He let out a sigh. "I went down a club to compensate for my new swing. It looks like I may need to go down another."

Tony chipped on and two-putted for bogey. I three-putted and also scored a bogey.

The twelfth hole was a short par three with a sand trap guarding the green. As with the last time I'd played here, my goal was to get the ball over the trap without it sailing too far over the green.

Tony's swing was good and he chose the right club. His ball arched high into the air and landed to the right of the pin. It rolled five feet, then came to a stop.

I hit and my swing felt terrific. The ball flew high in the sky and landed with a plop on the green's left side. It rolled about ten feet and stopped, no more than twenty feet from the pin.

"Wow," I said. "That felt great."

"You made a nice shot. I think your mind was elsewhere and you weren't trying too hard. Your natural swing was able to emerge."

We put the clubs in the bags then pulled out our putters. He told Carson we would walk the hole. Carson took off and we started toward the green.

"Tony, a few months ago, I asked why you didn't switch to running resorts full time and get out of the other businesses. You said you needed the other side to protect the resorts. Did something change?

"That's a fair question, and truth be told, it was your question that got me thinking more about it. In the old days, the resorts absolutely needed the protection of the other side. However, as Carlos showed us, it's the other side that is now the more vulnerable."

"Are you talking about competition from the cartels?"

"Yes, but it's not only the cartels. Society itself is changing."

"What do you mean?"

"Twenty years ago, we were the only place a serious gambler could go for a fair game. Now there are ten casinos within an hour's drive from here. We provide management and security for many of them, but it's in no way the same business."

"But the rest is doing okay?"

"It used to be we had good business in the soft drug trade. It was all used for recreation and the authorities would often turn a blind eye. Now, half the states have legalized the drugs that made up our business. The widespread availability has caused prices everywhere to crash."

"How can you respond to something like that?"

"The cartels have moved into importing heroin and fentanyl. The margins are still good since only a few states have decriminalized those, at least so far. The downside is those drugs are for more than pure recreation. They cause death and misery. It's why I've always resisted going in that direction. Besides, you have some firsthand experience at how eager the authorities are to stop that trade, at least in Arizona."

"I can understand why they want to crack down on those. But what about the ones in the middle? Like diet pills, painkillers, and sleeping pills. Those sorts of things."

"We've found narcotics to be a tough market for the past six or seven years. Street prices have remained very low. We suspect there is a separate source feeding these pills into Arizona."

"You make it sound like it's all become a no-win business."

"Not all is lost. There's still good money to be made off people's vices. But yes, times have definitely changed."

When we got to the green, Tony was away and two-putted for par. I lined up my shot and had visions of a birdie.

I gave it a solid stroke with the putter and it arched towards the hole, nicely breaking with the grain of the grass. Unfortunately, it stopped less than six inches before landing in the cup.

Tony shook his head and shared my pain. "Golf can indeed be a frustrating game," he said. "But every once in a while, you'll make the most beautiful shot. It's the search for the perfect shot that always keeps me coming back."

We drove toward the tee boxes for the thirteenth hole and got a welcome surprise. Johnny was waiting for Tony in the back of the big green cart. Even more of a surprise, Gabriella was driving. Two more unfamiliar goons sat in a separate cart, maybe twenty yards away.

"I didn't expect to see Johnny and Gabriella here today," I said as we drove to the boxes."

"Johnny and I will play the rest of the round together. He's been brushing up on his game. He wasn't overly eager at first, but I reminded him that no one can run a serious business in Scottsdale without being at least competent on the golf course."

"And Gabriella's his bodyguard?"

"Who else? For the time being, she'll split her duties between Max and Johnny. But, as we move forward with the split, Max won't need anyone like her. She has unique skills that will be valuable to Johnny's organization going forward."

Seeing Tony come around the corner, Johnny got out of the cart and walked over to the tee box. Once we stopped, I got out of the cart, walked over to the big man, and gave him a hug.

"Congratulations on the new position," I said. "I think I've gotten to know you pretty well since the first time at Junior Baker's Blues Club. I know you'll do great."

"Thank you," he said. "I'll admit, it still feels a little strange. It will be a long transition, but overall, it's a welcome change."

The foursome playing ahead of us were still on the green. Tony started talking business with Johnny, so I walked over to where Gabriella was sitting in the cart.

As always, her eyes were scanning the area. Her black Ferrucci Spy bag was on the seat next to her.

"I see you'll be getting a new job as well. Congratulations."

"Thank you," she said. "Is not so much new job, but new boss. It's okay. I like Johnny and I protect him."

"Once they complete the split of the company, it doesn't sound like we'll be seeing each other as much."

"Maybe not as much, but we will still see each other. Max and I have known each other for years. I no let him get too far out of my sight. But I no worry, he now has you to keep track of him."

I dropped my voice a little, even though the other men were too far away to hear. "Have you heard anything more about the guy Major Malakov talked about? Viktor?"

"Viktor Pyotrovich Glazkov," Gabriella said. As she mentioned the name, her face seemed to harden and a look of determination came into her eyes. "He will be problem."

"How can I help?"

"Unless you can tell me where he is currently living, there is nothing you can do. I have been putting off this day for many years. But it's okay. I knew I would need to take care of him someday."

"Will Max be able to help?"

Gabriella smiled. It was one of the few times I'd seen it happen. It softened her face and she became absolutely gorgeous.

"Max has offered several times to go with me and hunt Viktor. He is good man and I know his offer is honest. But Viktor is my problem. I will take care of him as soon as I am able."

"You don't think he'll send someone out here first?"

"No, that is not his method. He will spend many months gathering information on me and planning, the same as I will."

Tony came back to where Gabriella and I were chatting.

"Laura Black," he said as he put his hand on my shoulder. "It's been an enjoyable three holes. Now that I'll have more free time, we'll need to plan a full round together sometime soon."

"I'd love that, Tony. Call me anytime."

A little way down the path, a man in a Blue Palms uniform waited for me in a cart. He transferred my clubs to his vehicle and then drove me back to the golf valet.

~~~~

Since I was too late to follow Michael Palmer from the hospital, I parked down the street from the townhouse and waited. At about twelve forty-five, he came down the road and pulled into his driveway.
~~~~

He's right on time.

He got out of his car and unlocked the front door. Once he was safely inside, I made myself comfortable.

After about ten minutes, I called Sophie.

"How was golf with Tough Tony?" she asked.

"It wasn't bad. My game is terrible, but it was nice to be able to talk with him. I also got a chance to talk with Gabriella."

"How's she doing?"

"She's good. But that's what I wanted to ask you about. Would you use the secret software to do a deep dive on someone?"

She let out a long sigh. "Fine. Who is it?"

"The name is Viktor Pyotrovich Glazkov."

"Jeez, you'll have to send me a text. There're too many consonants for me to spell it correctly. Isn't this the assassin guy who's after Gabriella?"

"Yes, and before you ask, I'm definitely not getting involved with someone as crazy as that. Still, I thought maybe we could give her any information the secret software has on him."

"There's a white van parked down the street, filled with government agents, and you want me to start running searches on terrorists?"

"Is he any worse than Carlos the Butcher? We did a search on him and it didn't seem to stress you out."

"Not worse, but maybe different."

"I think you're worrying too much. If they don't want you to know about stuff like this, I'm pretty sure they'll just pull your access."

"Well, maybe. I'll punch it in and hope for the best. I'll let you know if anything comes back."

~~~~

I sat outside the townhouse and continued to wait. At one-thirty, the blonde was still a no-show. At two o'clock, she still hadn't arrived.

As long as I wasn't doing anything, I decided to take Gina's advice and call Kristy's husband. I figured if anyone would know what was going on, it would probably be him.

I didn't want to talk with him at the house, since Kristy might be there. I knew I couldn't get honest answers if she was with us. I looked up Andrew Darby's office number and called to make an appointment.

I was connected with Julie, a pleasant-sounding woman who was his admin. She apparently knew who I was and connected me right away.

"Mr. Darby? I'm Laura Black and I've been looking into the mishaps with your wife's business. Would you mind if I stopped by your office and spoke with you about it?"

"Not at all," he said. "Kristine's been telling me about you. I'm glad she has someone to help straighten things out. Would tomorrow morning at ten-thirty work?"

"Sounds good. I'll see you then."

I disconnected, then punched in the number for Suzi Lu. The phone rolled over to voicemail. This didn't surprise me since I knew she split her time between being a professor of computer science at ASU and being the professional dominatrix, Mistress McNasty. I left a message for her to call me.

~~~~

A little before three, Doctor Palmer came out the front door, then turned and locked it. He quickly got into his car and pulled out of the driveway. I was a little too far away to know for sure, but I think he looked annoyed.

I pulled out of my space and followed at a discrete distance. I didn't think he'd be looking for a tail, but I tried not to be too obvious about it.

I'd been hoping Michael and the blonde might have some alternate place where they would meet for the afternoon. If they did, I'd see if I could plant cameras there as well. But he only drove north on Hayden Road and headed straight to the hospital.

I sat in my car and looked out over the parking lot. The place was a constant buzz of activity, but Doctor Palmer stayed in the hospital.

Chapter Six

I sat in the parking lot for another twenty minutes, but it soon became obvious Michael Palmer wasn't going to be meeting with anyone for sex. I drove back to the office and logged into my computer. I quickly scanned the video files that had accumulated since the day before.

I first established that no one had used the bedroom the previous night to sleep in. This confirmed my belief that the townhouse was nothing more than a meeting place for the blonde.

When I scanned the files from earlier in the morning, I saw the blond had been there again, with yet another man. They arrived a little after nine and were gone by eleven forty-five.

This man liked to take a more active role than Doctor Elmaghrabi had. They must have changed to a new love position at least a dozen times during the forty-five minutes they were active on the bed. It was like watching a sex instruction video.

Damn.

I took a couple of non-compromising screenshots of the new guy, but he didn't look familiar. I deleted the videos of the new guy with the blonde and made my notation in the logbook. I then went through the videos of Michael Palmer.

He'd spent most of his time sitting on the bed playing with his phone. After about half an hour had passed, he disappeared, only to reappear five minutes later, holding a glass of wine.

After a second glass of wine, he started to get annoyed and began to pace around the room, often stopping to glance out the window. After two hours, he took off.

Feeling a little discouraged and annoyed, I went up to reception. Gina was already gone for the evening, but Sophie was sitting at her desk, typing something into her computer.

"How's Lenny been?" I asked.

"About an hour ago, he came out. I think he'd been in his office crying. He bitched at me for about ten minutes, then went back into his office. But he was out here again a few minutes ago, and he's back to being his usual cranky self."

"I left a message for Suzi to call me. Hopefully, she can give us a referral or at least some advice. Lenny is pretty easily distracted, and I think something like that would help smooth things over."

"What did you find out about the mix-up on the time last night?"

"I talked to Maggie, the scheduler at the Barrington. She all but came out and said Kristy was the one who made the change."

"Did she say if it was a phone call or email?"

"She didn't remember, but she thinks it must have been a phone call. It would have helped to know which it was."

"Do you think it was the scheduler who did it to sabotage the wedding? Maybe she's pissed off at Kristy about something?"

"I don't think so. It would only make her job harder. Besides, the Barrington isn't the only place where Kristy's weddings have gotten messed up."

"Well, what do you think? Did our client do it, then forget? If that's the case, there isn't a lot we can do to fix that. Maybe she should start taking Ginkgo Biloba? My grandmother took that for years, and she always said it helped her remember our names."

"I don't know what the problem is. At least not yet. I'll need to get some more information."

"Wouldn't it be hilarious if Kristy scheduled two weddings at the same place at the same time?"

"How would that be funny?"

"Oh, for the brides, it would be a disaster. But if you were going as a guest, it would be a lot of fun to watch everyone run around and try to straighten things out. It's always entertaining to watch as a bride completely loses it."

"Remind me not to let you plan any of my parties."

"That's probably a good idea. I'd be too tempted to have fun with the arrangements. When's the next wedding?"

"It's Saturday night over at the Tropical Paradise. There's a break for Christmas, then the next one is Tuesday at the Saguaro Sky."

"Well, you'd better figure out what's happening soon. Otherwise, your neighbor's wedding is going to be a disaster."

"You don't want to see Grandma Peckham lose it?"

"No, I like her. My fingers are crossed you can solve this before things go completely to hell." She then looked at me. Is anything else wrong? It looks like someone kicked your puppy."

"The blonde didn't make it to her appointment with Michael Palmer this afternoon," I said. "He came to the townhouse right on time, but she was a no-show."

"That's not good. If they don't get together again, we don't have any evidence. Has she been over there with anyone else since yesterday afternoon?"

"Yeah, she was with a new one this morning."

“Any idea who it was?”

“Not a clue,” I said as I handed her the screenshot.

Sophie looked at it for a few seconds before shaking her head and handing it back. “No idea,” she said.

“Next time I’m there, I’ll install a camera outside the house. Then we can keep track of who comes and goes.”

“If she was already with someone this morning, maybe she didn’t want anyone else this afternoon?” Sophie mused. “Or maybe she was too tired and couldn’t keep the appointment? After all of the men she’s had, I bet she’s starting to get sore.”

“She didn’t look tired or sore in the video,” I said. “Plus, for an operation like hers to work, she’d need to keep to a strict schedule. Michael Palmer has her on Tuesday and Thursday afternoons. Doctor Montoya has her Wednesday mornings and Doctor Elmaghrabi seems to be Wednesday afternoons. Now we have a new guy on Thursday mornings.”

“I can’t even try to say Elmaghrabi,” Sophie said, again fumbling the name. “I’ll just call him Doctor Sloppy Seconds.”

“That’s so gross,” I groaned. “And we still don’t know how many men she has over during the week.”

“Well, she’s had five sessions over there since Tuesday morning. And you said it looked like she was supposed to have one more today with Michael. It wouldn’t surprise me if she also has men over on Monday and Friday. Who knows, maybe there’s a big gang bang on the weekend.”

“I was thinking, all the other guys she’s been with are doctors at the hospital. Maybe this new one is too? Do they have any sort of listing of who works there, maybe with pictures?”

“The website only has pictures of the top people, but if she keeps to her habit of only being with senior management, we might get lucky."

Sophie typed into her computer for a few seconds and the executive management page for the hospital popped up. A dozen men and a handful of women were listed. Everyone was wearing a suit or something equally as nice.

"There's Doctor Montoya. He's near the top, and here's Sloppy Seconds," Sophie said as she pointed to the monitor.

"Where's Michael Palmer?"

"He's at the bottom," Sophie said as she scrolled down. "He's only the head of surgery. That sounds pretty impressive, but in the big scheme of the hospital, I guess he's only a cog in the machine."

"Hold on," I said as something caught my eye. "Scroll back up."

As Sophie moved halfway up the page, we both saw the picture of a smiling man in a navy suit with a red tie.

"What do you think?" I asked as I handed the screenshot picture to Sophie again.

She looked at the man on the computer screen, then back at the picture in her hand.

"It sure does look like him."

I looked at the caption below the picture on the monitor. "Henry Burnham, Chief Financial Officer."

"He's not a doctor?" Sophie asked as she looked at his qualifications.

"I guess you don't have to be if you're the one in charge of the money."

"Damn, it looks like our blonde girl is nailing about half of the executive staff over there. I wonder if the men know about each other?"

"You'd think it would be pretty obvious," I said. "But men can be pretty dense when it comes to things like that. If she tells each one the townhouse is her private sex crib, and she's only using it for them, how would they know the difference?"

"And so far, we only know about the men she has Tuesday through Thursday."

"Yes, and it doesn't seem right. I mean, the whole thing seems creepy, but it's weird how she keeps the top guys from the hospital rotating through her bedroom."

The door to Lenny's office opened and I saw Sophie tense. Lenny came out and dropped several files on her desk.

"I'm done with these," he said. "Make sure to put them away this time. The place is still a mess."

"Hey," she said, "do you see how much cleaner the office has been over the past month? I've gotten a lot of the files put away. What we need is someone to come in here and take care of stuff like this."

Lenny sniffed, ignoring Sophie's comments. "Since Christmas Eve is on Saturday and Christmas is on Sunday, that shouldn't affect either tomorrow or Monday, right? I hope you're both planning on being here and not wanting any extra time off."

I envisioned Lenny as Ebenezer Scrooge, telling Bob Cratchit not to waste money on coal to heat the office.

Sophie shrugged. "I'm not going anywhere this year. I'll be here tomorrow, Monday too."

Lenny looked at me. "I'll be in town," I said. "I have a wedding to go to on Christmas Eve for the Kristy Darby assignment. That's about it."

"Good," he said. "This is our busy time of year. I want everyone to be available. Make sure Gina knows as well."

"Jeez, who schedules a wedding on Christmas Eve?" Sophie asked. "It would serve her right if no one showed up."

"Where are you with getting the video for the Jessica Palmer assignment?" Lenny asked, still ignoring Sophie. "Other cases are starting to come in and I'm going to need you to wrap this one up as soon as possible."

"The blonde is sleeping with half of the executive staff over at Scottsdale General," I said. "I can't see that as something random. What with the other cameras in the room, she may be blackmailing them."

"I don't care," Lenny said. "Don't worry about it."

"But if all of these doctors are being blackmailed, it has to mean something."

"We aren't getting paid to look into a blackmail ring. Don't waste your time on it."

"You don't care that it looks like someone's running a major sex and blackmail operation against the top people at one of the largest hospitals in the city?"

"I could care less. Maybe if you happen to come across something concrete, we can use it in the divorce trial. It could explain why Michael Palmer has been so moody the past few months. But don't make this into anything bigger than gathering evidence of our client's husband's infidelity. Got it?"

Lenny then turned and went back to his office, firmly closing the door behind him.

Sophie looked up at me. "We've got to find Lenny a new girlfriend. I don't know how much longer I can stand being in the office with him like this."

"I'm waiting for a call back from Suzi," I said. "I'm hoping she can help. Are you planning on doing anything tonight?"

"A couple of the girls are planning on going out later. I might tag along for a couple of hours. After the week I've had dealing with

Lenny, I could use some handsome men buying me drinks and telling me how amazing I am."

"Do you want to grab dinner first? Down the street for tacos would work for me."

"That sounds perfect," she said. "Let me turn off the computer."

~~~~

I woke up early the following day and stretched. As soon as Marlowe heard me stir, he got up and began to purr, nudging me with his soft face.

Knowing I wouldn't be able to go back to sleep, I went into the kitchen and fed my starving cat. I then made myself a pot of coffee and found I still had half a bag of little powdered donuts sitting on the counter.

Bag in hand, I went to the couch and flipped on the local news. Marlowe quickly finished his breakfast and came over to watch me eat.

His head swiveled back and forth as I took each donut out of the bag and ate it. In less than an hour, both the bag and the pot were empty.

I got dressed but didn't feel like doing anything with my hair, so I put it up in a ponytail. Looking at myself in the mirror, I'd decided to swipe on some eye makeup.

~~~~

I made it to the office a little before eight and walked to the front. Lenny wasn't in yet, but Gina was in reception, talking with Sophie.

"Good morning," I said.

"What's so good about it?" Sophie moaned. Judging by the circles under her eyes, it looked like she was nursing a hangover.

"How late were you out last night?" I asked.

"Only until about twelve-thirty. But I used an Uber, so I wasn't too worried about how many drinks I was having. It's going to take me a couple of hours to feel like myself again."

"Sophie was telling me about your assignment," Gina said. "It's strange how the blonde disappeared. From what I understand, she seems to be a rather highly paid escort."

"If she's the one who's arranged everything, she must be making a mint," Sophie said, sipping a big doughnut-shop coffee. "Even if there's some sort of middleman involved, I bet she still takes home three or four thousand a week."

"You're probably right," I pondered. "I really need to find a better job."

"Could she be the one blackmailing the doctors?" Sophie asked. "If those are her cameras, she'd have plenty of evidence by now. Maybe she's done and decided to move on?"

"If they're being blackmailed," Gina said, "I don't think she's the one doing it. She may not even know about it."

"If she doesn't know about it, what is she doing there?" Sophie asked. "Well, other than making a ton of money."

"The people in charge may only be gathering evidence to keep the men quiet about something," Gina said. "As in, 'behave, or we'll release the evidence we have on you.' But I would guess they haven't sprung the blackmail threat yet."

"Why do you say that?" I asked.

"Once blackmail is threatened, the men will usually stop voluntarily providing additional evidence. Going to the townhouse to visit the blonde wouldn't be nearly as much fun if you knew several people were watching you."

"Why are you here today?" Sophie asked me. "I thought you'd be back at the townhouse before the first guy showed up."

"I'm heading over there in a few minutes," I said. "I'm also meeting with Kristy's husband at ten-thirty. But I first wanted to review the video files to see if anyone was using the townhouse last night."

"Good luck today," Gina said. "Call if you need anything."

"You can call me too," Sophie said. "But not until after lunch. If Lenny doesn't show up, I'll be taking a quick power nap."

"Power nap?" Gina asked. "Is that really a thing?"

"Yeah," Sophie said. "I read on the internet that lots of CEOs take power naps to help them focus. Besides, if you call it a power nap, it makes it sound like you're doing it for the good of the company and not because you're sleeping off a hangover."

~~~~

I went back to my cubicle and turned on the computer. I quickly scanned through the videos, but it was soon obvious no one had been in the townhouse since Michael Palmer had left, yesterday afternoon.

If the blonde followed her usual pattern, she'd have the first guy of the day over at the townhouse sometime around nine. I wanted to get there early enough to see the face of whoever went in with her.

~~~~

I made it to my familiar parking space at eight forty-five. Fortunately, the white BMW roadster hadn't arrived yet.

I sat in my car and waited. Ten minutes later, the black Mercedes of Doctor Manuel Montoya pulled into the driveway.

The doctor sat in his car for about twenty minutes, then got out and tried the front door. Finding it locked, he returned to his vehicle.

~~~~

As I sat in my car and waited for something to happen, Sophie called.
~~~~

"Hey," she said, "I was curious if our blonde girl is with a new guy today or if she's with one of her regulars."

"Well, it's Doctor Montoya this morning. But he's still sitting in his car in the driveway, waiting for her. He's been there for over half an hour."

"She's a no-show again today?"

"It looks like it."

"That's no way for her to run a business. She'll lose clients if she keeps this up."

"I thought you were taking a power nap this morning?"

"I was going to, but Lenny came in. Fortunately, he has a hearing at ten-thirty. I think I can stay awake until then. Oh, I got the report back on that name you gave me. That Viktor Glazkov guy."

"That was quick. It usually takes at least a full day for a deep dive."

"I know. It was freaky fast."

"And?"

"And it was a whole lot of nothing."

"There can't be nothing. What did it say?"

"All it said is that he was an industrialist from the Crimean region in the country of Ukraine. According to the software, he's retired and living somewhere on the Black Sea, exact location unknown."

"That's it?"

"I put the printout on your desk. But seriously, the entire report is only a few paragraphs.

"I figured there'd be more. According to Max, this guy was a big-time terrorist and Gabriella spent months trying to take apart his organization."

"Don't blame me. All I do is type it in."

"Well, I do appreciate it. Good luck getting your nap in."

I disconnected with Sophie and watched the doctor sit in his car. I wondered how long he'd wait before he realized the blonde wouldn't show up. My phone buzzed with an unknown Scottsdale number.

"Hello," I said when I answered.

"Miss Black?"

"Kristy?" I asked.

"No," the woman said with a laugh. "This is Julie, Mr. Darby's admin. He's running a little late this morning. He wanted to know if you could meet with him at eleven rather than ten-thirty."

"Oh, sure. It looks like my morning will be completely open. Let him know I'll see him then."

After Doctor Montoya had sat in the driveway for another half an hour, he seemed to reach his limit. He started his car and took off.

~ ~ ~ ~

I drove over to Andrew Darby's office and arrived just before eleven. It was located at El Dorado Square, a high-end business park on Scottsdale Road and Lincoln Drive.

When I pulled into the parking lot, I scanned the map to find the business. From what I could see, Darby Capital Management, LLC, took up the entire top floor of a two-story building.

After parking, I walked up the stairs of the correct building, then walked along the balcony until I found the reception lobby. I told the woman at the desk who I was, and she buzzed Andrew's admin.

After a minute, a pretty woman about thirty-five years of age came out. She introduced herself as Julie and led me to Andrew's office.

As Andrew stood and walked around his desk, he had the bright smile and intelligent eyes that I've come to associate with successful Scottsdale entrepreneurs. I was somewhat surprised when it appeared Andrew was in his mid-forties, approximately fifteen years older than Kristy.

Julie left, and I took a seat in front of Andrew's desk.

"I'm glad you're helping Kristine find out what's going on," he said. "She puts so much of her time and energy into the business. She's beyond frustrated with all of the problems that have come up."

"Your wife's been a wedding planner for about nine years?" I asked.

"Eight or nine. It started out merely as a way to help her friends while Kristine was in college. She's always fancied herself as a party planner. It's steadily grown since then."

"From what Kristy told me, you think she works too hard."

"I do think that. She seldom has a chance to relax. Her business takes up most of her time. She not only works during the day, but nights and weekends as well."

"Do you have any idea what's going on?"

"I wish I did. Kristine thinks someone's purposefully doing this to her. But if so, they're doing it in a very untraceable way."

"What do you think?"

"Kristine always has fifteen or twenty weddings going on at once. Each wedding is a dynamic puzzle of thirty or forty pieces that all need to fit together exactly. It would be understandable if she occasionally makes a mistake along the way."

"Have you told her that?"

"Not in those words. What I've suggested is that she cut back to one or two weddings a month. If it goes back to being a fun hobby, I think a lot of these problems will smooth themselves out."

"Well, until I can prove otherwise, I'm going on the assumption someone is actively sabotaging her."

"I understand. Let me know how I can support you. Julie also knows about the problem. If you need to get ahold of me, go through her. She has my schedule and will set up an appointment."

~~~~

After a quick lunch, I again drove by the townhouse. By now, I was starting to worry about the blonde.

Although I knew nothing about her, it seemed sort of strange how she hadn't shown up for her dates. Plus, after discussing the possibility of blackmail, I wondered if she really could be the mastermind behind it all or if she was only another victim.

Unfortunately, when I drove past the townhouse, it again appeared to be empty. I wondered if there'd be anything inside that would shed light on what was happening.

On impulse, I parked and grabbed my lockpicks. Throwing caution to the wind, I put on my baseball cap but left my clipboard in the car.

I again went around to the back of the townhouse and worked on the lock. Since this was the second time I'd picked it, I was able to pop it open within four or five minutes.

A quick look showed nothing had changed in the empty kitchen or living room. I climbed the stairs and went into the master bedroom.

At first glance, everything was the same as I had left it. The stench of the blonde's perfume was still mixed with the scent of a dozen different beauty products.

But this time, the room had a dead and unused feeling. For some reason, I felt it more here than in the rest of the house.

I checked my cameras and they were all still in place. On a hunch, I searched where I'd seen the other cameras a few days before, but they were gone.
~~~~

A cold and creepy feeling swept over me. I'd assumed the people who monitored the other cameras would only view them when the blonde was in the room with the men. But since they'd cleaned out the place, they must have seen me as I'd installed my own tiny spy cameras.

Damn.

If the blonde knew someone else was taking videos of her, it could explain why she took off. Unfortunately, it would likely take some time for her to establish a new love nest.

Since I still didn't have any hard evidence of Michael being unfaithful, I'd need to go back to following him from the hospital. Hopefully, he'd continue his pattern of seeing the blonde every Tuesday and Thursday afternoon, even if they had to meet somewhere new.

Jeez, I can already hear the lecture I'm going to get from Lenny over this.

My mind worked on the problem as I used my visit to replace the batteries in the cameras with fresh ones. It was unlikely the blonde would be back anytime soon, but I didn't want to waste the opportunity.

By now, I was getting good at changing the tiny cells. In less than ten minutes, I'd completed the switch in the three cameras that ran on batteries.

As I checked to make sure the cameras were still pointing in the right directions, I heard the sound of the front door opening.

Great, now she shows up.

Since the stairs were the only way out, I knew what I had to do. Letting out a sigh of frustration at once again having to hide, I quickly walked across the hallway to the spare bedroom.

Once inside, I quietly closed the door to within an inch or so of latching. The room was completely unfurnished and I knew I'd be sitting on the floor for the next three hours. I wasn't looking forward to it.

I heard the sound of footsteps coming up the stairs. One person at first, but they were soon joined by another.

I guess the guy is here as well. I wonder which one it is this time?

The footsteps reached the top of the stairs, then went into the master bedroom.

The sound I heard next set off warning bells. It sounded like a third person was coming up the stairs.

Could somebody be following the blonde?

My hand drifted down and I quietly began to unzip my shoulder bag. The rest of my body froze as I listened.

I heard the new footsteps come into the hallway, then they also went into the master bedroom. But instead of arguing or yelling, I listened to the murmuring of two men quietly talking.

I again heard the sound of footsteps in the hallway, and I hoped they'd simply go back down the stairs. Instead, the door to my bedroom was shoved open. Three men in leather jackets, gloves, and motorcycle helmets rushed into the room.

The first guy had on a yellow helmet. He grabbed at me, but I was able to dodge out of the way.

I pulled my pistol out of my bag as the second guy in the room threw himself against me. This one was wearing a blue helmet.

I fired off a desperate shot, but the bullet went wide, embedding itself into the wall. Blue-helmet guy latched onto the arm holding the gun.

As I struggled to free myself, the third man, the one with the red helmet, came at me. I gave him a hard snap kick to his knee. This immediately dropped him, but I had no time to gloat.

Blue-helmet still had the arm holding my gun, so there was no way I could aim it. Yellow-helmet again lunged at me and grabbed my other arm. I tried to struggle away, but they were holding me firmly.

Red-helmet, the guy who I'd kicked, got up and limped over to me. He was clearly in pain and I felt happy I could do at least that much. Shaking his head, he reached over and plucked the pistol from my hand.

As I struggled with the men, I tried to swivel my body to take out another one with a kick. Unfortunately, they were too strong and I couldn't do anything except thrash about.

"What do you jerks want?" I fumed at them. I was breathing hard and pissed that they'd attacked me.

"Hold her steady," red-helmet said in a thick Southern drawl as he took off his helmet. He was maybe thirty-five years old. He had a thin oily face, bulging eyes, and long stringy mouse-brown hair.

He pulled a bright pink stun-gun from his pocket and held it up for me to look at. There was a picture of a smiling cartoon kitty on the side of it.

"This is a stun-gun," he said. "It produces a high voltage electrical charge. It's non-lethal, but depending on where I apply it, it can be extremely painful."

He activated the stun-gun and a bright spark sizzled and danced across the electrodes. The spark made a loud snapping and crackling noise.

"Did you enjoy kicking me?" he asked with a smirk. "I bet you did. Well, I imagine this will shut you down for a while." Without further warning, he shoved the sparking tip of the stun-gun into my stomach.

An intense burning pain shot out in all directions and I felt my legs buckle. I collapsed to the floor, unable to control my movements.

I seemed to drift into a dream state and found it hard to focus my thoughts. As I lay on the floor, jerking and spasming, the man who had stunned me pulled a small black case from his coat pocket.

The case contained a syringe and a vial of clear liquid. While the other two men held my quivering body to the floor, I watched as he stuck the needle into the bottle. He extracted some of the liquid, then squirted a few drops out from the tip.

The man bent down and looked at me. His face was so close to mine, I thought he was going to kiss me. "Sweet dreams, angel," he said in his Southern accent. "We'll meet again soon."

I felt the slight pinch as he jabbed the needle into my leg. Then a burning sensation as the drug was injected.

I waited a few seconds, but nothing happened. I felt a brief surge of hope. My mind raced as I devised an escape plan.

I should probably pretend to fall asleep, then pick my time to get away from these creeps.

But even as I was formulating my plan, I felt intense drowsiness creep over me.

I fought it as long as I could. I told myself if I passed out, I might never wake up again. But in the end, the drug overcame me and I slipped into darkness.

Chapter Seven

"What do you know about Scottsdale General Hospital?" asked the man with the pink stun-gun.

I had awakened to find myself firmly tied to a metal chair in a small cinderblock room with an oil-stained concrete floor. The place had a musty chemical smell.

The face of the man who'd asked the question completely filled my field of view. He was close enough for me to count the pores on his nasty thin face and smell the tuna fish he'd had for lunch.

His long brown hair was pulled back in a ponytail, and his eyes bugged out of his face, giving him an almost cartoon-like appearance. Another man stood behind me, holding my head so I couldn't turn it away.

"I don't know anything about Scottsdale General," I said, slurring my words like a drunk. "Other than the guys there have a weakness for skinny blondes."

My stomach still ached and twitched from the first contact with the stun-gun. It was making it hard to think clearly.

The man held up the stun-gun for me to look at as he activated the switch. The smiling cartoon kitty on the front of the bright pink device seemed to be at odds with the pain and torment the weapon was designed to cause.

An intense white spark popped and flashed between the two electrodes. The man slowly brought the stun-gun to within an inch or so of my face, just below my left eye.

The snapping noise was deafening and brought a fresh wave of fear. My cheek soon grew uncomfortably warm while I waited for him to shove the device against me.

"Now then," he said calmly. "Let me ask you again. What do you know about Scottsdale General Hospital?"

At times like this, I wonder why I've decided to stay with the law office. Since I started working as an investigator, I'd been harassed, kidnapped, and tortured. I've been knocked unconscious and threatened with harm more times than I could count.

How did this escalate so quickly? I was only taking pictures of naked people having sex.

"We saw you come into the bedroom and find our cameras," the man with the stun-gun said. "We watched as you planted cameras of your own. We know you've been parked outside of the house, gathering evidence of who goes in and out."

"Yeah, so?" I asked. I still had no idea what he was getting at.

"This is the last time I'll ask," he patiently said. "What do you know about Scottsdale General Hospital?"

"I don't know anything about the hospital," I said. "I'm only here to get pictures of one of the guys having sex with the blonde so his wife can divorce him."

The man shook his head, as if he was disappointed. "Untie her and stand her up," he said to the guy who was holding my head. He then made twirling hand motions to hurry things up.

The man behind me didn't say a word. He quickly undid the ropes holding me to the chair, but didn't take off the bindings holding my wrists together behind my back.

I lunged forward to try to break free, but a third man grabbed me from behind by the hair. Then both men picked me up by my arms.

When I looked down at their hands, I saw they were both wearing thick rubber gloves. As soon as I saw this, I knew what was about to happen and my mind went numb with terror.

The man with the stun-gun again activated it. This time he held the sparking tip a few inches away from my stomach.

“Anything come to mind?” he asked. “Are you feeling a little more forthcoming now? Is there anything you’d like to tell me about?”

“You’ve got it wrong,” I said, trying my best to sound reasonable. “I’m only here to take videos of a guy for a divorce.”

“Wrong answer,” he sang out in a high falsetto voice.

The man then shoved the sparking stun-gun into my stomach. Intense searing pain shot through me. The man held the burning weapon against me as my body went into convulsions, still supported by the two men.

Time seemed to stop as he held the burning device against me for what must have been five or ten seconds. When he, at last, pulled it back, every muscle in my body was cramping, and my mind had gone blank.

“Put her back in the chair,” he said with a laugh. “I don’t think you’ll have to worry about tying her down.”

As they dropped me onto the chair, I began to slide off it. One of the men walked behind me and again grabbed both sides of my head, holding me upright.

Bright lights seemed to pop in front of my eyes, and tears slid down my face as my body was racked with spasms. I tried to take in a deep breath, but it hurt too much to do so, and I was reduced to panting.

“Now then,” the man with the stun-gun said. “Where were we?” Even in my confused state, I could tell he was thoroughly enjoying himself.

He moved the stun-gun to within an inch of my mouth. "I'm going to ask you again," he said, trying to sound like he was making a very reasonable request. "If you don't tell me what I want to know, the next one is going into your face. I've been told it's excruciating."

He activated the weapon and the spark again jumped and sizzled between the electrodes.

"What do you know about Scottsdale General Hospital?" he asked.

"I don't know anything," I said, my voice barely above a whisper.

"Such a pity," my questioner said. "Unfortunately for you, I can keep this up all day long."

I closed my eyes and waited for the pain to start. Instead, the man turned off the stun-gun.

I heard the sound of heels on the concrete floor. I slowly opened my eyes and watched as a woman came into my field of view.

She was in her late fifties, stocky, and dressed like a businesswoman. She had on a white button-down blouse and black slacks. Her hair was chopped short and she wore almost no makeup. She looked vaguely familiar, but I couldn't place her.

"Well?" the woman asked, sounding impatient. "She's the one who broke into the house and planted the cameras? Right? What does she know?"

"She doesn't know anything," the man with the stun-gun said. "She would have talked by now."

"I see," the woman said, sounding annoyed. "And how many more times do you plan on stunning her?"

"Oh, I don't know, five, maybe six. After that, the batteries will be drained."

The woman shook her head. "Benny, I know how much you enjoy

doing that, but if she knows nothing, there's no use in simply torturing her. What did you do with her car?"

"Two of my men are ditching it in the desert, a little north of Wickenburg. When the police find it, they'll assume she was headed up to Vegas and got kidnapped or maybe murdered."

"Good, we need to have attention drawn away from us."

"What should I do with her?"

The woman looked down at me and pondered the question for a moment. "Once it gets dark, get rid of her."

"Alright," he said. "Do you care how it's done?"

"I could care less. Go ahead and have your fun. But dump the body a long way from here. Use that place we found out in the desert. I don't want her connected with us."

The man leered at me and snorted out a sick little laugh. "It'll be my pleasure."

I immediately knew what he was thinking. This wasn't going to be quick or pleasant.

At a gesture from Benny, the two goons behind me hoisted me to my feet. My legs were still wobbly from the shocks I'd taken earlier and they didn't bother to untie my hands. I couldn't do more than weakly struggle as they dragged me down a dirty cinderblock hallway.

About halfway down the corridor, we passed a large room, and I caught a glimpse inside. Several tables were set up where half a dozen middle-aged women were busily working. I only was able to look for a few seconds before being pulled away.

I couldn't see what they were doing, but cardboard boxes and white plastic bottles were scattered everywhere. From the activity in the room, the operation seemed to be substantial.

One of the men opened a metal door at the end of the hallway, and they dragged me inside this new room. It seemed to be some sort of general storage for the business.

As they carried me inside the new room, I saw a dirty mattress lying on the floor in the corner against the back wall. They hauled me over and dropped my limp body onto it.

"Don't go anywhere," one of the goons said with a laugh. "It sounds like you'll have some company real soon."

"Go to hell, you jerks," I weakly said.

"If you want something fun to think about," the goon said with another laugh. "Benny always likes to use the stun-gun on his women a couple of times before he gets started."

"Yeah," the other guard said with a smirk. "That way, they don't struggle so much."

He closed the heavy steel door with a clang. Then I heard the sound of the bolt being slid into place.

Damn.

~~~~

I sat on the filthy mattress with my back against the wall for almost twenty minutes while feeling gradually returned to my legs. I knew I had to hurry if I had any chance of getting out of this.

Benny and his pink stun-gun would be back any minute to act out his sick urges, then kill me. But no matter how I contorted my body around or tried to will my legs to work, it was a painfully slow process.

~~~~

When I could finally more or less stand without falling over, I searched my prison cell. It was a typical storage room like you'd find in any business. There were two sturdy metal shelves filled with boxes of copier paper, files, old adding machines, and all manner of office supplies.

One of the shelves held a guillotine-style paper cutter. It was sitting a little higher than was comfortable to reach. Still, I turned and was eventually able to lift the handle.

Slipping the rope holding my hands together underneath the blade, I rubbed the bindings back and forth across the cutting edge. I had no idea how sharp the trimmer on an old paper cutter would still be, but it was all I had.

I couldn't see if I was doing anything to cut through the rope, but I kept going. When it didn't feel like I was accomplishing anything after the first two or three minutes, I began to rub faster and harder.

So, okay. Maybe I'm starting to panic.

I kept waiting for the metallic grinding sound of the sliding bolt. I knew the door would then fly open. I could only imagine how my escape attempt would enrage the man and how it would only make my bad situation worse.

With a fresh burst of panic, I continued to feverishly scrape the binding back and forth against the metal. Suddenly, my hands flew apart as the blade severed the cord. I brought them out in front of me and shook my arms to force some circulation to return.

I quickly rearranged some of the boxes on the shelf against one of the walls. I climbed up the sturdy metal structure until I was sitting on the top shelf and could reach the ceiling's drop-down acoustic tiles.

As I was about to reach up, my head started to spin. I had to steady myself to keep from falling back to the floor. It seems the drug they'd injected me with hadn't entirely left my system, and the climb up the shelving unit had left me dizzy. I knew I had to hurry, but I waited another two or three minutes for my equilibrium to return.

Carefully, I lifted one of the tiles and stuck my head up to look around. Light fixtures and electrical cables stretched out as far as I could see. Some birds had made nests in the ceiling space and everything was covered in a layer of feathers, straw, and pieces of pink insulation.

The cinderblock walls separating the rooms did not extend all the way up to the roof of the building. Instead, they ended about a foot above the level of the drop-down ceiling.

I stood on the top of the metal shelf and hoisted myself up. By doing this, I was able to sit on the top of the cinderblock wall that separated the storage room from the room next to it.

I carefully lifted an acoustic tile from the new room and looked down. This room appeared to be an office area. There were four desks, computers, tables, and file cabinets.

It must have been past closing time since the lights were off and the room was empty. Fortunately, when I looked down, a row of file cabinets was pushed against the wall, directly below me.

I swung my half-numb legs around and replaced the ceiling tile from the storage room I had just left. Hopefully, this would present them with a mystery as to how I'd escaped from the room. I then carefully let myself down to the file cabinets.

A round metal-bladed fan sat on the top of one of the cabinets and I knocked it over as I dropped down. The sound was loud and I hoped it didn't carry outside of the room.

I reached up and slid the ceiling tile above the file cabinets back into place. My hope was to further hide how I'd escaped from the storage room.

I climbed down off the file cabinets. There was a window with a metal grill over it in the room and a door leading out to the parking lot.

The door didn't seem to be alarmed and had a latch to open it from the inside. Looking around to make sure no one had seen me come into the room, I opened the door and slipped through.

~~~~
~~~~

I found myself outside in a manufacturing and industrial part of town. Wrecked cars and heaps of rusted scrap metal were piled all around the massive dirt lot.

Keeping an eye out for anyone trying to follow me, I crept between two of the dirty buildings. I didn't have a clear idea where I was, so it didn't matter which direction I went.

The sun was going down, so I knew that way was west. It seemed as good a direction to go as any. My only goal at this point was to put as much distance between me and the creeps as possible.

I crossed a street, which seemed to be more dirt than pavement, then went down a narrow alleyway formed between a low cinderblock building and a high-bay garage. I glanced around again, but fortunately, no one was trailing me.

I was limping and couldn't go faster than a slow trot. My legs were still weak and my stomach ached, but at least my muscles had stopped twitching; I took this as a good sign.

Crossing over to a new street, I saw a familiar warehouse, about a block down. There were three large faded pictures of vegetables on the side of it. One was a dancing tomato, one was a smiling stalk of celery, and the third was a singing ear of corn.

The warehouse told me I was on Mary Street, a little north of the Salt River. I turned right and walked up to Curry Road.

Knowing I had to get off the street as quickly as possible, I anxiously thought about where I could go. I had no money, no identification, and no phone.

After being stunned twice and having crawled through a dirty ceiling, I probably looked like crackhead death warmed over. Because of this, I was thinking the helpless-woman ploy probably wouldn't work.

I suddenly had an inspiration. I remembered what I did the last time I'd found myself in this exact situation.

I made it over to Scottsdale Road. Keeping off of the sidewalks as much as possible, I walked north until I saw Jeannie's Cabaret.

Scottsdale has several strip clubs and they all seem to do a brisk business. Out of all of them, Jeannie's is the one that starts to approach what I'd call classy.

While walking through the parking lot, I tried to detangle my hair and straighten myself up the best I could. I didn't want to be prevented from going in.

I walked up to the front entrance, where a red velvet rope was strung between two poles. On either side was a huge bouncer. Both were dressed in black tuxes with tails.

The men gave me the once over. There was a long silence, and I was sure they weren't going to let me in.

Crap.

"Um, I heard after six at night, there isn't a cover charge for ladies," I said, giving them my best smile.

"Yeah, that's right," one of the bouncers said in a rough, gravelly voice. "From now until Sunday night, there's no cover at all for the ladies."

This seemed to have the decision come down in my favor. After talking with me, it would have been awkward for them to stop me from going in.

The other bouncer unlatched the velvet rope and held it to the side. "Welcome to Jeannie's," he said.

Beyond the rope was a hallway lined with mirrors and thousands of tiny lights on the walls and ceiling. A thick red carpet led the way to the interior, where I could hear the pounding beat of classic rock music.

It took a few seconds for my eyes to adjust to the dim light of the club. There were four small stages and one larger one connected to the back by a catwalk. A woman was dancing on each of the five platforms.

The club was about half full. Most of the crowd appeared to be guys who had stopped by after work, but there were also a surprising number of women. It was still too early for the drunken multitude that would descend on a Friday night.

I looked around and was relieved to see my friend Danica Taylor-Sternwood standing at the bar, waiting for a drink order to come out. I'd become friends with Danica about a year earlier while on an assignment.

There was an empty barstool next to the waitress station and I collapsed on it. "Hi, Danica," I said.

Danica glanced my way and it was apparent that she didn't recognize me. She paused a moment before I saw the recognition in her eyes.

"Laura?" she asked. "Is that you? What happened? You look terrible."

I nodded my head. "Long story, but it's been a rough day. I just escaped from some jerks who've been holding me at a business south of Curry in that industrial area."

"Oh my God," Danica gasped. "Are you alright?"

I had to think about it for a moment. I did a quick mental check of all my body parts. Finally, I nodded my head. "Yeah, I'm a little sore, but I think I'll be okay."

About a year earlier, Danica had also been kidnapped and held in a business in the same industrial park. Fortunately, she'd been rescued by Gina before the men who had taken her could do more than bruise her in a couple of sensitive areas. When I searched her face, I could see she was reliving the horrible memories.

"You always seem to be in danger," she said as she shook her head. "Have you ever thought about finding a different job?"

"All the time. Can I borrow your phone?"

"Sure, um, it's in my locker. I'll be right back." She then made some hand signals to the woman tending the bar to give me a drink and charge it to her.

Danica took off for her locker while the bartender poured out a scotch from the bar gun. When I took a sip, it had a nasty plastic aftertaste, but I gratefully finished it in a long gulp.

I then remembered I probably still had some of the sleeping drug in my system and probably shouldn't toss alcohol on top of it, but it was too late. I also knew that sometime soon, I'd want to have another drink or two with Max to help me forget about this.

Danica came back, holding out her phone. She then picked up a tray of drinks and took off.

I punched in Sophie's number and hoped she wasn't in the middle of a date. If she was, she might not answer, and I'd have to go with some sort of plan B.

"Hey, Danica," Sophie said when she answered. "It's been a while. How are you doing? How's married life?"

"Sophie," I said. "It's me. You wouldn't believe the shitty day I've had today."

"Laura? Oh, I have no problem believing you're having a bad day. But why do you have Danica's phone?"

"I'm at Jeannie's and I borrowed it. Could you come get me? I need to swing by my place and grab a spare set of keys, then I need to go up to the desert somewhere past Wickenburg to look for my car."

"Wickenburg? Seriously? That's more like a road trip than a simple pick-up. You do know that, right?"

"I know. But if you could do it, I'll make it up to you."

"Well, you're in luck," she said with a laugh. "Now that I'm down to only dating one guy, I seem to have a lot of free evenings."

"Thanks, Sophie. You're a lifesaver."

"I know I am. Now, don't forget, you owe me big time."

~~~~

Sophie walked into the club about twenty minutes later. As she did the last time she'd been here, she spent a few minutes checking out the guys, who were looking at the dancing women.

"Damn," she said as she came over to where I was sitting. "There's something about walking into a room full of horny guys that gets my blood going. You can actually smell the desperation in here."

"Well, before you get going too far, keep in mind we're leaving in a few minutes."

"Fine, but don't forget, you owe me. Where's Danica?"

"She's over there," I said, pointing to the catwalk.

Sophie went to the stage and waved. Danica walked to the edge of the platform and bent over so they could talk. After a few moments, Sophie came back, a massive smile on her face.

"Danica says she's worried about you," Sophie said. "But I told her that a shitty day for you is pretty much par for the course."

I was about to protest, but Sophie was right. "Let's get out of here."

~~~~

As she drove over to my place, I told Sophie about what had happened since I'd gone into the townhouse earlier in the afternoon. She only shook her head.

"You really did have a crappy day," she said as she reached over and pulled a feather out of my hair. "Are you going to call the police this time?"

"I actually thought about it, but I don't think it would do any good.

I'd fill out a lot of paperwork and answer a lot of questions. The police would go out to the business where I'd been taken to be tortured. They'd interview some of the people who work there. All of them would deny I was ever at the business and say they had no idea what I was talking about."

"You're probably right about that."

"I have no way of proving anything and it'll be my word versus theirs. If you were the police detective looking into my story, what would you do?"

"Well, are you at least going to tell Max? You know he'll want to know all about it, especially if this has something to do with a rival gang."

"I thought about that too. But honestly, I'd have to answer just as many questions with him as I would with the police. Plus, you know he'd want to go out and do something about it. I don't think I want to be responsible for a lot of people getting hurt. I'll tell him, but maybe not everything."

"Still, it seems a little messed up that someone can do that to you and there's nothing you can do about it. Lenny should give you hazard pay."

"You're singing my tune."

~~~~

I scanned the parking lot at my apartment, looking for anyone who didn't belong. When everything looked clear, I got out.

"I'll have Grandma let me into my place. Then I'll grab my spare set of keys and we can go."

"Oh, I'll go with you," Sophie said as she grabbed her purse. "I haven't talked with Grandma for a while. We can gossip about her wedding planner."

We walked into my apartment house and took the elevator to the
~~~~

third floor. I was glad Sophie had decided to come along. I didn't think anyone would come at me in the hallway to my apartment, but you never know.

When we walked up to Grandma's door, we could hear an episode of *The Big Bang Theory* playing on her television. I knocked and the TV volume went down.

After about fifteen seconds, the peephole briefly went dark. We heard the sound of deadbolts being unlocked and chains being slid off latches as Grandma opened the door.

She looked us over and I could feel her eyes linger on me. Grandma shook her head slightly, as if she was somehow disappointed. She then turned to Sophie with a smile.

"Why, Sophie," Grandma said in her always cheerful voice. "Isn't this a nice surprise? Come on in. I wasn't expecting to see you until the wedding."

"Hi, Grandma," Sophie said as she gave her a hug. "It's good to see you again. I'm looking forward to the wedding. Especially after hearing all about your wedding planner and the wacky things that have been going on."

"Isn't it the craziest thing?" Grandma asked. "But I know Laura will have everything straightened out before the ceremony. Won't you, dear?" She then looked at me with her sweet smile.

"I'm working on it," I said. "Sophie can fill you in. Could I borrow your key to my place? I need to grab my spare set. I'll be right back."

"Why are you walking so funny tonight?" Grandma asked. "Did something happen again?"

"I took a couple of stun-gun hits to the stomach. It's taking me a while to shake it off."

"Really? Stun-guns? Was this on purpose?"

"No, it happened as part of an investigation I'm working on."

Grandma shook her head. "I didn't think so, but I never know anymore. Young people do the craziest things nowadays. Well, do be careful, dear."

"I'm trying," I said.

"Um," Sophie said. "While you're at your place, you should probably change your clothes and comb out your hair. And if you think we might actually end up somewhere, later on, you may want to think about retouching your makeup."

"I figured," I said. "How bad is it?"

"You sort of have the crying-raccoon thing going on."

I went over to my apartment and opened the door. I found my spare set of keys and tossed them into a shoulder bag I'd grabbed from the closet. I also dug through my drawer and pulled out my old twenty-five caliber pistol.

After Sophie's comments, I was curious about how bad I looked. I went into the bathroom and glanced in the mirror.

What I saw sent a shock of panic through me. My hair was sticking out at all sorts of weird angles and there were feathers and bits of insulation from the ceiling still stuck in it.

Worst of all, Sophie had been right about my makeup. My eyeliner and mascara had smeared and had started to drip down my face. It was little wonder why it took Danica a few seconds to recognize me.

Fighting down the urge to hop in the shower and start again from scratch, I put on a new outfit, brushed out my hair, and quickly fixed my makeup. Within about fifteen minutes, I was back at Grandma's.

Sophie and Grandma were sitting on the couch, drinking tea. Marlowe was on Sophie's lap and seemed to be asleep.

"I was telling Grandma about the strip club," Sophie said. "Do you know Grandma used to be an exotic dancer?"

"You were?" I asked. I know I probably sounded a little skeptical, but I couldn't help it. The thought of Grandma Peckham dancing naked on a stage wasn't registering.

"Oh yes," Grandma said. "This was back when I was living in England and in college in Cambridge. I'd make pin money by dancing at a back-alley club called The Alligator. It was a notorious place back in the day."

"What was it like?" I asked.

"It's nothing like it is today, of course. We wore knickers, nylons, and a garter. We also wore pasties with long tassels on them."

"So, nobody got completely naked?" I asked, hopefully. I really didn't want the thought of a naked dancing Grandma to be in my mind.

"Land sakes alive, no. Back then, if anyone had actually taken off their clothes, they would have been arrested."

"It sounds like a fun place to work," Sophie said.

"I don't like to brag," Grandma said. "But I was rather famous at the club for being able to swing one of my tassels to the right and the other to the left. Watching those tassels spin around always drove the men wild with lust. They'd hoot and toss shillings on the stage, all night long."

Chapter Eight

We got back into Sophie's car and headed out to the Loop 101. I sighed, knowing what I had to do next. I gave Max a call.

"Hey," I said when he answered. "Where's my car?"

The line was silent for a full five seconds before Max spoke.

"You don't know where your car is?"

"It's a long story. I'll tell you about it later. But right now, I need to find my car. I heard it was up north of Wickenburg, somewhere out in the desert."

"Okay," he said. "I'll find out and give you a call."

"You still have the tracker on my car, don't you? Can't you just look it up?"

"It's not like it's an app on my phone. But it should only take a few minutes."

True to his word, Max called back five minutes later. "Your car is in a big dirt parking lot on the side of Highway 93, about fifty miles north of Wickenburg."

I had a feeling I knew where he was talking about. "Does this big parking lot have a name?" I asked.

"Not really. All it says is Nothing."

"Nothing? It figures."

"You know the location?"

"Yes," I said with a laugh. "Nothing is where my car broke down when Susan Monroe and I were driving to the Black Castle Casino. It's where that jerk Jonathan LaRose picked us up."

"Do you think there could be a connection?" he asked, sounding concerned. "I could have somebody meet you there."

"No, I think it's only a weird coincidence. But I'll call you when we get my car."

"Any idea when you'll get there?"

"It'll take us almost two hours from here."

I looked over at Sophie, whose eyebrows were creased with concentration, a slight smile on her lips. I then glanced down at the speedometer, which was pushing eighty. "Um, or maybe more like an hour and a half."

~~~~

During the long drive, the sun slowly went down. There were enough clouds on the horizon for us to be treated to a gorgeous Arizona desert sunset. It sort of helped make up for some of the crappy events of the day.

Sophie drove out to Wickenburg and only slowed enough to not get a ticket as we went through the town. We then entered the deep desert, and she again opened up the Volkswagen.

Sophie tuned her satellite radio to the Bon Jovi channel and started singing along to the tunes. We quickly sped through the fifty miles of cactus and Joshua trees and finally made it to our destination.

Nothing, Arizona consists of a huge dirt lot and a single yellow cinderblock building. The structure must have been a gas station or a convenience store at one time, but it was now only a broken and empty
~~~~

shell with graffiti sprayed all over it. A faded sign on a tall pole announced the name of the town.

We drove around to the edge of the lot, where several abandoned cars were more or less lined up. The windows were bashed out of most of them. My car sat between two old sedans that I vaguely remembered being here the last time I'd been to Nothing, a month and a half earlier.

"You know," Sophie said. "It's probably a good thing you're still driving your old piece of shit car. If you had your new one, someone would have stolen it by now. But one look at your disaster of a car and people will assume it's been sitting here for a couple of months already."

"Shut up," I grumbled. "I'm already having a hard enough day without your brilliant observations."

Sophie pulled a flashlight from her glove compartment. I switched it on, and we used it as we got out and walked around my car. Fortunately, it hadn't been here long enough for anyone to damage it further.

I used my spare set of keys to open the vehicle and quickly confirmed the interior was empty. Walking around to the trunk, I saw the faded red bungee cord that holds the lid down had already been unfastened. Leery of what I might find, I slowly opened it up.

With a sigh of relief, I found my purse. The bad guys had simply tossed it in the trunk without trying to hide it. I opened it and was surprised to see my wallet, keys, phone, and even my pistol were still in the bag.

"Did they leave anything in your wallet?" Sophie asked.

"Um, about ten dollars," I said as I leafed through a five and a handful of singles. "But I only had thirty or forty to start with. I suppose I should be grateful they were staging this as a kidnapping and not a robbery."

"See," Sophie said with her cheerful smile. "Things will only get better from here."

"Thanks for driving me up here," I told her as we got ready to leave.

"Just remember this when I ask you to do some monster favor for me sometime down the road."

I started up my car and confirmed I had enough gas to make it back to Wickenburg. I gave Sophie a thumbs-up and we both took off.

As we sped back through the desert, I looked at the clock. Since it was only nine-fifteen, I knew Max would still be in his daily wrap-up meeting.

I voice texted to let him know I had my car and was heading back. I also asked him to call me when he had a chance.

~~~~

The lights of Wickenburg were coming into view when the theme to *The Love Boat* started playing on my phone.

"I'm glad you got your car back," Max said when I answered. "Of course, I'm rather curious how it ended up in the middle of the desert."

"I'm looking into the husband of a client for Lenny. The guy's a doctor over at Scottsdale General. It started out with the usual naked pictures for the divorce. But I'm learning he's only part of a larger operation somebody is running on several of the doctors and administrators at the hospital."

"What kind of operation?"

"Sex and possible blackmail. But I don't know if it's anything more than that."

"I take it the people running the operation found out you were spying on them?"

"Yes, and they weren't very pleased about it."
~~~~

"Are you alright?"

"Yeah, I'm fine. A little twitchy, but I'll be alright."

"Do you need my help with anything?"

"Maybe. I have a weird question. Do you know anything about Scottsdale General Hospital?"

"Like what? Are these the people behind the blackmail?"

"I'm not entirely sure, but it seems possible. Several members of the executive staff seem to be caught up in a sex ring that makes no sense unless there's blackmail involved."

"Scottsdale General has a somewhat shaky reputation," Max said. "They seem to keep hiring people who get caught stealing narcotics. Unfortunately, before they're caught, the drugs they steal eventually make it out to the street. The leaks from the hospital seem to be sizeable. Tony's often said it's one of the reasons we've never been able to properly get into the business."

"You'd think after the first time someone stole drugs, they'd monitor the people they hired a little more closely."

"You'd think. Maybe it's hard to get good people to work in a hospital pharmacy."

"Um, would you mind if I come over to your place tonight?"

"Really? This is the first time you've asked to come to my house. Is something going on?"

"Well, I might still have some people looking for me and I'd rather not stay up all night listening for noises."

"Are you sure you don't want some help with this? Gabriella told me she's feeling a little fidgety. Nothing's happened over here since she got the chance to shoot Major Malakov in the face. You know, she'd probably think it would be fun to have something new to look into."

"No, I only need somewhere to stay for tonight."

"I have an idea," he said. "Tomorrow is Christmas Eve. We can go over to your place tomorrow morning, pick up some things for the rest of the weekend, and then go back to my place. That is, if you'd like to spend the weekend with me."

"I haven't been thinking a lot about Christmas, but that sounds perfect."

~~~~

I got to Max's a few minutes after eleven. When he opened the door, I gave him a hug and walked straight to his bathroom. Within a few seconds, my clothes were lying in a pile on the floor.

I took a hot shower to wash my hair and remove the grime that had accumulated after being stunned twice and then crawling through a nasty ceiling. I would have stayed in the shower longer, but I was so tired I could hardly stand.

When I got out, I towel dried my hair and wrapped one of Max's thick bath sheets around me. I then walked into the bedroom and collapsed on the bed.

I was enjoying the softness of his sheets and would have quickly fallen asleep, but I heard Max talking to me. He was standing next to the bed, and I knew he was looking down at me.

"What?" I asked as I opened one eye and looked up at him.

"Did you want to take the wet towel off before you pass out?"

At this point, I really didn't care one way or another. But I nodded my head and Max helped pull off the towel. He then crawled into bed next to me and I vaguely remember putting my head on his shoulder before falling asleep.

~~~~

When I woke up the following day, it took me a second to realize where I was and how I'd gotten there. The big bed was empty and the house was quiet in a way my apartment never was.

I went to Max's closet and looked around for something to wear. I finally found a red silk kimono. I put it on and went searching for coffee.

I found Max busy in the kitchen. He was sorting out ingredients for breakfast and I could smell he'd already made a pot of one of his french roasts.

"Good morning," he said as he gave me a long hug. He then stepped back and eyed me up and down. "You look good in silk. Feeling better today?"

"Much better," I said as I poured out a mug, ignoring his comments about how I looked in the thin, clingy silk. "Sorry, I fell asleep on you last night. Yesterday was a long day."

"I could tell. I'm glad you made it over here while you were still awake."

"Where's Beatrice?"

"She's off for the weekend," Max said as he started whipping eggs to make an omelet. "She's spending Christmas with her sister down in Tucson."

"So, we're all alone?"

"All weekend. Think you can handle that?"

"I'll manage," I said with a huge smile. "When do you want to head over to my place? That is, unless I'll be running around here naked all weekend."

"It's a thought, but I have us scheduled to be over there at ten. I'll have someone do a security sweep before we get there."

Max and I sat on his couch, drinking coffee and eating breakfast. The view out of the picture window, watching the city slowly waking up, was lovely.

I remembered what Sophie had told me about her search for Gabriella. This seemed as good of a time as any to bring it up.

“Um, I think I once told you we have a source within the government where we could find out a lot of information on someone?”

“I remember. You said it was how you got the intel on Carlos Valentino.”

“Well, we tried to get information on the guy who’s hunting Gabriella, Viktor Pyotrovich Glazkov.”

“I take it your source didn’t have anything on him?”

“Not a thing. All we got was that he was a retired industrialist in the Crimean region of Ukraine.”

“That’s not right. If it’s a real intelligence source, they’d have to have more than that…” Max mused. His voice trailed off as he seemed to think about it. “Okay, I think I might know what the problem is.”

“What?”

“I don’t think our government knows his actual name. When I was active in the region, all I had was a codename. They only referred to him as the Snow Ghost.”

“So, how do you know all about him?”

“From Gabriella. The Snow Ghost wasn’t a major threat to our side, but he was decimating hers. That’s why she was taking them out. I didn’t learn the whole story until much later. I doubt that our government ever put together that Viktor Glazkov and the Snow Ghost are the same person.”

“Really? I’ll see if Sophie can come up with anything on the Snow Ghost when she returns to the office on Monday.

~~~~
~~~~

We pulled into the parking lot for my apartment and I saw a black SUV in the corner. As we parked, the door to the vehicle opened and Carson got out.

"Good morning," he said as he walked over to us.

"Did you find anything?" Max asked.

"No, I did a couple of perimeter sweeps and checked out the interior. I didn't see anyone who looks like they don't belong here."

"Alright, stay outside while we go upstairs. The parking lot is the obvious entry point. Give me a call if you see anything."

"Copy that," the big man said.

"Hi, Carson," I said as I waved.

"Ma'am," he said with a nod. As with Tony, it was pretty obvious he wasn't going to say anything else with Max standing next to us.

We took the elevator up to my floor and entered my apartment. I loaded up my overnight bag with a couple of outfits and some things from the bathroom. I also stashed my old twenty-five caliber pistol back in the drawer.

Hoping I wasn't forgetting anything important, we stepped into the hallway and I locked my door.

"I should tell Grandma Peckham I'll be out for the weekend," I said. "I don't want her to worry."

I knocked on my neighbor's door. When she opened it, she was wearing her purple jogging suit.

"Well, good morning," she said. She then saw my boyfriend standing next to me in the hallway. "Hello, Max," she said. "It's good to see you again. Come on in. Could I make you a cup of mountain oolong tea?"

"Not today," he said. "We're just on our way out. But thank you."

"Were you planning on being here this weekend?" I asked. "I was planning on spending a couple of days over at Max's. I wanted to make sure someone would be around for Marlowe."

"Other than running around doing some final things for the wedding, I'll be here all weekend. I'm supposed to spend time with Bob's family and do Christmas morning, but that hopefully won't last more than a few hours. I'll be glad to take care of Marlowe."

"Thanks. I'd hate for him to be lonely over Christmas."

"Oh, whenever you go somewhere, I think the main reason he cares is because only one of us is feeding him. He keeps looking at me like I should feed him more to make up for it."

"I'm looking forward to the wedding," Max said. "Is everything still on track? I heard there were some challenges with your wedding planner."

"As far as I know, everything's still good from my side," Grandma said. "Is everything's still going well on your end?" she asked, looking at me.

"Nothing's changed since last night," I said. "There've been a few challenges that have come up, but Kristy and I are doing our best to make sure things go smoothly next Saturday."

"Well, my fingers are crossed about the wedding," Grandma said. "Oh, when you come back on Monday, stop by my place. I have something for you. It's only a little Christmas present."

As soon as Grandma mentioned presents, I remembered I had her and Max's gifts back at my place.

"Hold on," I said. "I'll be right back."

I went back to my place and found Max's bags of coffee beans. They weren't wrapped yet, so I spent a few minutes looking for a gift bag to put them in. The closest I could find was one that said Happy Birthday, but I figured it would be close enough.

I'd already wrapped Grandma's present, two sets of soft fluffy towels that matched the colors of her bathroom. Presents in hand, I relocked the apartment and went back next door.

When I got back to Grandma's, I could tell something weird had happened. Grandma was looking into space and seemed to be on the verge of crying. I set her present down and looked at her.

"Grandma?" I asked. "Is everything alright?"

"Oh," she said as she sniffed back a tear. "Everything's fine, dear."

I looked between Grandma and Max. "Well?"

"I asked Grandma where they were going for their honeymoon," Max said. "She said with the wedding happening so quickly, they didn't have anything left over for a trip. So, I offered them four nights at one of the casitas at the Blue Palms with a full food and beverage comp."

"Wow," I said. "Nice wedding present."

Max pulled out his phone and dialed a number. "Hey, Cassy, it's me. Which of the casitas are still open for New Year's Eve? I'd like to set up a four-night complete comp package. That's right. New Year's Eve through the fourth of January. Put it into my discretionary cost center."

He listened for a moment. "Okay, that'll be perfect. Hold on." Max looked at Grandma. "What will your name be next month?"

Grandma looked at him blankly for several seconds. Then she broke out into a sweet smile. "Henderson," she said.

Max got back on the phone. "Mary and Bob Henderson. They'll arrive late on New Year's Eve, probably one or two in the morning. Also, set up the honeymoon package in the room. Champagne and strawberries, monogrammed bathrobes, the works. Perfect. Thanks, Cassy."

"Okay," Max said as he disconnected. "You're all set. Head to the

Blue Palms after the wedding reception next Saturday and they'll have everything ready."

I looked at Grandma and saw a tear sliding down her cheek. "You've got yourself a keeper," she said.

~~~~

We went back down to the parking lot. Max let Carson know everything was alright and he could head back to the Blue Palms.

Carson gave me a nod and said, "Ma'am," which I took as his way of saying goodbye. He then climbed into his SUV and took off.

~~~~

We were about halfway to Max's house when my phone rang with the Mazda dealer's number. I hit the speakerphone answer button. "Hello?"

"Miss Black?" a woman asked. "This is Mia. I wanted to let you know your car's in. It's ready to go anytime you want to pick it up."

"That's great," I said. "It's Christmas Eve. How late are you open?"

"Until one," she said. "If you think you might be a little later, I could see if someone would stay until you got here."

I looked over at Max, but he was already pulling into a parking lot to turn the car around.

"We'll be there in fifteen minutes," I said.

~~~~

We drove over to the Scottsdale Auto Show at Pima and the Loop 101. This is a group of seven or eight auto dealerships bunched together in one place along the highway. It's where Max and I had spent much of our Thanksgiving weekend, looking for a new car.

We parked in a visitors' space and went into the showroom. A woman came over and I recognized her as the one who had sold me
~~~~

the car. Unfortunately, I'd completely forgotten her name.

"Laura," she said as she held out her hand.

"It's good to see you again," I said, hoping my forgetfulness hadn't been noticed. "I hear the car came in."

"It came in yesterday afternoon," she said. "It's right over there."

She pointed to a shiny white Miata convertible, sitting by itself in the middle of the showroom floor. A red and yellow "Sold" sign was posted on the windshield.

"Oh, it's so beautiful!" I knew I was squealing, but I couldn't help it.

"It's all prepped and washed," the saleswoman said as we walked around the car to admire it. "We even filled the tank."

"Thank you so much," I said as I signed a paper saying I'd received the vehicle.

Two of the salespeople opened a set of double-glass doors and I drove my car out to the parking lot. It felt so wonderful to be sitting in a shiny new convertible. I completely loved it.

I followed Max as he led the way to his house. About halfway there, Rihanna's *S&M* started playing on my phone.

"Hey, Sophie," I said when I answered. "I just got my car. Oh, my god, you have to see it. It's so beautiful."

"Wow, that's great news. Are you still sure you don't want to ditch your old one? If we'd have known, we could have just picked your purse out of the trunk last night, and you could have left your old POS sitting up at Nothing."

"Shut up. You know I'll want to use the old one when I'm working. Think what would have happened yesterday if I'd been driving the new Miata."

"That's true. It would be over the border by now."

“Anyway,” I said. “You called me. What’s up?”

“Um, do you remember one of the doctors the blonde chick was nailing? Isaac Elmaghrabi, or however you say it?”

“Yeah,” I said. “I can’t forget that name, Doctor Sloppy Seconds. She had him on Wednesday afternoon.”

“Well, I’ve got some bad news. They just fished him out of Tempe Town Lake.”

“Seriously?”

“Serious as a heart attack. According to the paper, they think he jumped off the Scottsdale Road bridge sometime last night. The body washed up on the shore near Tempe Beach Park. A couple of ASU students were out rollerblading when they found him.”

“Damn.”

“I know. The newspaper’s saying it’s the curse of Scottsdale General.”

“What’s that?”

“According to the article, about once a year, one of the top people at Scottsdale General will commit suicide. It must be a crappy place to work. Even worse than our law office.”

“Why would someone who makes that much money commit suicide?” I asked. “It seems pretty stupid if you ask me.”

“Maybe this has something to do with the blackmail? Maybe they told him about the evidence they had on him and he decided to go for the big-sleep option.”

“I don’t know. But the whole thing still seems pretty messed up.”

~~~~

“I need to head over to the Tropical Paradise for Kristy Darby’s next wedding,” I reminded Max as we were cuddling on his couch.
~~~~

"I'll need to be there by four."

"I'll be glad to come along, if you don't mind the company. While you're busy with the wedding, I'll work on some projects I have going on."

~~~~

A little after three-thirty, we climbed into the Miata and took off. I was disappointed the temperatures were only in the sixties. It was too cold to put the top down. If Max hadn't been in the car with me, I probably would have lowered it anyway and turned on the heater.
~~~~

Chapter Nine

We pulled into the valet line at the Tropical Paradise. Our doors were opened, and we both got out. The attendant got into my car and took off. As he did, I stopped and stared in wonder.

Like most of Scottsdale's resorts, the Tropical Paradise has seven or eight parking slots next to the front entrance. These were used to display some of the fancier cars the customers arrive in.

Tonight was no different. A red Ferrari, an orange Lamborghini, and a white Rolls Royce were lined up for display.

The thing that shocked me was that the attendant drove my Miata to the slot closest to the entrance, then efficiently backed it into place. Even though I knew he only did it because I was with Max, the sight of my shiny white car sitting in the display parking area was a little emotional. After so many years of having the crappiest vehicle on the street, seeing my Miata parked next to a Lamborghini amazed me.

~~~~

After a quick hug, Max took off for his office and I walked over to the Wedding Grotto, the site for the ceremony. Like most of the venues at the Tropical Paradise, it was a beautiful intimate space. Counting out the white chairs, there looked to be seating for about a hundred and twenty guests.

Kristy was already checking on the accommodations, her tablet in
~~~~

her hand.

"Well?" I asked. "How does it look?"

"So far, everything's good. The flowers are perfect, the seating is just as we ordered, and the alter looks great."

"What about the officiant?"

"The bride has a friend who can perform marriages in Arizona. He's back with the wedding party getting ready."

"Is there anything else we need to check?"

"Of course," she said with a laugh. "But I've covered the things that could be major problems, at least at the ceremony. Next on my list is making sure the setup in the reception ballroom is complete."

I followed Kristy for the next twenty minutes, and it became apparent everything looked good. The ballroom looked sophisticated and stylish, with fifteen tables fully set with elegant stationery, immaculate place settings, and gorgeous flowers.

While Kristy checked on the bride, I walked back to the Wedding Grotto and sat in one of the white seats. In the silence, I was able to really get a sense of the venue.

Even though no one else but me was in the space, it was exciting to know what was about to happen here. It made me think back to my wedding and how full of hope and optimism I had been that day.

As I thought about the ceremony, I was surprised I felt a touch jealous of the bride. I'd only met her a few minutes before, but I was suddenly envious of her getting married.

What the hell?

Ever since my divorce, I'd been telling myself I never wanted to get married again. But was that still true?

When I was with Reno, I occasionally fantasized about living with him and growing old together. But that's all they ever were, occasional fantasies. So, why had I suddenly become emotional at the thought of getting married again?

~~~~

The ceremony went off without a hitch. About halfway through, as they started to say their vows, I stopped paying attention to the ceremony and started thinking about the reception and everything that could go wrong.

It was a little strange, looking at the event as a planner and not as a guest or someone in the wedding party. In my mind, it was starting to become a checklist, with forty or fifty things that all had to happen at the correct time and in the proper order.

I was beginning to see why Kristy carried a tablet with her the entire night. I was also starting to see how trying to plan a dozen weddings at once could lead to mix-ups and confusion.

As the wedding party exited the Grotto, Kristy and I went to check on the reception. We walked back into the ballroom, and Kristy took in everything at once.

To me, it all looked beautiful. But I noticed her stiffen and suck in a breath.

"What's wrong?" I asked.

"The DJ isn't here yet," she said, sounding annoyed. "I've worked with her before, and she's usually set up by the time the guests start to arrive."

"Do you have her number? I'll call and make sure she's only running a little late."

"Thanks," she said as she texted me the number. "Her name is Rainbow Raven. While you do that, I'll go back to the kitchen and make sure nothing else is wrong."

Tablet in hand, Kristy took off through a door in the back. I called the number, and a woman answered.
~~~~

"Hi," I said. "I'm looking for Rainbow Raven."

"You've got her," the woman said in a bright and cheerful voice. "What can I do for you?"

"My name is Laura Black and I'm helping out Kristine Darby tonight. Are you still on your way over here?"

The phone went silent for a few seconds. "Um," she said. "Are you talking about the wedding at the Tropical Paradise?"

"That's right."

"But, um, I was told the gig was canceled. Something about the bride getting cold feet."

"No, it's still going on. How soon can you be here?"

"Crap," she said, sounding genuinely distressed. "Are you serious? This totally sucks, and I'm really sorry, but I won't be able to make it tonight. When the wedding canceled, I drove out to my sister's in Riverside to do Christmas. It's like a five-hour drive back."

Damn.

"Who told you the wedding was canceled?" I asked.

"It was Kristy. I got an email from her, like three or four days ago."

"Do you still have it? I'd like to see it."

"Sure, if you give me your address, I'll forward you a copy. Are you saying Kristy didn't send it?"

"I don't think it was her. If you got an email, someone might have hacked their way into her account."

"Wow. Tell Kristy I feel terrible about this. But when I got her note, I assumed it was legitimate."

I gave Rainbow my contact information then went to look for my client. I found her in the kitchen, still looking over the dinner preparations.

"Kristy," I said. "Rainbow's in California and isn't coming. She said she got an email, presumably from you, saying the wedding had been canceled."

"What?" Kristy asked, clearly upset. "You've got to be joking. Why would I tell her the wedding was canceled? This is great. Now you're saying someone's hacked into my email account?"

"Rainbow will be sending me a copy of the email, but it looks like it."

Kristy looked to be on the verge of crying. "I can't have a reception without music," she muttered. "There's no way."

"Do you have anyone else that can fill in?"

"On Christmas Eve?" she asked with a laugh. "I was lucky to get Rainbow, and I had to book her six months in advance."

"Okay," I said. "Let me try one more thing."

I pulled out my phone and called Max.

"Hey," he said when he answered. "How's the wedding going? Does everything look okay so far?"

"Actually, no. Someone emailed the DJ and told her the event was canceled. Now she's out in California. People are starting to roll in, and they're standing in a very quiet ballroom."

Max seemed to think for a moment. "This is sort of a longshot, but I might be able to help. One of the team members who's working tonight as a valet also moonlights as a DJ. I was thinking about that as he parked your car. I don't know what types of music he's into, but I could see if he wouldn't mind getting his equipment and working a wedding instead."

"Would you ask? It would save us a huge problem. Call me back when you get an answer?"

Five minutes later, my phone rang with the theme to *The Love Boat.*

As always, hearing the ringtone made me smile.

"Rafael said he'll be glad to do it," Max said. "As luck would have it, he worked a Christmas party last night and still has the equipment loaded in his van. Although, he's asked for his usual DJ fee on top of what he was going to make working here tonight."

"I'm sure Kristy will pay him. She's pretty desperate. Um, are you good with paying someone who won't be working for you tonight?"

"Having you for a girlfriend is going to be expensive," he said with a laugh. "I think I'm going to have to resign myself to that."

"Thanks," I said. "You've pulled us out of a jam. I'll make it up to you."

"Really? Well, I can think of one or two ways. Perhaps later tonight?"

"You're so naughty," I said with a grin. I knew a blush was spreading across my face.

"Don't you know it."

~~~~

Fifteen minutes later, a man in a Tropical Paradise valet uniform pushed a cart, loaded with equipment, into the ballroom. Kristy and I hurried over to meet with him.

"Thank you so much for agreeing to do this," Kristy said as she held out her hand and handed him a card.

"No problem," he said as they shook, and he handed her a card of his own. "I'm Rafael Torres, but I go by DJ Chronos. What happened to your music tonight?"

"There was a weird miscommunication," Kristy said. "And I suddenly didn't have a DJ."

"Good thing I still had my equipment in the van from last night," he said. He then looked a little embarrassed. "Um, the only thing is,
~~~~

I'm still set up for a Mexican Christmas party. I don't have a lot of traditional wedding reception music with me."

"No problem," Kristy said as she held up a thumb-drive memory stick. It's got every song the bride requested. Play whatever you want off of this. As long as you get in the Chicken Dance, the Cha Cha Slide, and the Hokey Pokey, we'll be okay."

"Eeewww, seriously?" he said with a laugh. "In that case, maybe I'd better introduce myself as DJ Rafael. I don't want word getting out that DJ Chronos was playing the Hokey Pokey."

Rafael pushed his cart to the stage to set up. Now that the crisis was over, Kristy seemed to deflate.

"I hope this is the only problem we're going to have," she said. "I don't know if I can handle another crisis tonight."

"Does everything else look okay?" I asked.

"So far. I usually don't have any problems with the catering or the facilities over here. Unfortunately, it seems like I have a bigger problem than simply being disorganized. It's pretty obvious someone is actively trying to sabotage me."

"I was thinking the same thing," I said. "If someone's emailing your vendors and canceling events at the last minute, we could have a serious problem. As soon as you get home tonight, make sure to change the passwords for all of your accounts."

"At least I know it's not me. All this time, I was starting to wonder if I was losing my mind."

~~~~

As the reception was winding down, Kristy walked over to me. "Well," she said. "Other than the DJ, everything went okay tonight."

"Did the bride ever say anything about the last-minute switch?"

"No, at least not to me. Of course, the fact that she started doing
~~~~

tequila shots as soon as she walked in the door might have had something to do with it."

We both looked over to one of the tables, where a very drunk bride was being attended to by several women wearing matching bubblegum-colored taffeta dresses.

"I hope changing the passwords on my accounts will help stop the problems," Kristy said.

"It will probably help," I said. "But I don't think it'll stop them. We still need to find out who's sabotaging your events. Until we do that, the issues will likely continue."

~~~~

When I woke up the following morning, I realized I was at Max's house. I also noticed I wasn't alone in the bed.

"Good Morning," Max said as he wrapped his arm around me. "Merry Christmas."

"Merry Christmas yourself," I groaned out as I flopped over on his chest. "What time is it? It feels late."

"It's almost nine. It's been a while since I've slept in this late."

"Wow, me too. We should get up."

"Is there anything you need to do today?" he asked.

"Um, not really. There aren't any weddings today, and nothing will be going on with my other assignment."

"Why don't we stay in bed?" he asked as he kissed my forehead. "We don't need to get up until you get hungry."

"I'll probably need coffee before food. But staying in bed with you all day sounds like a wonderful way to spend Christmas."

~~~~

I woke up early Monday morning at Max's. After we had a lovely breakfast, I drove back to my place to get ready for the day. Before I went up, I checked the parking lot and the hallways for bad guys, but nobody seemed to be around.

Since it was the day after Christmas, most people had the day off, and traffic was light. As I drove to the office, I took a few quiet moments to think about my assignments.

Unfortunately, it wasn't one of the days that Michael Palmer was scheduled to have the day off. I wasn't even sure he'd be seeing the blonde anymore, now that I'd blown their operation.

On the other hand, Kristy didn't have another wedding until the next day. So far, I wasn't any closer to finding out who was sabotaging her events.

The more I thought about it, the more I realized I had nothing.

~~~~

"How was Christmas?" Sophie asked as I walked up to reception. "Did you spend the entire weekend with Max?"

"Yes, except for the wedding on Christmas Eve. He also had to go up to the Blue Palms for a couple of hours yesterday morning. They had a problem. Apparently, someone poured red dye into one of the main pools."

"That sounds festive."

"True, but Max wasn't amused. They had to drain the pool, have a bunch of people out to clean it, and then had to fill it again."

"Doesn't he have a staff to take care of things like that?"

"It was the manager of the hotel who called to notify him. But Max wanted to take a look for himself. He grumbled all day about the overtime."

"How was the new French roast coffee? Did he like it?"

"We had the first one today."
~~~~

"And?"

"It was okay. Honestly, they all taste pretty much alike to me. But Max went on about it, so he was either being polite, or he really liked it."

"Or maybe both? What did he give you?"

I pulled my hair back so she could see my ears.

"Damn," she said. "Diamond earrings? Are the ones on the sides rubies?"

I nodded. "Max knows about the jewelry I already have. He said I needed something to complete the set."

"Jeez, that'll do it. Hey, did you hear the latest on Doctor Sloppy Seconds?"

"No, we didn't have the TV on all weekend."

"You bad girl," Sophie said with a smile. "Anyway, it was in the paper this morning and I was talking with Lenny about it. They just released the initial autopsy results of that Doctor Elmaghrabi guy."

"Okay, what did they find?"

"Apparently, it wasn't exactly a suicide. His skull had been bashed in before he was tossed off the bridge. From what I read, he was still alive when he hit the water but drowned immediately after."

"Do they have any suspects?"

"The newspaper article didn't list any. It was mostly about the curse of Scottsdale General."

"How can a hospital have a curse? Besides, if he was murdered, it's hardly due to a curse."

"Hey, after everything you went through with the Seven Sisters, you should be the last person to not believe in curses."

"Fine, but it still doesn't make any sense."

"What are you going to do about the Palmer assignment?" Sophie asked. "I don't think they're going to use the townhouse anymore, now that you've blown their cover."

I slowly shook my head. "All I can do is follow the doctor around. Hopefully, he'll still see the blonde. I only hope they don't start going to random hotels. I could get videos of them going in and out of the room, but you know how pissy Lenny gets when that's all I can come up with."

"He's pretty specific about that. He wants naked bodies in high definition."

"I suppose it gets our clients better settlements, but still."

"Yeah," Sophie said with a laugh, "I know what you mean. By the way, I was thinking about your old car."

"What? You've come up with some new place you want me to abandon it?"

"No. I've been thinking about what you said about keeping that POS for surveillance and stuff."

"And?"

"And, I think it's a great idea. A Miata isn't exactly subtle for surveillance. Although, I'm glad you got the white one. I know you'd first thought about getting a red one, and that would have been even worse."

"Why am I expecting a but?"

"But I'm thinking your old car is becoming a little too distinctive for surveillance. With the red Bungie cord holding down your trunk and the mirror that's only sort of held on with duct tape, it sticks out like a minister at a strip club."

"Actually, I was thinking the same thing. As soon as I can find a couple of hundred extra in the budget, I'll start to get those things fixed. Oh, I talked with Max about that Viktor guy."

"What did he say?"

"He doesn't think the government knows Viktor's actual name. I have a new alias for you to punch into the secret software."

"You just love having me do searches on radicals and extremists, don't you? Well, if you come in tomorrow and I've disappeared, you'll know what happened. The government will have me stashed in some sort of black ops interrogation facility out in Nevada."

"I think you worry too much."

"The white van is out there again today, and I'm running searches on terrorists like they're my best friends. But okay, fine, whatever. What's the new name?"

"Snow Ghost. He lived in Ukraine, or Georgia, or maybe Russia, somewhere in that part of the world. I know he was active like twelve to fifteen years ago."

"Are you sure you don't mean Space Ghost? I used to love watching that show."

I gave her my best annoyed look.

"Jeez, what's with the look. I'd think you'd be happy I run all these names for you."

"Of course, I appreciate it. I'll tell you what. You type the request in, and I'll buy you lunch the next time we go out."

"Fair enough," she said. "It's a deal."

Lenny opened his office door and came out to reception. He didn't look any better than he did before Christmas.

"Where are you on the Jessica Palmer assignment?" he grumbled at me. "You left me a message about being kidnapped again. What happened this time?"

"On Friday afternoon, I was in the townhouse. Since the blonde hadn't shown up for her last two appointments, I wanted to see if I could learn anything. Three guys followed me into the place and grabbed me. They took me to some sort of scrap metal business south of Curry Road."

"Jeez, Laura," Lenny said, sounding annoyed. "You've got to be more careful. It seems like you get abducted almost every month by someone."

"It's not like I try to get kidnapped."

"Well, you look okay," Lenny said as he looked me up and down. "Do I want to know the details of how you got out of that? We aren't going to have the police over here asking about a lot of dead bodies, are we?"

"No, we won't have the police over here," I fumed. "And yeah, I'm fine. Thanks for asking." I know I sounded a little pissy, but once again, I was amazed and somewhat hurt at Lenny's total lack of empathy.

"Good," he said, still completely unaware I was upset. "So, where are you on getting the video of Michael Palmer?"

"At the moment, I'm not anywhere. The people running things at the townhouse saw me when I planted my spy cameras. I'm pretty sure they've closed up shop and changed locations."

"What? Are you saying you're back to square one? That's freaking great."

"I'm not any happier about it than you are."

"Alright, you're going to need to start over. Go park yourself at the hospital and follow Doctor Palmer. If he keeps the same schedule, he should meet with her again tomorrow afternoon, but we can't count on the timing for that."

"That's assuming they're still going to have the blonde meet with the men. Now that their operation has been found out, they might pull the plug on it."

Lenny shook his head. “They must have some reason they’re using her to have sex with all of the men. Assuming that reason still holds, they’ll probably want the activity to continue. As long as the men themselves don’t know about the cameras, the organizers probably won’t tell them anything about why they’re making the switch in locations.”

“I’ve also been thinking about Doctor Elmaghrabi,” I said.

“Sophie told me about that. What about him?”

“They’re saying he was murdered. I think we might have some information the police would want.”

“Oh, really?” Lenny asked, sounding doubtful. “And what information would that be?”

“Well, I had a video of him with the blonde last week. Something big’s going on, and it’s tied up with the activities at the townhouse. The murder probably also has something to do with the people who took me. I’m sure everything’s connected.”

“But you no longer have the video?”

“No, it didn’t seem relevant at the time and I deleted it.”

“You now see why we have that policy,” Lenny said as he gave me a knowing nod. “Keeping stuff like that can only cause us problems.”

“But shouldn’t I go to the police and let them know what I saw?”

“And tell them what? You had a video of the murdered guy in bed with a pretty woman from the previous week?”

“Well, yes.”

“Was he there under coercion or threat?”

“It didn’t appear so.”

“This woman. Do you know who she is?”

“Not yet.”

“And she’s since disappeared?”

“We haven’t seen her since Thursday morning.”

“Do you have any direct evidence that the woman was involved in a plot to murder him?”

“Um, not exactly, but it all seems completely suspicious.”

“The detectives will want to know how you got the video. They’ll also want to know why you were taking pictures of the murder victim having intimate relations with the blonde in the first place.”

“What we’re doing is legitimate.”

“That’s true. But our first duty is to the client. I don’t want to have her name associated with a murder investigation.”

“But shouldn’t we at least tell the police about what we know?”

“Why? Do you think they’re going to thank you? What do you think they’re going to say when you tell them you destroyed the evidence? All you can tell them is what you remember seeing on a video. You only looked at it once and I imagine you didn’t take the time to carefully watch the entire encounter.”

“No, it was over two hours long.”

“So, you really don’t even know what was on the video you erased.”

“Not the whole thing.”

“Look,” Lenny said. “I know you want to do a good deed and help save the world. But a first-year law student would chew you up if you tried to go on the stand with that.”

“But the murder?” I asked.

“We don’t have any idea what’s been going on at the townhouse, and really, I don’t care. We’re not the police and it’s not our place to get in the middle of a murder investigation. Get the evidence of Doctor Palmer being unfaithful and get out. That’s all I want.”

Lenny turned to go back to his office, and the phone in my back pocket started to buzz. I pulled it out and saw it was the Scottsdale Barrington. I went into the main conference room to take the phone call.

Hopefully, this isn't another problem.

"Hi," the woman said. "This is Maggie Simms. I'm the scheduler over at the Barrington."

"Of course," I said. "What can I do for you?"

"I've been concerned about what happened to Kristy's wedding last week. I spent most of yesterday afternoon trying to piece together what happened. I was thinking she probably made the change to the serving time through an email. I told you I keep all of the emails in a separate folder for each wedding, but I didn't have a record of the change."

"I remember. You seem very organized."

"Well, not organized enough. I went back through my records and found the email. It was in a folder for a different wedding. This one occurred exactly one year earlier. I keep track of my folders by date, and I put it in the right date, but the wrong year."

"That's actually good news," I said. "Someone also sent an email to the DJ at Kristy's wedding last Saturday night at the Tropical Paradise. The email said the wedding was canceled, so she took off for California."

"Oh no," Maggie said. "Were you able to find another DJ on such short notice?"

"We got lucky on that one and found someone willing to play for us. Kristy's changed the passwords to her accounts. We're hoping this will make the problems go away."

"I hope you're right. But honestly, that may only force the person to become more devious. There are all sorts of ways to sabotage a wedding."

Chapter Ten

I disconnected with Maggie and went back to Sophie's desk.

"I keep hitting dead ends on the blackmail ring," I said. "I was thinking, maybe I should approach it from a different angle."

"How so?" she asked.

"When the creeps had me in their torture chamber, a woman came in. She seemed to be in charge of the operation. I'm sure I've seen her somewhere before."

"Any idea where? Is she from the Black Death?"

"I don't think so. It was from somewhere more recent."

"Do you think she's another doctor? Everyone we've dealt with so far is on the senior staff at Scottsdale General."

"Maybe, but I wouldn't think one doctor would be blackmailing another one. It doesn't seem very doctor-like."

"There's one way to find out," Sophie said as she pulled up the website for the hospital. "Let's take a look."

I stood next to Sophie as she brought up the page for the executive staff. By now, it looked like a who's who of my life over the past week.

I quickly scanned down the list and stopped when I saw a smiling picture of the woman who had come into the room to both stop my torture and order my death.

Damn.

"It's her," I said, pointing to the screen. "In this picture she looks a lot nicer, but it's the same woman."

"Lillian Abbot," Sophie read. "I don't think she's a doctor. The letters after her name are CSCP. She's the Director of Supply Chain, whatever that means."

"I think it means she's in charge of everything the hospital buys."

"Oh, that sounds reasonable. I can see a hospital buying a lot of stuff. Still, why would she want to blackmail the rest of the executive staff?"

"I don't know, but I'd love to find out," I said. "Could you do a deep dive on her with the secret software?"

"I figured. I'll run the standard checks at the same time. Since she ordered you dead, we should probably find out what her deal is."

"There was also the jerk who kept jolting me with his pink stun-gun. Lillian called him Benny."

"I'll see what I can find out. I don't suppose you have a last name or a license plate, anything like that?"

"Unfortunately, I was too busy trying to escape with my life."

"Yeah, I suppose that would keep your mind preoccupied."

I then got another thought. "Is it possible to run a search on the hospital itself? Maybe it's not one specific person?"

"I don't see why not. I'll run the standard searches on it, then I'll ask the secret software. I'll let you know when I get everything back."

"Most of the top people at the hospital seem to be involved in whatever is going on. They're either involved in running it or being blackmailed because of it. If we're going to narrow this down, it might be easier to find out who's not involved."

"Well, the only top person who doesn't seem to be tangled up with anything yet is the head of the hospital."

"Who's that?"

"It's J. Barrett Knight," Sophie said as she pointed to the top picture on the web page. "He's listed as both the President and the CEO."

"You say his name like I'm supposed to know him."

"You don't know who J. Barrett Knight is?"

"No, should I?"

"He's one of the Knight brothers of the Wolfe-Knight Foundation."

"Oh, okay, I've heard of them. They're the ones who do the charity events around the Valley."

"Yup, the same group."

"But if one of the Knight family is head of the hospital, maybe whoever's blackmailing the executive staff is only doing it to get to the Wolfe-Knight Foundation."

"That would make sense," Sophie said. "They have tons of money. I bet they'd rather pay someone off than have a nasty sex scandal go public."

"The other possibility is that they're blackmailing him as well and we don't know about it yet. I mean, who knows who the blonde has at the townhouse on Mondays and on the weekends? It could be anybody, even J. Barrett Knight."

My phone buzzed again. This time it was Suzi Lu.

"Hi, Suzi," I said when I answered. "It's been a while since we've talked."

"Laura," she said, sounding happy. "It's great to hear from you. I'm doing really well. I was thinking about you the other day when John and I were talking about his retreat up by Strawberry."

"There are times I wish I had a bunker up in the mountains," I said with a laugh. "It would be great to have somewhere to go where no one had a clue where I was."

"As you know, I never want to know the details of my clients' personal lives. But John mentioned his responsibilities at work are going to be increasing. I can tell he feels pride and a sense of accomplishment at his new position."

"Yes, I also heard about that. I know he'll do great."

"So, what's going on with you?" Suzi asked. "Did you come across another computer file that needs to be cracked?"

"Hold on a second," I said as I looked over at Lenny's door, then motioned Sophie into the main conference room. She grabbed her tablet and walked with me into the room. I closed the door, put the phone on the table, and turned on the speaker.

"You're on speakerphone with Sophie and me," I said. "No, I wanted to ask you about the dominatrix side of things."

"Really?" she asked with her great laugh. "Are you planning on turning to the dark side? I'd be glad to give you some pointers. I might even have some old equipment and books I could let you have."

"No, it's about my boss. Do you remember him from when you were over here?"

"Of course, Lenny. I remember him. He seemed very eager to please. I was actually a little surprised when I didn't hear from him again. I figured he'd want to audition to become one of my boys."

"Well, he's currently going through a break-up and he's taking it pretty hard. I figured if he had someone who could get him through it, maybe it would help."

"Of course. Helping a client go through a tough situation is one of the things I'm best at. Unfortunately, I'm not taking anyone new at the moment. I haven't for several months."

"You aren't getting out of the business, are you?"

"No, not at all. But I already make more money than I can spend, and I'm finding it satisfying to spend more time with each of the clients I already have. I've started to find a good balance. I think my clients appreciate it as well."

"You wouldn't happen to know anyone who's taking on new people, would you?"

"As a matter of fact, one of my protégés, Countess Carla, the Cruel, is currently looking for another man to join her circle."

"That would be great. I know it would do Lenny a world of good. How do we go about this?"

"The process is simple. There first has to be an interview where both sides can get a feel for one another. If there isn't some level of personal chemistry, it would never work out."

"Isn't that what you were doing the day I met you downstairs at the apartment house? You were using that man as a footstool to see if he had the ability to obey you."

"That's right. He passed the audition and is one of my regulars now."

"When can we do the interview?" I asked. "The sooner, the better."

"Well, we had a cancellation for tomorrow afternoon. Would Lenny have any free time?"

Sophie pulled up Lenny's schedule on her tablet and pointed. "Um," she said, "he's free from one until three, if that works for you."

"Perfect," Suzi said. "We'll see you tomorrow afternoon."

"Okay," I said. "We'll see you then."

I disconnected and looked up at Sophie. "Crap, we've pulled the trigger. I only hope this doesn't backfire too badly on us."

"Don't worry about it," she said. "Really, how much worse can this make it?"

"Setting a dominatrix loose on Lenny? Sure, what could possibly go wrong?"

"Well, maybe. But it'll be interesting to watch."

"I need to tell Gina what we've done," I said.

I went to the back offices where Gina was at her desk, typing in a report.

"What's wrong," she asked when I sat at my desk and looked at her.

"Um, Mistress McNasty and her protégé, Countess Carla, the Cruel, will be over here tomorrow afternoon at one o'clock. They'll hold an audition to see if Lenny is worthy of Carla taking him on as a client."

"Well," Gina said. "I don't see how that can make it any worse."

"That's what Sophie said. But somehow, I get the feeling this may not work out quite as we envision."

~~~~

Gina and I were still chatting about the assignments when Lenny walked back. It was apparent he was looking for me.

"Hey," he said as he got to my cube. "I just got a call from Jessica Palmer. With the death of that doctor over the weekend, Elmaghrabi, they're promoting Michael Palmer to the position of Chief Medical Operations Officer."

"That was quick," I said. "They haven't even buried the man yet."

"According to our client, they only informed her husband a few minutes ago. You should probably head over to the hospital and keep
~~~~

an eye out for Doctor Palmer. If he's still seeing the blonde, he might want to go out and celebrate with her."

Lenny went back up to reception. I looked at Gina.

"Well?" I asked.

"If what you've been saying about the blackmail ring is true, it sounds like they're using the carrot and stick approach with the men over there."

"What do you mean?"

"If the guys cooperate, they get promoted and have access to a beautiful woman. If not, they get bashed over the head and tossed off a bridge."

"Lenny thinks I should drop anything having to do with the blackmail and concentrate on getting the sex video."

"He's not wrong. That's all we're getting paid for."

"But the husband of our client is caught up in something big. I know she wants to divorce him, but what if he ends up going to prison? Divorced or not, I don't think she'd like to see the father of her kids in the penitentiary."

"That's true, but be careful. It sounds like you're dealing with some nasty people on this."

Gina took off to work on her assignments. I sat back in my chair and tried to think.

From my conversation with Max, he thought Scottsdale General had a shaky reputation. Still, he didn't know any of the specifics about what was going on over there.

If I was going to get to the bottom of it, I needed to get a fresh perspective on the place. I pulled out my phone and called Danielle.

I've always had a complicated relationship with Danielle Ortega. She started out as my friend, then was an enemy, then became my friend again.

Further complicating things, she had recently assumed leadership of the Arizona branch of the Black Death, the deadly drug cartel out of Mexico.

"Hey, Danielle," I said when she answered.

"Laura," she said, sounding happy to hear from me. "I'm glad you called. I was thinking about you. From what I understand, everything is good with you, Tony, and Max."

"Yes, everything seems to have settled down over there. Thank you for your advice on that."

"What's up today? Are you calling to remind me about the wedding?"

"Well, yes. That was one of the things. Grandma's starting to get excited about it."

"I really like her," Danielle said. "I'm looking forward to going. Are Sophie and Gina still planning on being there?"

"Yes, and don't forget, you're my cousin from Albuquerque. You'll have to sit at our table."

"It sounds like fun. Is everyone bringing a date?"

"I think so. Gina has a new boyfriend and Sophie is down to one."

"Really? I never thought she'd have only one. It sounds like there's a story behind that."

"There is, but I'll let her tell it. Are you still seeing Roberto?"

"Yes, it's been almost two months already. We still get along, so I'm hopeful."

"Wow, time flies."

"I know. What are you getting Grandma for a wedding present? I have no clue what she needs."

"That one was tough," I said. "I ended up getting them a gift certificate for dinner at Different Pointe of View. It's one of my favorite places in town, and I think they'll like it as well."

"Maybe I'll stop by sometime before the wedding and ask her what she wants. What else did you want to talk about?"

"This may seem like a weird question. But do you know anything about Scottsdale General Hospital?"

"Like what?"

"I'm not entirely sure. I'm in the middle of an assignment for work, and I seem to have stumbled across a serious sex and blackmail ring. Everyone seems to be connected with the executive staff of Scottsdale General."

"You have the most interesting job," she said with a laugh.

"Interesting isn't the word I would use. Have you heard anything about the hospital?"

"About sex and blackmail? No, nothing like that."

"Have you heard about anything else?"

"Nothing directly, but Carlos used to grumble about them. He said they were making it harder for us to get into narcotics."

"Max said they keep hiring employees who eventually get caught stealing drugs."

"I've heard the same thing. You'd have to question why the hospital would employ people like that."

"But even if there were three or four people sneaking drugs out, you wouldn't think the amount making it to the street would be very high."

"I don't know," Danielle said. "But we've never had a lot of luck with selling pills. The street value is too low to make a profit on it."

"That also confirms what I've been hearing," I said.

"I'll see if I can find out anything on them and let you know. In either case, we'll see you Saturday night at the Scottsdale Barrington."

"We'll save a place in the pew for you."

~~~~

I had packed up and was about to head up to the hospital to see if Michael Palmer would meet up with the blonde, when my phone buzzed. It was Sophie.

"Are you still here?"

"Yes, I was about to leave."

"Well, come up here first."

I walked to the front, where Sophie was pulling some paper from her printer.

"Hey," she said. "I've got the first results back on the hospital. I did several web searches and checked out their credit rating, stuff like that."

"What did you come up with?"

"Not a thing. They're clean as a whistle."

"That doesn't make any sense. Didn't they have anything on all of the people they caught stealing drugs?"

"Well, yeah. There are actually several articles about that."

"And?"

"And the police say Scottsdale General is a model for other hospitals in how they control their drug inventories."

"Really?"

"The police say the hospital has put in so many safety measures, they recommend other hospitals adopt the same policies."
~~~~

"Max said the hospital has a shaky reputation and Danielle said they were having a harder time getting into narcotics because of them. What do you think?"

"I think we'll need to decide how we're going to handle the wedding," Sophie said.

"What's there to handle?"

"We're going to have Max and Danielle sitting at the same table. They might each bring along a bodyguard or two. Gina still doesn't know about Danielle being head of the Black Death. The whole situation could become awkward."

"I don't think anyone will want to talk business," I said. "It's a wedding."

"Well, I hope so. I trust Danielle and everything. But I remember what happened the last time the Black Death came to a wedding." Sophie then made hand gestures to mimic an exploding wedding cake. "Boom."

"Do you seriously think Danielle would plant a bomb at a wedding she's going to?"

"Probably not. But if she takes off unusually early, I might step outside for a few minutes while they serve the cake."

~~~~

Taking Lenny's advice, I drove up to the hospital campus on Haden Road and found Michael Palmer's car. It was parked in the doctor's lot, as it had been the first time I'd looked for it.

I sat there for the rest of the afternoon. A little before six, Doctor Palmer walked to his car and took off.

I followed two cars back until it was apparent he was simply heading home. By this point, I was getting hungry, and I peeled off.

I went to a Filiberto's for a drive-through beef taco and a carne
~~~~

asada burrito. I then drove home to Marlowe.

~~~~

The following day, I arrived at the office a few minutes after eight. Marlowe had been in a fidgety mood the night before and had spent much of the night playing with his tail.

Unfortunately, he'd been on the bed with me while he'd been doing this. Needless to say, I hadn't gotten a lot of sleep.

"I got the secret software reports back on the hospital," Sophie said as I meandered up to her desk.

"Great," I said with a touch of sarcasm. "What do they say? Does the government also think the hospital is clean as a whistle?"

"Not exactly. According to the secret software, Scottsdale General is currently being investigated by both the FBI and DEA for running a major narcotics ring."

"Wow. Really?"

"There's page after page of it. They suspect it's been going on for years."

"Well, Max and Danielle both said the place seems a little shaky, and I understand a big hospital would have a lot of drugs flowing through it. But you'd think a hospital would be about the worst place to run a drug ring."

"Why's that?"

"It's like you found in the newspaper articles," I said. "They'd have all sorts of accounting and reporting requirements, stuff like that. You'd think they'd need to be pretty strict about keeping everything straight."

"From what I read in the report, the records from the pharmacy at the hospital have never been right."

"How could something like that be messed up?"
~~~~

"Well, they had an office fire a little over five years ago that destroyed a lot of their records. Then, they had a warehouse fire three years ago that supposedly ruined a lot of the pharmacy's drugs."

"Seriously?"

"They'd supposedly just gotten in a big shipment and were storing everything in the warehouse. The hospital wrote off the entire thing as being destroyed."

"Seems like a lot of bad luck for one hospital."

"That's not all of it. Last year, they reported some sort of ransomware that supposedly corrupted their inventory files. They also seem to have a string of fall-guys."

"What do you mean?"

"It's the people we keep hearing about. Five times in the last four years, the hospital has turned in someone they say had been stealing drugs. In every case, they gave the police video records of the person actually committing the theft. The hospital is saying these people and the thefts are the reason why their accounting records are so messed up."

"You'd think the cops would be able to piece together what's happening over there."

"It looks like they suspect what's going on but haven't been able to actually prove anything."

"Have the reports come through on Lillian Abbot yet?"

"The regular reports say she's clean. She has no criminal background, hasn't had a parking ticket, nothing like that, and her credit's good. Only, it's sort of weird."

"How is it weird?"

"The records on her only go back a few years."

"Is that unusual?"

"I can usually find records on someone at least back to high school. But with her, there's nothing. I can't even find the college she went to."

"Maybe she changed her name after a divorce?"

"Maybe, and Abbot is a relatively common name, so I might have completely missed it."

"Did you do a deep dive?"

"Yes, but the secret software reports on her haven't come back yet."

"I'll keep my fingers crossed."

"Speaking of the secret software, I made a call this morning on the office phone, and it was making some weird clicks," Sophie said.

"What kind of weird clicks?"

"Like maybe someone's running a wiretap on it."

"Are you still worried about the Men in Black?"

"You don't think I should be? I read stories in the news all the time about people disappearing when they get too close to the truth."

"By the news, are you talking about the tabloids you get in the check-out line at the grocery store?"

"Hey, the news in those papers is as good as anything I've seen lately on the networks. If you want to hear a lot of crazy conspiracy theories, just tune in to the nightly network news."

~~~~

I drove up to Scottsdale General and sat for almost three hours watching Michael Palmer's car. I decided that if I was going to continue to do this for a living, I'd need to take up knitting or something else to keep me busy while I sat around doing nothing.

I had just started thinking about food when Sophie called.
~~~~

“Hey,” she said. “Are you coming back to the office? Suzi’s supposed to be here sometime this afternoon.”

“I’ll be down there in twenty minutes,” I said. “So far, Michael Palmer hasn’t gone anywhere but to work since last Thursday.”

Chapter Eleven

I walked up to the front to find Gina huddled with Sophie at her desk, looking down at a report.

"Hey," Sophie said as I walked up. "I got the secret software reports back on Lillian Abbot."

"And?"

"And you know how I said there weren't any old records on her?"

"Yeah, what did you find out?"

"Well, it turns out, before about seven years ago, Lillian Abbot didn't exist."

"She had to exist somewhere," I said.

"We've spent the last two hours punching everything we know about her into the secret software to see if we could get a match," Sophie said.

"But we hardly have any information on her at all," I pointed out.

"True," Gina said. "Fortunately, the website picture of her is in high-definition. Sophie was able to use the facial recognition feature of the database."

"Well?" I asked.

"According to what we've been able to piece together," Sophie said,

"Lillian Abbot is an alias for a woman named Ruth Skaggs."

"Really? What else did you find out?"

"She's been a criminal for most of her life. She also spent three years in prison for running a narcotics ring out of a medical clinic in Vicksburg, Mississippi, where they had the big Civil War battle. After her release, seven years ago, she disappeared and is currently wanted for multiple parole violations."

"Are there any pictures of her?" I asked.

"Several," Sophie said as she displayed them on her monitor. Most of the photos were of the woman in prison orange.

"Yup," I said. "It's the same woman. How did the hospital miss that when they ran her background check?"

"We're thinking they didn't miss it," Gina said. "Maybe they even hired her *because* of it."

"What do you mean?"

"Think about it," Gina said. "If you wanted to make a lot of money by setting up your hospital to be a secret narcotics ring, you'd want to hire someone who already knew how to do it."

"Whoever brought her in would need to be pretty high up in the hospital," I said. "Covering up something like that would take a lot of authority."

"Well," Sophie said as she brought up the executive staff of Scottsdale General on her monitor again. "The only person who seems to be above it all is him." She then pointed to the President and CEO.

"J. Barrett Knight?" I asked. "We talked about him the other day. It doesn't make any sense. His family pours millions of dollars into every charity in Scottsdale you can think of. I don't see how he could be involved in any of it."

"Fine," Sophie said. "You come up with a better explanation."

"What about the guy who attacked me? His name was Benny."

"I cross-referenced everyone who works at the hospital with the name of Benjamin or Benny," Sophie said. "I found a guy who's listed as a warehouse manager called Benjamin Todd."

"Do you have a picture of him?"

"Here you go," Sophie said as she pulled up a photo that had been taken as a police mugshot.

As I looked at the picture, the face was several years younger, and the hair was shorter, but I recognized the man as the one who had taken such pleasure in torturing me.

"That's him," I said. "What do you know about him?"

"According to the secret software, he was born and raised in Vicksburg. He was working in a local clinic there when Lillian Abbot set up her narcotics operation. This was back when she was known as Ruth Skaggs. He has a long list of minor criminal convictions, mainly assaults, DUIs, bar fights, things like that."

"He didn't get fingered for his part in the drug ring?"

"It doesn't look like it. He seems to have escaped undetected when Ruth Skaggs headed to prison."

"He seems like a slippery little creep," I said. "I could see him talking his way out of a situation."

"Well, you said he was bad news," Gina said.

"I take it Lillian hired him when she became the Supply Chain director for the hospital?"

"It doesn't say who hired him," Sophie said. "But he started about three months after Lillian Abbot joined the executive staff."

"I'd say that's close enough for a connection."

~~~~
~~~~

After lunch, Gina and I gathered at Sophie's desk while we waited for Suzi to call. I was still stressing about the meeting while Sophie seemed to be like a kid waiting to open a big present. As usual, Gina was calm and was simply taking in the situation.

My phone rang and I pulled it out of my back pocket. It was Suzi Lu.

"Hi, Suzi," I said. "You're on speakerphone with Sophie and Gina."

"Laura, I'm with Carla. Will this afternoon still work for the introduction? We'll need at least half an hour when we won't be disturbed. Forty-five minutes would be better."

"We're ready for you," Sophie said. "Anytime between one and three-thirty should be good. It's only the four of us here, and we don't have any clients scheduled for the rest of the afternoon. All Lenny is doing is preparing for a hearing on Friday."

"Perfect," Suzi said. "Thanks, Sophie. We're half a block down the street. We'll be there in two minutes."

I disconnected, and Gina looked at me. "You still seem uneasy about this," she said in her motherly tone.

"I really hope this works out," I said. "The last time we set Lenny up with someone, it turned out to be a real roller coaster ride."

"Yeah, but I gotta see what happens," Sophie said. "I've been looking forward to this all day."

"Well," Gina said. "At least this will be interesting."

Sophie hit the intercom button. "Boss, would you mind coming out to the front for a minute?"

The door to Lenny's office opened and he walked up to Sophie's desk. "What?" he asked, clearly annoyed.

As if expecting a new client, he looked around, but it was only the three of us. "Where's the client?" he asked.

"Um," I said. "This isn't about a new client."

"Okay," he said, sounding irritated. "So, what is it then?"

The front door opened and Mistress McNasty strolled in. She was wearing a tight red leather shirt, unbuttoned down to her navel, and a pair of black leather pants. She held a riding crop and was slapping it against the palm of her hand.

Behind her walked a woman, maybe thirty-five years old. My first impression was the woman was an Amazon, like in Wonder Woman.

Where Suzi is of average height and thin, the woman with her was at least six feet tall and athletic. She had long red hair that curled halfway down her back. She was wearing black leather pants and a tight blue leather shirt, which was opened to expose an ample amount of doctor-assisted cleavage.

Her boots had a three-inch heel, which made her even more imposing. She looked erotic and intimidating, sort of like Gabriella, but with less feeling of outright danger.

Lenny's mouth dropped open, and his eyes bugged out in surprise. "Mistress McNasty?" he asked weakly.

Lenny stood in the middle of the reception area while the two women slowly circled him. I could smell their perfumes mingling as the air slowly swirled around the office.

It didn't take long for Lenny to become self-conscious as the women assessed him. He seemed to shrink as he looked back and forth between them.

Suzi looked Lenny over with mild disdain. "Slug," she said. "It has come to my attention that a proper woman has recently dismissed you from her life. No doubt it was because you're so weak and disgusting."

Lenny's eyes became slightly unfocused and he got a look of confusion on his face. "Um, yes, mistress," he quietly said. "How did you know?"

"It's my business to know these things. As it so happens, you did me a service several months ago. I wish to repay my debt by introducing you to Countess Carla, the Cruel. Perhaps she can make a man out of you."

"Mistress, you didn't tell me he was this pathetic," Carla said to Suzi as they continued to circle. "I mean, just look at him. It will take weeks to achieve even basic discipline with him. I really don't know if I want to put in the effort. The final results will be miserable, at best. I have my reputation to think of."

"I realize he's wretched and completely loathsome," Suzi said. "Still, he does have one or two qualities that give me a faint glimmer of hope. I think he can be trained to at least obey you."

"I have my doubts," Countess Carla said as she shook her head. "But as a personal favor to you, Mistress McNasty, I'll interview him. That is assuming he can afford me. One look at the sorry state of this office and I'm already having second thoughts."

"Oh no," Lenny said, now excited as he looked back and forth between the two women. "I have plenty of money. I just never spend any of it fixing up this place. It pretty much looks the same as it has since the nineteen-eighties. The carpet hasn't been replaced for over twenty years."

Gina and Sophie looked at each other. "Eeewww," they both said in unison.

"Worm," Suzi said. "Do you have someplace private where Countess Carla can judge you?"

"Um, yes, mistress," Lenny said as he looked back and forth between the two stern faces. "We can use my office." His voice was shaking and I couldn't tell if it was from fear or excitement. Maybe it was a bit of both.

Lenny led the women into his office and closed the door. The three of us stood in a slightly shocked silence for several seconds.

“Wow,” Sophie said. “That was amazing.”

“This will certainly take Lenny’s mind off Elle dumping him,” Gina said.

“Yeah, but did you see the look on his face?” I asked. “I still hope we haven’t created another monster with this.”

“I thought it was hot,” Sophie said. “I wouldn’t mind if those two women started walking around me and talking about my need for some firm discipline.”

“Eeewww,” Gina and I both said.

“Hey,” Sophie said, slightly annoyed. “Don’t yuck on my yum.”

We walked closer to Lenny’s office, but all we heard was the quiet murmur of voices. After the excitement we’d just had, it was a little disappointing.

Ten minutes later, the office door opened and Suzi came out.

“It’s looking good so far,” she said. “Carla will have a mini-session with Lenny to see if he can follow orders and obey her without question. Assuming it goes well, the sessions after this will be at her dungeon.”

“Is there anything we should do to help?” Gina asked.

“Actually, there is. Pretend you don’t know where he’s going when he disappears at the same time every week. In fact, don’t even mention this happened at all. It will work out best if Lenny keeps this as something separate.”

“We can do that,” I said.

“With all the talk about Lenny’s money, should we be worried?” Gina asked.

“No, Carla is good. Lenny won’t be allowed to give her anything of value, other than the agreed-upon fees for their sessions. Now, these fees can be as high as both parties agree to, but she’ll keep it reasonable and the price will be arranged ahead of time. She's not trying to cheat him or trick him in any way."

"You don't know Lenny," Sophie said. "If he falls for her, I can see him going completely overboard."

"That can happen, and you'll all need to help keep an eye on him," Suzi said. "Especially during the first few months. A new client will sometimes try to show his appreciation by attempting to give expensive gifts. Carla wouldn't accept one if he tried, but be alert if he buys anything to give to her."

"What will she do if Lenny insists on giving her presents?" Gina asked.

"In that case, let Carla know. She'll focus his gifts on something positive. Is there anything you can think of that would benefit him? Some worthy cause or charity he's been wanting to get into?"

Sophie looked around the office. "Redecorating this crappy place would be a start, especially after that crack about not replacing the carpet in twenty years. Maybe then we'd attract a higher class of clients."

"That would be perfect," Suzi said, smiling broadly. "Something like that would benefit everyone, not just Lenny. I'll be sure to let Carla know."

From inside Lenny's office, we heard Carla shout: "Obey me, slave."

This was followed by the distinctive sound of a hand striking flesh and then Lenny yelping like a small dog. He started to make a hurt, whimpering noise. It was actually kind of creepy.

"Do you think everything's going alright in there?" Gina asked, her eyebrows raised.

"Oh yes," Suzi said with a laugh. "I've been waiting for it. Lenny needed to experience something painful to drive home the concept that he's not in control when he's in the presence of his mistress. Don't worry. She'll never do anything to permanently damage him."

~~~~

Twenty minutes later, the office door opened, and Countess Carla, the Cruel, stepped out. She was smiling brightly and I could tell she had enjoyed herself.

She made eye contact with Suzi and nodded her head. At this, Suzi also broke out in one of her infectious smiles.

"Very well," Suzi said. "We're done here. Lenny will be acceptable. Remember everything we talked about. And make sure to call if there's anything I can do to help."

"Thank you so much for the referral," Carla said to us in a quiet voice. "He seems like a total sweetheart."

We looked at each other and Gina wrinkled her nose. Sweetheart wasn't a term anyone had ever used before about Lenny.

The two women took off through the front door. A minute or so later, Lenny came out of his office looking dazed, but happy. He was holding a glass of Beam on the rocks.

The entire left side of his face had a bright red mark from where Countess Carla had slapped him. From the size of it, she had put some force behind her swing.

"Wow," Sophie said, ignoring Suzi's advice not to talk about the session. "What happened to you?"

"Um," Lenny said. "I didn't answer a question quickly enough, so Countess Carla slapped me. Only, she called it a correction." He reached up and felt the red mark on his cheek. "It hurt, but it also felt kind of good at the same time. It's hard to describe."

Sophie nodded her head, as if she completely understood. Gina and I only looked at each other.
~~~~

"Sophie," Lenny said. "I'm going, um, golfing this Thursday morning, from nine to noon. And, I'm also going golfing every Thursday from nine to noon, from now on."

"Okay," Sophie said with a knowing smile. "I'll put it on your calendar."

"I'll be in my office for a while. Make sure I'm not disturbed for at least half an hour. I need a couple of cigarettes."

~~~~

On the way up to the wedding at the Saguaro Sky, I swung by Scottsdale General to see if Michael Palmer's Porsche was still there. If he was still seeing the blonde, but in a different location, I knew I still had a hope of getting a video.

Even if the blonde wasn't going to be with the men anymore, I was hoping he had some sort of backup concubine he'd be with on a regular basis. Unfortunately, the Boxster was still in the lot.

Michael seemed to be working at the hospital for the day. I stayed as long as I could, then took off for the wedding.

~~~~

I arrived in the guest parking lot at the Saguaro Sky a little after three o'clock. The wedding wasn't scheduled until five-thirty, but I knew Kristy was worried about it going off smoothly and would already be here.

As always, whenever I come up to the Saguaro Sky, I felt that special closeness to the resort. In my own small way, I knew I had helped shape it into what it has become.

The wedding would be held in the White Chapel. I knew from previous visits that it was a lovely venue that held about a hundred guests.

The reception was scheduled at the Hohokam Ballroom and Terrace. This was the same space where the cougars had thrown a graduation party for Annie, back in June, when she'd graduated from college.

Half of it was inside and decorated as a fairytale ballroom. The other half was outside on a tropical patio, overlooking a waterfall and one of the resort's larger pools.

I walked to the White Chapel and looked around for Kristy but couldn't find her anywhere. The chapel itself was dark and completely empty. Except for the pews and the altar, the room had no decorations at all.

Confused, I walked to the Hohokam Ballroom. When I got there, Kristy was walking out. The look on her face confirmed there was a problem.

"What's going on?" I asked. "The chapel doesn't even have the lights on. Nothing's been decorated yet."

"That's not the worst of it," she said. "Take a look in there. Nothing's been set up. The wedding ceremony is in two hours, and the tables aren't even in the ballroom yet. I'm going to find Camille and find out what's happening. She's head of events here."

"What can I do?"

Kristy thought for a moment. "Go out to the loading ramp and look for the florist. They're supposed to be here in about fifteen minutes. Assuming they show up, help them move the wedding flowers to the chapel and the reception flowers in here."

"And then?"

"Come find me. Camille has her offices on the mezzanine floor, above the main lobby."

Kristy took off to find out what was going on, and I went into the ballroom. As she had said, the venue was utterly empty.

The lights were off, and the big room echoed as I walked through it. I walked out to the patio, and it didn't have so much as a table or chair on it.

I left the ballroom and went to find the florist. When I made my way back to the loading dock, the delivery van was pulling up. I introduced myself and helped them load flowers onto some oversized plastic carts.

Wheeling the flowers through the resort, we took the first load to the White Chapel. We dropped them off in front of the alter, then went back and loaded up the remaining arrangements. I led the way to the ballroom, where we dropped everything off against a back wall.

~ ~ ~ ~

I'd made it halfway back to the resort's business offices when I ran into Kristy. She looked terrible.

"Well?" I asked. "What happened?"

"I found Camille. When I asked her why nothing had been set up, she said I'd canceled the wedding."

"She said you canceled?" I asked. "That makes no sense."

Kristy shook her head in defeat. "I've got eighty people who'll be here for a wedding in an hour and a half, and nothing's ready. Did the flowers come?"

"Yes, they're in the chapel and the ballroom."

"Okay, that's one problem avoided. I've already dropped off the stationary. Fortunately, there isn't much to do in the chapel other than the ribbons, the guest book table, and the flowers."

"Do you need me for that?"

"No, the wedding party should be arriving soon. I'll rope the bridesmaids into helping me decorate the chapel before the pre-ceremony pictures. They won't suspect anything's wrong. They'll think it's all part of the fun."

"What can I do?"

"Camile is working to find people to set up and work the reception. If you could go back and help her, it would probably speed things along. Plus, if you have any friends who wouldn't mind helping us tonight, now would be a good time to start calling."

"Let me see what I can do," I said. "While you're setting up the chapel, why don't you call the other vendors and make sure they're still coming."

"That's a good idea," she said. "But if anyone else calls off, this whole thing is going to quickly fall apart."

~~~~

I went back to the business offices and searched until I found Camille's office. It was empty, so I found Jackie's office instead. When I got there, Jackie was having a discussion with a woman about the cancelation.

I knocked on the door frame, and Jackie looked up.

"Oh, hi Laura," she said. "I'll be with you in just a minute. We're having a bit of a crisis today."

"If it's about the wedding, I'm part of that."

Jackie laughed and shook her head. "I should have known. Laura, this is Camille Conner. She's our events manager. Camile, this is Laura Black. She works as an investigator for a law office in Old Town Scottsdale."

Camille and I shook hands, but she was obviously upset and distracted.

"Do you have any idea what happened?" Camille asked. "My day was going great until ten minutes ago when Kristy came in here asking why nothing had been set up. When I told her she'd canceled the wedding, it was obviously news to her."

"Someone's been sabotaging Kristy's weddings," I said. "They've hacked into her email and have been sending out last-minute
~~~~

cancellations to her vendors."

"Breaking into an email account is pretty hardcore," Jackie said. "Somebody must really be upset with her."

I frowned and started to think about what had happened. "As soon as Kristy realized what was going on, she changed all of her passwords. How were you told the wedding tonight was canceled?"

"I got a voicemail from Kristy yesterday morning," Camille said. "At least, I thought it was from her. She said the wedding would be canceled for today, and she'd call later to reschedule."

"Do you still happen to have the voicemail? I'd like to hear it."

She shook her head. "After she said it was canceled, I deleted the message. It didn't seem important to keep it."

"Is there any way we can still do the wedding?" I asked hopefully.

"Well," Camille said, doubt in her voice. "The venues are still available, but nothing is set up. That alone usually takes a couple of hours. I also haven't scheduled anyone to work the event. For something this size, we'll need a total of at least ten people. Twelve would be better."

"Will you be able to get enough people in to make it go smoothly?"

"Honestly? I don't think it's possible. The week between Christmas and New Year's is a horrible time to call people in at the last minute. If they're not already here working, most of them are traveling."

"What needs to be done?" I asked.

"Well, there's the general setup of the chapel and the ballroom. We also have to set the dining area up for approximately eighty guests. We're talking twelve tables. Each one needs linens, place settings, flowers, and stationery."

"I helped bring in the flowers so that part's covered. Kristy already brought in the stationary."

"She's using her own caterer so the food won't be affected," Camille said. "But we'll also need to set up the gift and cake tables."

"I think we can do that. What about the appetizers and dinner?"

"The hard part will be finding enough servers," Jackie said. "We'll need at least five. Six would be better. I can probably pull one or two in from the other restaurants, but keep in mind, this is our busiest time of the year. I'm already short on staff."

"What else will we need to cover?"

"Can you run the music for the ceremony?" Jackie asked, looking at Camille.

"No problem. I've had to do it before."

"Perfect," Jackie said. "So, I think the bartender is the only other skill position we'll need."

"Can you start calling and see who we can get?" I asked. "I'll be working the event, and Kristy will be there to help direct everyone. I'll call Sophie and see what she's up to tonight. She likes weddings."

"Okay," Jackie said. "I'll see who's on-site that can help out. But don't be surprised if you see team members from housekeeping and the maintenance crews in to help."

As I walked back to the ballroom, I pulled out my phone and called Sophie. "Hey, chica," I said when she answered. "Kristy has a major problem over here. Somebody called the resort and canceled the entire wedding."

"Oh, crap," she said. "What are you going to do? Are they going to have to postpone the wedding? Seriously, I don't know how you would even try to reschedule an entire wedding."

"Fortunately, the venues are still available, but Jackie doesn't have anyone to do set-up or work the reception. It's all hands on deck. Are you available tonight?"

"Jeeeeze," she moaned. "You know, this makes twice in one week you've asked a big favor from me. You're starting to pile them up."

"I know, but can you come over here?"

"Oh, I suppose. It'll be better than sitting at the desk for the rest of the afternoon. And since it's actually work-related, Lenny can't get too upset over it."

"Okay, only try to be here as soon as you can. We're crazy tight on time. Jackie's pulling people in from wherever she can."

"I'll call Gina," Sophie said. "If she's not going somewhere with Jet tonight, I'll make sure she comes in as well. It'll help spread the pain around."

Chapter Twelve

I went back to the ballroom, and the lights were now on. A good-looking man in his late twenties, wearing a resort maintenance uniform, was rolling a big round table in from a back room.

"Where can I find the chairs?" I asked.

"They're on carts in the back," he said, flashing me a beautiful smile. "I'll show you where they are."

A woman from the business office arrived and helped us gather everything from a storage room. It was slow going, but we were eventually able to bring out the supplies.

Kristy came in with a copy of the reception layout and directed the placement of everything. Once everyone had their instructions, she took off to supervise the pre-ceremony pictures.

Sophie arrived and immediately attached herself to the cute guy from maintenance. She helped him finish bringing out the rest of the tables. They then took off to bring in the portable bar and gather the carts of alcohol, mixers, and supplies.

Jackie had also arrived, followed a few minutes later by Gina and Jet. Gina made introductions to Jackie. From the way Jackie looked him up and down, she was impressed with Gina's new boyfriend.

"Thank you both for coming out," Jackie said. "Right now, we're setting up the guest dining tables. We already have the first one completely done, and you can use it as a reference. We have eleven more to go."

Gina and Jet got to work setting up the tables. As I suspected, they worked remarkably well together. I then helped Jackie set up the banquet, gift, and cake tables.

We were working steadily and seemed to have established a rhythm when I checked the time. It was already after six o'clock.

I knew the ceremony was finishing up, and eighty hungry and thirsty people were sitting in the chapel. I looked around at the half-finished room and felt a sense of dread.

The door to the back opened. I had visions of guests pouring in, a half-hour early. Instead, it was a younger guy. He wore a flashy outfit with several gold necklaces and pushed a cart full of sound and lighting equipment.

"Hey, Jackie," he called out. "Should I set up in the usual place?"

"Santiago," she said with a wide smile. "It's good to see you. Yes, the same place as last time." The DJ then wheeled his cart to a spot in the back of the ballroom and began to unload the equipment.

I walked over to Jackie. "We have less than half an hour until everyone starts to come in. Is this going to work?"

"The caterer has arrived and is getting ready in the kitchen," she said. "We might even get the ballroom and terrace set up before everyone walks in."

"So, we'll be okay?" I asked hopefully.

Jackie shook her head. "I have someone trying to call in additional staff, but so far, no one is even answering the phone."

"How bad is this going to be?"

"Even with Gina, Jet, and Kristy, we still don't have nearly enough people."

"Camille will be back in a few minutes, once the ceremony finishes."

"Yes, and we also have a server coming over at seven o'clock from one of the restaurants. Sophie's volunteered to be the bartender, so that will help. We also have a woman from housekeeping who's in the back changing into a server's uniform. But honestly, this is going to be a slow-motion nightmare."

Even as she said this, the back door to the ballroom opened. We both looked up, again afraid the guests were starting to arrive. Instead, Pam, Elle, Shannon, and Cindy walked in.

Each of them was dressed for a night on the town, complete with perfect hair and makeup. As they got closer, the familiar scent of several mingled high-end perfumes surrounded us.

"Is this the right ballroom?" Elle asked with a broad smile. "We heard you were having a crisis and needed some help."

"Oh my God," I said. "Thank you so much for coming out. You're saving us from a complete disaster."

"Ladies, thank you for coming over," Jackie said. "Laura's right. You're helping prevent a catastrophe. I didn't know if anyone had gotten my voicemails or not."

"Annie's visiting her parents in Colorado," Pam said as she walked over to hug Jackie and me. "Sonia probably would have come out as well. But she's spending a couple of weeks down on Saint Thomas for Christmas."

"Wow, that would be a great place to spend the holidays," I said.

"It's her favorite island in the Caribbean," Cindy said. "She owns a house overlooking the bay at Charlotte Amalie."

"In case you haven't heard, Sonia's started dating a pole vaulter from the ASU track team," Shannon said with a laugh. "She wanted to take him down to Saint Thomas over his Christmas vacation and show him a good time."

Gina saw the cougars arrive and brought Jet over to introduce him to everyone. From the way the girls looked him over, they all approved as well.

Sophie also saw the cougars come in. She waved and yelled out "hello" from across the ballroom. But she was still setting up the bar with the good-looking guy and didn't seem inclined to leave him.

"I don't know what Jackie's told you about tonight," I said to the ladies. "But we'll be serving appetizers and dinner for about eighty people. Will that be okay with everyone?"

Elle started laughing. "Laura, you're so sweet. But we weren't always rich. I worked my way through college as a waitress."

"I spent two years working at a Denny's," Pam said. "It's a skill you never lose."

"And I've hosted larger parties than this at my home," Shannon said with a laugh. "Tonight will be a piece of cake."

~~~~

By six-thirty, the ballroom was finished, the bar had been stocked, and we were outside, finishing up on the terrace. We were as ready as we were going to get.

The guests all seemed to arrive at once. Half of them went to find their places at the tables while the other half went to the bar. The DJ started playing some upbeat music, and we were suddenly in the middle of a lively party.

With Kristy directing in the kitchen and Camille leading the servers, the hors d'oeuvres and dinner went relatively smoothly. The only hitch was when some of the guests started asking the cougars out on dates as they circulated through the room carrying the trays of appetizers.
~~~~

I'd been concerned over Sophie's ability to handle so many people at once. But she turned out to be a natural.

It was an open bar, but she'd placed a big tip jar on the counter. She'd also unbuttoned the top two buttons on her blouse. After doing this, most of the men would toss in a dollar or two every time Sophie made them a drink.

I went back several times to see if she needed help, but she said she only required me to keep everything stocked. As I walked through the crowd, several people commented that her drinks were strong but delicious.

I went out to the patio a few times to gather up the hors d'oeuvre plates and the glasses. The guests from up north were walking around in short sleeves without seeming to notice the cold. The Scottsdale natives were huddled around one of several industrial-sized heaters, which had been strategically placed around the patio by the good-looking maintenance man.

While I served the dinners then cleaned up afterward, I overheard several men comment that the resort must have brought in a group of professional models to work the reception. Each of the men seemed appreciative and impressed.

~~~~

By nine o'clock, everyone had enjoyed a piece of cake, the newlywed couple had their first dance, and the dinner was winding down. Kristy, Camille, and Jackie called everyone together and thanked them for their help.

Gina and Jet said their goodbyes and took off. They'd made an effective team and looked cute together.

The DJ turned up the volume on the music, and the guests were starting to drift out to the dance floor. As the cougars and the servers began to go their separate ways, Elle walked over to me.

"Laura," she said. "Now that we've done our good deed for Jackie,
~~~~

we're going out. Why don't you come with us tonight?"

"Thanks, but I can't. I'm actually here working on an assignment. Someone's been sabotaging Kristy's weddings. Tonight is only the latest example. I'm trying to figure out who's doing it and stop them."

"Sophie was filling us in on all of the crazy things that have been happening with Kristy's events. Whoever's doing it almost succeeded in ruining the wedding tonight. I'm glad we were available to help you and Jackie out."

"So am I. Um, I heard you and Lenny didn't work out."

"No, and I do actually feel terrible about how I acted the other night. But he came out and told me he loved me and wanted to go on a vacation with me. I was a little hesitant about dating a guy long-term in the first place. When he said that, it sort of freaked me out a little."

"Yeah, we heard about it. Lenny can be a little awkward around women at times."

"Is he doing okay? I probably hurt his feelings, and I never meant for that to happen. But when he said those things, I had a little bit of a panic attack. I had to leave while I could still breathe without hyperventilating."

"He'll be alright. Dating is a relatively new thing for Lenny. I think it's going to take him a while before he gets the hang of it."

~~~~

I followed Kristy around for the rest of the reception and helped keep the bar stocked for Sophie. Even though some of the guests had already taken off, the ones who'd stayed seemed to be making full use of the open bar.

Sophie worked like a machine, but she had a broad smile and seemed to be having a great time. She'd unbuttoned the third button down on her blouse, and her tip jar was close to overflowing.

~~~~

I had a hard time waking up the following day, but Marlowe was insistent. I managed to get dressed without incident and made it to the office by eight.

Gina wasn't in, but Sophie's and Lenny's cars were in the back. I walked up to reception, where Sophie was smiling and scrolling through her tablet.

"Good morning," she said brightly.

"You're in a good mood. Thanks for coming out last night. I know I keep asking favors of you, but I was getting desperate."

"Don't worry about it," she said. "I had a lot of fun. In fact, I was thinking, maybe I should talk with Jackie about moonlighting as a bartender on a regular basis."

"Why would you want to do that?"

Sophie opened her desk drawer and handed me a thick stack of dollar bills, held together with a rubber band.

"What's this for?" I asked.

"They put almost five hundred dollars in the tip jar last night. I'll send two hundred to Jackie to hand out to the people working with us, but that still leaves almost a hundred for each of us."

Damn, maybe I should moonlight as a bartender as well?

Sophie looked at me as if she were about to say something. "What?" I asked.

"It's probably nothing," she said as she shook her head. "But it was weird."

"What was weird?"

"Lenny, this morning." Her eyes flicked to his closed office door.

"What about him?"

"He was nice to me. I'm not sure why, but it kind of gave me the creeps."

"Lenny's never nice to us. I wonder if it has something to do with Countess Carla?"

"Maybe," Sophie said. "But it was still totally weird."

~~~~

I went back to my desk and opened the video files from the townhouse. I didn't think Michael had been back since the previous Thursday, but you never know.

I went through file after file. I'd watch the video for a few seconds, fast forward for a while, then watch it again. Unfortunately, each file was the same. Scenes of an empty bedroom in an empty townhouse.

After reviewing all the files, I went up front and knocked on Lenny's door.

"Hi, Laura," he said as he looked up from the yellow legal pad he was scribbling on. "Come in, sit down. What can I do for you?"

"Well, now that the blackmailers know about the cameras, it doesn't look like the blonde will be using the townhouse anymore. I went through the videos of the past few days, and the place hasn't been used since last Thursday."

"I was afraid of that," Lenny said, looking a little sad. "It's unfortunate, but it looks like you're going to need to run surveillance in the parking lot of Scottsdale General. It seems a little hopeless. You could be waiting weeks for Michael Palmer to drive to a mistress who may no longer exist."

"It's possible," I reluctantly agreed.

"I guess it can't be helped," Lenny said as he ran his fingers back through his hair. "But in the meantime, I suppose you'd better go back and pull the cameras out of the townhouse. If Michael Palmer figures out we have surveillance in his bedroom, it will be twice as hard to get videos the next time he's with a woman."
~~~~

"Okay," I said. "I was also thinking. Jessica Palmer told us she had a friend in the surgery scheduling office. Why don't we have Jessica call the office back? Maybe we can learn what days Michael has scheduled off for the next few weeks."

"That's a wonderful idea," Lenny said with a smile. "We have a lot of new cases coming in, and we're going to be super busy around here. On the days he's scheduled to work at the hospital, maybe I can give you one or two of the new ones. Hopefully, you'll have time to work everything in."

I left Lenny's office and saw Sophie looking at me.

"Well?" she asked. "Is he still acting all nice and everything?"

"Yeah, and you're right. It's a little creepy."

"I told you. I'm not sure if I can get used to this or not."

"I wonder how long it'll last?"

I went back to my cubicle and called Jessica. I told her what I needed with Michael's schedule. She said she'd find out and get back to me.

~~~~

Ten minutes later, Jessica called back with the bad news.

"I called the scheduling office," she said. "Michael doesn't have any days scheduled off for the next month."

Damn.

"Is that set in stone, or can they change it?"

"No, they change it all the time. But right now, there's nothing."

I disconnected, and less than a minute later, my phone rang with a new call. This one was from the Saguaro Sky.

"Laura?" the voice on the phone asked. "This is Camille. I got your number from Jackie. I still feel horrible about the wedding mix-up last
~~~~

night."

"Hi, Camille. Don't worry about it. It wasn't your fault, and it ended up being okay. The bride didn't know the difference and everyone seemed to have a great time. Thank you for your help to make it happen."

"I'm glad everything worked out. Listen, I was thinking about what happened. I told you I deleted the voice mail from Kristy the other day, but I realized I still have the number where the call came from. Would that be helpful?"

"Wow, yes. That would be great."

"I'll forward it to you. I've worked with Kristy for years. I feel terrible that someone is doing this to her. But at least it explains why her weddings have been having so many problems over the last few months."

I disconnected and walked back to Sophie's desk. By the time I arrived, my phone had buzzed with the text.

"Could you run a phone number for me?" I asked. "Camille found the number for the person who called her to cancel the wedding."

"I guess. Just don't ask me to look up any more international terrorists, drug kingpins, or known assassins."

"Are you still worried about the government?"

"Well, yeah. That white van is still out on the street. After all the crazy searches I've been doing lately, I'm hoping to get a chance to lay low for a while."

~~~~

I had some free time and decided to go to the townhouse. Since the blonde seemed to have no further interest in the property, Lenny was right. I needed to go back and gather up the cameras.

Figuring it would be safe enough to sneak back in and pick them
~~~~

up, I parked on the street where I had before. This time I remembered to grab my clipboard. Walking to the back of the townhouse, I was able to quickly pop open the lock.

I hadn't been in here since I'd been attacked by Benny and the jerks. It was a rather creepy feeling going back up the stairs.

When I walked into the master bedroom, I was a little surprised to see that the place had been cleaned up. All of the items belonging to the blonde were gone.

I hadn't noticed anyone in the room on the video files, but I probably would have missed it if they were quick. It made me curious if the blonde was the one who had cleaned up the place or if it had been Michael Palmer.

Of my spy cameras, I was able to recover three of them. The little stuffed bear was missing. I guess whoever had cleaned up the room had decided to either take it or toss it.

I went into the bathroom, which had also been cleaned out. The only thing left was a hairbrush sitting next to the sink. When I looked down at it, I stopped. Instead of the long blonde hair I would have expected, the strands in the brush were a light brunette.

I pulled a few of them out from the brush, and they were all at least eight inches long. Far too long to be Michael Palmer's.

Well, damn.

~~~~

I drove back to the office and made a beeline to my cubicle. I turned on the computer and pulled up one of the folders containing video files from the townhouse.

Since I'd already looked at the files from earlier in the week, it didn't take me long to find what I was looking for.

Even though the sex and blackmail operation had stopped, Doctor Palmer had apparently decided not to let his townhouse go to waste.
~~~~

At nine in the morning, he had been back in the master bedroom, this time with a new woman.

I was somewhat surprised they weren't still in the bedroom when I had gone over there. I must have just missed them.

His new paramour looked to be in her late twenties, had shoulder-length brunette hair, and wore glasses. She didn't have the toned body of a professional escort. She instead looked more like the girl next door.

I fast-forwarded through the file, occasionally stopping to get a sense of what they were doing. One thing I noticed, again and again, what this woman seemed to lack in terms of skill, she more than made up for in enthusiasm.

~ ~ ~ ~

I strode up front to reception and marched to Sophie's desk.

"What are you so happy about?"

"I've got a video of Michael Palmer with his new mistress. It's in full color and high definition."

"Really, what happened?"

"I guess with the blonde out of the picture, he decided to tap into a new source."

"Well, thank God for that. This assignment has caused you no end of trouble."

Without knocking, I opened the door and walked into Lenny's office. He looked up from a document he was flipping through.

"Yes, Laura," he said, a pleasant smile on his face. It was a little unsettling. "What can I do for you?"

"Good news," I said. "I have a video of Doctor Palmer being unfaithful.

"Really?" Lenny asked, surprised. "That's wonderful news. What happened? Did the blonde show up again?"

"No, it was a brunette this time. They were over there this morning."

"Do you have any idea who she is?"

"I've never seen her before. But this one doesn't look like an escort."

Lenny thought about it for a minute and shook his head. "Alright, let's put this down as a lesson learned. Next time you do this, make sure to put a camera outside as well. That way, we can get the license plate of whoever we film. It'll keep the whole thing a lot cleaner."

I so hate that there'll be a next time.

"Yeah," I said. "I was thinking the same thing."

"Very good," he said. "We'll need to have Jessica Palmer come in so we can give her the news and move forward with the divorce. Would you mind seeing if Sophie can set up something for tomorrow afternoon?"

"Okay, no problem."

"But first, you'd better send me a link to the video. I don't know every important woman in Scottsdale, but I know most of them. Let's make sure this new paramour's not on the city council before showing the video to anyone else. I wouldn't want to embarrass any of our friends."

~~~~

"Hey," I said as I walked up to Sophie's desk. "We need to set up a meeting with Jessica Palmer, sometime tomorrow afternoon."

"I can do that. You're going to break the news about her husband being a creep and everything?"

"Yup, another assignment in the books."
~~~~

"Actually, I'm glad you're here. I got the results of the phone number you gave me. I didn't even have to use the secret software. All I did was Google it."

"Great. What did you find out?"

"Well… I don't think you're going to like it."

"Okay. I won't like it. What did you find out?"

"The phone call was made from Darby Capital Management."

"From Kristy's husband?"

"It looks like it. He must have broken into her email and has been sabotaging her all this time."

"Oh, Jeeze," I said. "I hate being pulled into the middle of a family squabble."

"I know what you mean. I like Kristy. I don't want to see her headed to a divorce over this."

"Wait a minute," I said. "Camille said there was a woman's voice on the message."

"When Kristy changed her passwords, Andrew must have gotten someone else to make the call."

"But why would Kristy's husband do something like that?" I mused.

"Maybe he was jealous because she was doing so well?" Sophie asked. "Or maybe, he was upset over Kristy always being gone nights and weekends. Who knows with men?"

"I suppose I'd better go and see him. I'm really not looking forward to this."

As we were talking, Sophie got up and walked to the window. She looked up and down the street, then seemed to stiffen.

"Is your white van still there?" I asked.

"Now it's parked in front of the big fountain with the horse sculptures."

"Have you been able to see who's driving it?"

"The windows are tinted too dark for me to get a good look."

"But you still think it's the Men in Black?"

"Who else would it be?"

~~~~

I went back to my cubicle and called Darby Capital Management. I needed to sit down with Andrew and find out why he was doing this to his wife. I also needed to make sure the sabotage would stop. After the usual delay with the front desk, I was transferred to Julie.

"Hi, Julie," I said when she answered. "It's Laura Black. Is Andrew available today? I'd like to come over and meet with him."

"Oh, hi, Laura. Unfortunately, he's at an investor's meeting all day. But he'll be back first thing in the morning. Just come over whenever it's convenient for you. Unless he's on the phone, you can go right in."

I hated putting off the meeting but was sort of relieved at the same time. I really hated being in the middle of someone's marriage problems.

"Okay," I said. "I'll be over in the morning."
~~~~

Chapter Thirteen

The following day, I made it to work a few minutes after eight. It was Thursday, and I was hoping to get there before Lenny took off for his first session with Countess Carla, the Cruel.

Unfortunately, his car wasn't in his space in the back. I knew I'd probably missed him.

"Did Lenny leave already?" I asked Sophie when I walked up to reception. "I wanted to take a look at him before he went over to Carla's dungeon."

"Yeah. Lenny was in here early to set up a bunch of work for me to do. He bounced outta here about fifteen minutes ago."

"How was he? Did he seem okay with going through with it?"

"Are you kidding?" Sophie asked. "He was like a kid on Christmas morning."

"Well, I hope it helps. I didn't know how much longer I could have dealt with him moping around the office."

"Did you go over and talk with Kristy's husband yet?"

"Not yet. I'm heading over there when they open the office."

"Let me know what happens? I'm curious as to what sort of sorry-ass excuse he'll come up with."

~~~~

I drove up Scottsdale Road to Lincoln and turned into the El Dorado Square business park. I got lucky and found a space in front of the Darby Capital Management building.

From the reception lobby, the woman there buzzed Julie. She appeared a minute later and walked me back to Andrew's office.

As I walked in, he stood, and we shook hands. He offered me a seat in front of his desk.

"Miss Black, it's good to see you again. What can I do for you today?"

"You might have heard, there was another problem at the wedding last night."

He frowned as he thought about it. "Yes, Kristine told me about it. She said someone attempted to cancel the entire wedding."

"Yes, and this time they almost succeeded."

He sighed and slowly shook his head. "How can I help?"

"Up until last night, the changes and cancelations to your wife's weddings have been made by someone who'd hacked into her email account."

"Kristine told me about that as well," he said. "I'm surprised somebody could do that. I thought they were making those harder to break into. What happened last night?"

"Once we discovered your wife's email account was the source of the problems, Kristy changed her passwords. But instead of the problems stopping, the instigator simply changed tactics. To cause chaos at last night's wedding, they called the resort directly."

I wasn't sure how to bring up what I'd learned, so I just plunged in.

"Mr. Darby, I'll be completely candid with you. It turns out the
~~~~

resort had a record of where the call canceling the wedding originated. It came from right here."

"What?" he asked, sounding genuinely surprised. "You think I was involved?"

"The last time we talked, you said you thought your wife worked too hard. You also said you'd like to see her cut down on the number of weddings she was involved with. From your perspective, having her out of the house nights, weekends, and holidays could have been an issue."

"I do think she works too hard. I also hate the fact that she's never home anymore, but I've never done anything to sabotage her work."

"Since you're married, the password to her email account is something you easily could have gained access to."

"Miss Black," he said. "I don't know how you can come in here and accuse me of doing anything to harm my wife...."

As I looked at him, he seemed to come to some sort of conclusion, and his face fell.

"Oh, no," he said quietly. He looked at me. "Um, the call that came from here to cancel the wedding, was it from a man or a woman?"

"It was a woman. I'm assuming you had somebody do it for you."

"Oh, you stupid twits," a voice called out from the door to the office. We looked over to see Julie glaring at us. "How can you both be so dense?"

"Julie?" he asked. "Was it you?"

"Of course, it was me, Andrew," she said in a matter-of-fact voice. "You've been miserable ever since that stupid wedding business took over Kristine's life. She's never at home, and even when she occasionally flits into the house, she doesn't make the smallest effort to be with you." She was starting to look fanatical.

"Oh, Julie," Andrew said, shaking his head. "Even if I wasn't happy at home, why would you do this?"

"Andrew, I knew you couldn't see what was happening, but it had gotten to the point where it started to affect your mood and personality. You were always the sweetest and the most wonderful person. I needed to do something to make it better for you," Julie said imploringly.

"How did you do it?" I asked. "How did you break into her emails?"

Julie rolled her eyes at me. "Kristine came over here about six months ago, so Andrew could take her to lunch. When she arrived, Andrew was in a meeting, so she borrowed my computer to check an attachment in an email. When Kristine read it, she went into a panic and took off. There was some problem with one of her weddings, of course," she sneered.

Julie shook her head and sighed, her voice switching to wistful. "I would give anything to have a quiet lunch with Andrew, and she just blew it off like it was no big deal. I mean, how could a proper wife even think about doing that to her husband?"

"Did you see her log in to her email account?" I asked.

"It was even better than that," she said with a nasty laugh. "Kristine was in such a hurry to rush out, she didn't log out. Plus, my computer remembered her password. I've been able to get into her emails ever since. Well, I could until she changed her password a few days ago."

"And that's when you decided to start calling directly?" I prodded.

"It was easy. People tell me all the time I sound just like Kristine. And from the emails, I knew the details of the events I was canceling. So, I thought, why not? If they heard Kristine's own voice canceling everything, how could she deny it? She'd have to stop being a wedding planner and go back to being a proper wife."

"You're saying you sabotaged Kristy's weddings to make things better for me?" Andrew asked.

"I thought if I could force Kristine into stopping her stupid wedding planning business, she would go back to taking care of you, as a proper wife should. I know if you were my husband, I'd treat you like a king."

Watching Julie was kind of like looking at one of those two-faced dolls switching back and forth: sweet and heartfelt one minute, angry and condescending the next.

"Did you do anything to sabotage the wedding happening on New Year's Eve?" I asked.

"Um, yeah," she said, gazing adoringly at Andrew. "I've called and left messages with the Barrington, the florist, the DJ, and the photographer that the wedding was canceled. You may want to call them and tell them it's back on."

"Crap, I hope it's not too late." I stared hard at Julie. "Can I assume you're going to stop doing anything to Kristy's weddings?"

She nodded her head. "Yes, I'll stop."

I looked at Andrew. "I need to work with Kristy to fix the next wedding. I'll let you work on how you want to straighten everything out with your wife."

"Yeah," he said as he shook his head. "That's going to be tricky."

"I also don't know where it goes from here. I suppose a lot of it will depend on Kristy. I get the feeling Julie broke about a dozen laws over the past couple of months."

~~~~

I got into my car and called Kristy. "Hey," I said. "I've got some news. I need to talk with you, right away. Where are you?"

"I'm at home."

"Okay, I'll be right over."
~~~~

When I pulled up to Kristy's house, the front door opened. She must have been watching for me to arrive.

"Hey," I said. "Let's go back to your office."

We went back to Kristy's den and sat at the small conference table. I took a moment to look out at the beautiful tropical oasis Kristy had created in the backyard. It was peaceful.

Kristy was looking at me expectantly, so I plunged right in.

"We found out where the call to cancel last night's wedding originated. It came from Darby Capital Management."

"From Andrew?" she asked as her face fell. "I can't believe he'd do anything like that.

"No, it wasn't your husband. It turns out it was Julie, his admin."

"Julie?" Kristy asked, clearly puzzled. "Why would she do something like that?

"It's pretty apparent she's had a crush on your husband for some time. Her jealousy, combined with resentment over you not paying enough attention to Andrew, drove her to try to ruin your business."

"Julie's been working with Andrew ever since I first met him. That was ten years ago. I wonder how close their relationship has been over the years?"

"Um, I'm not sure. I didn't sense anything was going on between them. Still, he didn't seem overly surprised when he found out it was her."

"Even if she was somehow in love with him, I still can't believe Julie's been the one sabotaging everything the entire time. It just seems too unreal."

"Well, your husband knows all about it now, and I think the problems will stop. But we still have to deal with the wedding on Saturday. According to Julie, she called the Barrington and canceled the venue. She also called the florist, the DJ, and the photographer."

"Crap," Kristy said. "I need to start calling right now and straighten everything out."

"Do you think we can pull everything back together in time for Grandma's wedding?"

"Since the wedding is on New Year's Eve, people might have already made other plans. But I don't care what it takes. I'll make sure it happens smoothly."

~~~~

I grabbed a quick lunch at the In-N-Out drive-through, then headed back to the office. Lenny's car wasn't in the back, but Gina's was.

I went to my cubicle and collapsed in my chair.

"You look like you've had an interesting day," Gina said.

"Yesterday afternoon, I got a video of Michael Palmer being unfaithful, and today I found out it was Andrew Darby's admin who's been sabotaging the weddings. I just came back from telling Kristy."

"Well, you've been productive," she said with a laugh.

The back security door opened and Lenny came shuffling in. The side of his face was bright red and he seemed to be walking a little stiffly.

"Wow," Gina said. "Are you alright?"

"Yeah," Lenny said with a wide grin. "Um, golf was great."

"Are you sure everything's good?" I asked. "You seem a little wiped out."

"Oh, I'm sure," he said, still grinning. "I'm going up front to my office. Don't bother me for a while unless it's something important. I'm going to have a Beam, a few cigarettes, and think about, um,
~~~~

golfing for a while."

Lenny walked up to the front. Less than a minute later, Sophie came back to the breakroom.

"Hey," she said. "Did you see Lenny?"

"It looks like Countess Carla really worked him over," Gina said.

"Yeah, but he seemed happy," Sophie said. "Maybe it will help?"

"How did Kristy react to the news that her husband's admin was the one causing all the trouble?" Gina asked.

"She handled it better than I probably would have," I said. "But I don't think she's dwelling on her husband yet. She seems more focused on cleaning up the mess Julie, the admin, caused."

"And this admin's been secretly in love with Kristy's husband this whole time?" Gina asked. "How long have they worked together?"

"According to Kristy, Julie's been with Andrew for over ten years."

"It sounds like she wanted more than to simply ruin Kristy's business. It sounds like she was looking for ways to sabotage the marriage. Once things calm down, I can see Kristy and her husband having a long talk."

"I agree," I said. "I don't think things at the Darby house will be settled for a while."

~~~~

Jessica Palmer was due to show up soon, so I walked back up front with Sophie.

"Hey," she said when we got to her desk, "on that Snow Ghost thing. While you were gone, I got a ton of stuff back from the secret software. It runs to like eighteen pages."

"Really? That's great. I don't suppose it says where he's currently living?"
~~~~

"You don't seriously think I read all eighteen pages. Do you?"

"Fine. Let me have them and I'll go through it. Buzz me when the client gets here?"

~~~~

I went back to my cubicle and called Max. "Hey," I said when he answered. "I have some news about Viktor."

"Really? You're very efficient. Should we do this over the phone or do you want to meet?"

"It probably would be better in person."

Max thought about it for a moment. "I hadn't planned on going home until after the nine o'clock wrap-up meeting, but I can do it from the house. Would you like to meet over there for dinner?"

"That would be perfect."

"I'll let Beatrice know. She always likes to cook for someone other than me."

After I disconnected with Max, I flipped through the report on Viktor. Gabriella had been right. The guy was seriously bad news. He ran a crime and terror organization that spanned the border regions between the countries of Ukraine, Azerbaijan, and Georgia.

I read through page after page of the attacks and atrocities his group had carried out. I could see why both sides had wanted to take him down.

~~~~

Ten minutes later, Sophie called to let me know Jessica Palmer had arrived. I joined her with Lenny in the main conference room.

"I want to see who he was with," she said. "Show me."

The conference room had a computer and I used it to bring up a video file on the TV mounted to the wall. I knew from viewing it before that this camera gave the clearest view of the activities on the bed.

Our client watched in silence for several minutes before she spoke. She was a lot calmer than I would have been in her place.

"I know that woman from somewhere," she said. "I just can't place her."

We let the video play for another four or five minutes. By this point, things on the bed were starting to get hot and heavy.

I noticed Lenny was watching as intently as our client. I even saw Sophie watching the video through the glass walls of the conference room.

"Oh, my God," Jessica said. "I remember who that is. That's Megan Hastings. She was a surgical intern at the hospital last year. I saw her two weeks ago, at the hospital's holiday party." Jessica slowly shook her head. "Bitch."

"Very well," Lenny said in his professional lawyer voice. "Now that we have proof of infidelity, we can move forward. Of course, even though his actions are clearly reprehensible, there's nothing illegal in what they're doing. She appears to be over the age of consent. But we can certainly imply we have additional videos of him at the townhouse. We'll stipulate as part of our negotiation that all copies of the videos will be destroyed. That is, if they play ball with us."

Our client nodded her head and I got up to leave. From here on, it would be Lenny sending a dozen letters back and forth to the opposing counsel, along with the tons of paperwork needed to start a contested divorce with kids. My part of this assignment was done.

"Thank you," Jessica said to me. "I don't know what you had to do to get a video like that. Actually, I really don't want to know the details. But now, I'll be able to go forward with this. My husband isn't just moody. He's a jerk, and I know I'm doing the right thing. It means a lot to me."

"Sure," I said. "I'm glad I could help."

~~~~

"What are you going to do about the hospital thing?" Sophie asked as I sat in the chair next to her desk. Lenny was in his office, and Gina was out. "With that big build-up with the sex, and the blackmail, and a warehouse full of drugs, I can't believe it's all over."

"I don't know what else I can do," I said. "I'm not the police, and I'm not sure how deeply I want to get involved in something like that."

"It just seems kind of disappointing," Sophie said. "The blackmail ring is still going on somewhere. Lillian Abbot and that Benny guy are still tossing guys off bridges and burying people in the desert. Even the curse of Scottsdale General will still be going strong."

"I know. I hate leaving a job half done, but I don't know what else I can do."

"Well, I suppose we shouldn't get too emotional over it. I'm sure Lenny is already thinking about how to load you up with another two or three assignments."

Great.

~~~~

I swung by my place to make sure Marlowe had food in his bowl and pick up a few things. I made it to Max's a little after six.

As he opened the door, I threw my arms around him in a long hug. It felt incredible as he hugged me back.

"You don't know how much I needed that," I said. "It's been a crazy day."

"Bad?"

"No, just crazy."

As we walked into the living room, I smelled something delightful coming from the kitchen.

"Laura," Beatrice said as she walked over to me. She was a plus-sized woman, in her late fifties, and had an accent I never could place. I always thought it sounded a little like Gabriella's. "I'm so glad you could come to the house. It's more fun than cooking only for Max."

"It smells wonderful," I said.

"I make you sarmale and mici tonight. You may have had them before, but never like I make them. You'll see."

"Um, it sounds great," I said, having no idea what she was talking about.

It turned out that sarmale were cabbage rolls filled with pork, and mici were grilled minced meat rolls. These were a bit outside of what I usually ate, but everything was delicious.

Max opened a bottle of red wine I'd never heard of before called Ramnista. Beatrice hovered and fussed until we told her several times how perfect everything was.

Once we had worked our way through dinner and had opened a second bottle of wine, Beatrice told us good night. She also warned Max not to clean anything up. She said she'd get to it first thing in the morning.

"You wanted to talk about Viktor?" Max asked when we were alone.

"What's your take on him? I know he's going to be coming after Gabriella."

"There isn't a lot to tell. Viktor Pyotrovich Glazkov is, or at least was, the head of a wealthy crime and terror syndicate that covered three countries at the intersection of Europe and Asia."

"I was reading about some of the things they did. They seemed to be responsible for a lot of misery in that part of the world."

"Gabriella led the team tasked by the Major and her government to eliminate them, one by one. She was about halfway through the operation when Major Malakov went nuts and went on his killing spree. At the time, Viktor swore vengeance on her."

"Fleeing from an enemy doesn't seem like Gabriella."

"It wasn't that she was running from him. We gave her an opportunity to come to the west and she took it."

"What do you think about what the Major said? Was he serious about calling Viktor and telling him about Gabriella?"

"I'm sure he was. I've never known him to bluff. And if Viktor now knows where Gabriella is, it could be a serious problem."

"I know she's thinking about going after him. She said she was looking for information that could help her."

"I take it that's the intel you came up with?"

"Yes," I said as I pulled the report out of my bag and placed it on the table. Max picked it up and started flipping through it.

"According to the report," I said, "he's currently living in a place called Sevastopol. I looked it up and it's on the Crimean Peninsula in the Black Sea."

"I've actually been there. It's a beautiful city and I can see its attraction to Viktor."

"But why there?"

"Sevastopol is in the Republic of Crimea. But the country is claimed by both Russia and Ukraine. As you can imagine, the local government's a mess and it's pretty easy to fly under the radar. Does the report list an address?"

"No, only the city."

"Still, it's a good start. There's no telling how out of date this information is, but it will definitely be useful. I assume it's alright if I share this with Gabriella?"

"That's a copy and she can have it. Of course, I'd appreciate it if she didn't let anyone know where she got the information."

"I don't think you need to worry about that. But I should also let my old unit commander know the actual name of the Snow Ghost. That way, the records of who he is will be complete."

"Maybe they'll want to do something official about him. It would save Gabriella some trouble."

"Yes, but I wouldn't count on it. I'm sure Viktor's fallen off their radar over the past few years."

"I suppose. Wishful thinking."

"I need to have the wrap-up meeting in a few minutes," Max said. "Of course, if you'd like, you could stick around and spend the night."

"Um, I hope you don't think it's too bold of me, but we've been drinking, and I shouldn't drive. And, um, I did happen to bring a change of clothes."

"Huh," he said. "It sounds like you came over here with some ulterior motives."

"Maybe one or two."

Chapter Fourteen

I woke up the following day and was pleasantly surprised to find myself in bed with Max. He rolled over and gave me a wonderful hug. This soon turned into kissing, which turned into something that threatened to keep us in bed all day.

~~~~

When we finally got up, I found it challenging to put myself together without my supplies. Still, I didn't think Max would appreciate it if I'd brought over a blow dryer and a box of products.

Maybe later.

Beatrice must have gotten up early. The kitchen was spotless, and there was a breakfast of eggs, toast, bacon, and French-roast coffee waiting for us.

As I sat with Max, sipping coffee and munching on toast, I started daydreaming. I was thinking that I could get used to this.

"What?" Max asked.

"What do you mean, what?"

"You were sitting there with a smile on your face."

"Who, me? No, you're imagining things."

~~~~

Max and I both took off at the same time. I remembered Lenny had a hearing all morning, so I decided to swing by the office before heading home. I figured it would be safe to visit Sophie without Lenny there giving me any new assignments.

When I walked up front, Sophie seemed to be in a good mood. She was reading the Surfline reports, singing to herself, and tapping her hands on the desk.

"What are you doing here?" she asked. "Both of your assignments are done. I'd leave before Lenny finds some way of giving you something new."

"I only stopped by to say hello. I'm heading to the grocery store. It's been weeks since I've had actual food over at my place."

Sophie's head perked up. "Oh, crap," she said.

"What?"

Sophie's eyes grew big and she stood up. "Look out the window, quick! It's the van."

I turned to see the white van come to a stop, double-parking directly in front of the office. The doors opened, and four serious-looking men climbed out.

"Jeez," Sophie moaned. "It's the Men in Black. Damn it. I knew it was them."

She then glanced at me, looking pissed. "If they take me away to their interrogation facility, just remember, most of this is your fault for making me run all of those stupid searches for you."

The front door opened and two men wearing golf shirts and sunglasses walked into the room. One stayed next to the door and kept watch over the room, while the second walked directly to Sophie's desk.

"Miss Rodriguez," he said to Sophie in a slow, monotone voice as he flipped open a case containing a very real-looking badge. "My name is Agent Anderson. I'm here to discuss your activities concerning some sensitive information you've had access to for the past year and a half."

"Hey, everything I've done is legit," Sophie said with a tone of defiance. "We got your secret software after we helped out the DEA with a big case. They said it would be helpful as we searched out information on the bad guys."

The man seemed unmoved by Sophie's explanation. "I'll be as candid as I can be, Miss Rodriguez. We've become quite concerned about your use of our database. In addition to the usual searches we expected you to perform in the normal course of your employment, you've run several searches on members of international drug cartels and on known terrorists."

"Well, yeah. I sometimes run across some names, you know?"

"During the course of our investigation into your activities, we've learned that your searches earlier this year helped local law enforcement in the confiscation of a large shipment of heroin from an international drug cartel known as the Black Death."

"Yeah, I did help with that one."

"A month ago, you performed a search on a terrorist known as Major Nikolay Malakov. We had him listed as being killed, a casualty of war, you might say, a little over ten years ago. As it turns out, the information we had was incorrect. It now appears as a result of the intelligence you gathered, this wanted fugitive was, in fact, turned over to the government of the United States to face justice."

"Oh, yeah. He was a jerk. I'm glad you've got him."

"Some of your most recent searches involved an international terrorist known to us only as the Snow Ghost. It has become apparent that a man you've recently performed a search on, Viktor Pyotrovich Glazkov, is, in actuality, this same person. Even our own intelligence community did not make this connection until you pointed them in the right direction.

"I guess I'm just a naturally curious person," Sophie said, trying to smile and look friendly.

"In addition, the searches you've performed over the last two weeks are helping us piece together the activities of a large narcotics distribution ring. This drug operation has apparently been operating for several years out of Scottsdale General Hospital."

"Well, good. They need to be shut down."

"Very well," he said, sounding impressed. "We still aren't entirely sure how you obtained these leads, but as a result of our investigation, we've tagged your account as a credible intelligence source. We'll still closely monitor your activities, of course. But I've been authorized to inform you that you are no longer considered to be a terror suspect or a drug cartel member."

"What?" Sophie yelled, clearly upset. "How could you think I'm a terrorist? I'm about the sweetest, nicest person you're ever likely to meet. If you weren't part of the government and would disappear me, I'd come over this desk right now and show you who's a freaking terrorist."

"Sophie," I said, trying to calm her down. "It's okay. They said you're no longer a suspect."

"Well, of course, I'm not a suspect," she said as she flipped her hair back. "I'm not a threat to the government. I'm only a threat to people who piss me off."

Sophie must have had a new idea. Her eyes opened wide with some sort of revelation.

"Hey," she said to the man still standing in front of her desk. "Did you have anything to do with installing a brain control microchip in my head a couple of months ago?"

The room went silent as the two agents looked at each other. Agent Anderson was wearing an earpiece and he seemed to be listening to someone for instructions.

"I'm sorry, ma'am," he finally said. "The government of the United States does not engage in mind-enhancing technology on civilians without authorization."

"Ha! I knew it!" Sophie shouted in triumph as she looked at me. "Didn't I say they broke into my apartment and planted a mind-control chip in my brain? You said I'd only passed out from being drunk that night. But maybe now you'll believe me the next time something like this happens."

"He didn't say he planted a mind-control chip in your brain," I pointed out.

"Yeah, but he didn't say he didn't. That sounds like a confession to me."

I was about to ask the man to tell Sophie the government had nothing to do with installing a microchip in her head. But the agent was already walking out the door.

As we watched out the window, all four men got into the white van and it took off down the street. The office suddenly seemed eerily quiet.

"Damn," Sophie said.

"What?" I asked.

"I wish Gina had been here. She's never going to believe me."

As Sophie sat at her desk, fanning herself, I got a call from an unfamiliar local number. When I answered, it was Roberto, Danielle's boyfriend and bodyguard.

"Um, hi, Roberto. Is everything alright?"

"Actually, no. Things are not alright. Danielle is missing."

Oh no.

I felt my heart sink. "How can I help?"

"I need some information from you. She said she was going to visit a friend of yours first thing this morning. Someone called Grandma. She wanted to ask her about a wedding present."

"That would be Grandma Peckham. She's my next-door neighbor."

"I thought I should go with her, but she insisted on going alone. She said Grandma knew her as your cousin and posed no security threat."

"That's right. It's a long story. When was the last time you knew where she was?"

"It was earlier this morning. She wanted to swing by your neighbor's place, then she was coming to the office for a meeting. Unfortunately, she never showed up. I've called her cell phone, but she doesn't answer."

"Let me give you the address of the apartment house. I'll meet you over there."

~~~~

As I drove to my apartment, I called Max.

"Hey," I said when he answered. "I don't have any details yet, but it looks like Danielle's missing. She was on her way to visit Grandma Peckham this morning. That's the last anyone's heard of her. I'm on my way home to talk with Grandma and see what I can learn."

Max let out one of those soft sighs he does when he gets annoyed. "Thanks for letting me know about this. I can see this getting complicated quickly. Do you need any assistance?"

"Not yet, but maybe later. I'm meeting Danielle's bodyguard over at the apartment."

"Keep me informed. This isn't good. Things are currently quiet between our two groups. I'd hate to think this could lead to something bigger."
~~~~

"But you didn't have anything to do with it."

"True, but things like this always seem to stir the pot. Everybody gets excited, and that's when accidents happen. I'll call Johnny. He'll need to know as well."

~~~~

When I pulled into the parking lot to my apartment house, Danielle's white Camaro convertible was parked next to my beat-up old Accord.

Roberto pulled into the lot, driving a black SUV. Another man was sitting beside him. Following closely behind was another big vehicle with four men in it.

Roberto stepped out, as did his passenger. The other men got out of the second vehicle and fanned around the parking lot.

Roberto walked up to me. "Laura, this is Sebastian. He works directly under Danielle as second in command of our group."

I shook hands with the man. I recognized him from the time I had covertly taken over as head of the group. Still, he was clearly distracted by events and barely looked at me.

"I think it unlikely that Danielle would be kept in a residence here," Sebastian said in a thick Spanish accent as he looked up at the apartment building. "Still, we will need to search any place where she could possibly be."

"Why don't you both come in with me while I ask Grandma about Danielle. You can look around and see with your own eyes that Grandma Peckham isn't a security threat."

We walked into the building with a man trailing us. Sebastian stationed him in the atrium.

I suggested taking the stairs, and Sebastian agreed. I kept my eyes open but didn't see anything unusual as we made it to the third floor.
~~~~

“I don’t want to overwhelm my neighbor,” I said. “We won’t get good answers if there are too many of us. Would one of you mind hanging back for a few minutes?”

Sebastian motioned for Roberto to go with me while he stayed by the elevator. We walked down to Grandma’s, still keeping a lookout for anything amiss. I knocked, and the door eventually opened.

“Why hello, Laura,” Grandma said as she eyed the man standing next to me.

“Grandma, this is Roberto. He’s Danielle’s boyfriend.”

“Well, it’s good to meet you. Come on in. How is Danielle? I’m looking forward to seeing her again on Saturday.”

“That’s why we’re here. She’s missing.”

“Oh, dear,” Grandma said. “What do you think happened?”

“We’re not sure yet. She was coming over here to ask you about wedding gifts, and no one has seen her since.”

“I’ve been out most of the morning, shopping at the Bashas’ on Indian School Road, but she didn’t come here after I came back. The only visitor I’ve had today was Marlowe.” She pointed to my cat, who was fast asleep on his afghan.

“Her car’s down in the parking lot, so we know she made it that far,” I said. “She might still be somewhere in the building.”

“Was she driving a white convertible?” Grandma asked. “I saw one when I came back. I’d never seen it here before, and it was parked next to your car. I thought you might have a visitor.”

Roberto started to fidget, and Grandma read his thoughts. “Roberto,” she said as she rested her fingertips on his arm, “I don’t think Danielle could be in here, but let’s look anyway.”

Grandma led us on a quick tour of her apartment. It didn’t take us long to go through the rooms, which were all neat as a pin. Danielle wasn't anywhere to be found.

"We're going to go to my place next," I said. "I don't think she could be there either, but at this point, we can't rule anything out."

We said goodbye to Grandma and went back out into the hall. Sebastian joined us, and Roberto shook his head.

When we got to my door, my heart sank. The wood along the frame was splintered. From the marks, a prybar had been used on it.

Damn it.

"Someone broke into my apartment," I said. "I don't know if they're still in there or not."

I got out my key to unlock the door. But even as I inserted it into the lock, I was able to simply push it open.

Roberto and Sebastian each pulled a pistol. I let the two guys with guns go in first, and I followed behind them.

We quickly went from room to room. We searched the closets, the shower, and anywhere else Danielle could be hiding. I even looked under the bed.

We quickly found she wasn't anywhere in the apartment. I was surprised but happy to see the damage to my place was minimal.

I was also relieved when I looked in my bedroom closet. My makeshift jewelry box on the upper shelf hadn't been disturbed.

I should probably put my jewelry somewhere better than in my closet, like in a safety deposit box.

"Danielle doesn't know about me getting a new car yet," I said. "When she saw my old car in the parking lot, she would have assumed I was at home. She may not have been as cautious as she usually would have been."

I had a sudden inspiration. "Roberto, when you last saw Danielle, was her hair up or down?"

"It was up," he said. "She had it in a sort of bun."

"I think I know what happened," I said. "I've been looking into some shady activities at Scottsdale General Hospital. The men running that operation may still be after me."

"And you think these men could have captured Danielle?" Sebastian asked.

"After they found out I wasn't here, they must have waited for me to come back home."

I pointed to the window, and the men looked out of it. They could see Danielle's white Camaro.

"From the window, they would have seen Danielle come into the parking lot and get out of her car. We both look so much alike. If her hair was up, they likely would have thought she was me."

"Yes," Sebastian said. "What you say seems to fit with what we are seeing. Is there anything else you can tell me about this?"

"If it's the same people, I think I might know where they're holding her."

I quickly described the operation that had been set up at the scrap metal business south of Curry Road. I also explained how I had previously been taken and what had happened to me.

Both men looked at each other. I could tell they wanted to act, but I could sense a feeling of frustration between them.

"What's wrong?" I asked.

"We've run into this sort of thing before," Sebastian said. "We have many men we can use for combat. But this is more of a hostage rescue."

"Do you have anyone in your group with training in this sort of thing?" I asked.

"Not really," Sebastian said. "Although kidnapping is a common tactic in our world, it is almost always a matter of wanting payment for their release. Trying to rescue someone is outside of what we normally do."

"Usually, when it is tried, many people die, on both sides," Roberto said. "Unfortunately, this usually includes the hostage."

"Um," I said. "I might have a solution, but it would involve using some people out of Max's group. Would you be okay with that?"

The men looked at each other. Roberto indicated it was Sebastian's decision.

"I would need to discuss this directly with them," Sebastian said. "And, we would need to be intimately involved, of course. But if they have people trained in hostage rescue, I'd be foolish not to at least listen to a proposal."

"Honestly, I'm not sure if Max will want to be directly involved in something like this. If things went bad, it would only increase tensions. But I know he wants to keep the truce between your two organizations."

"We'll go back and start to make plans," Sebastian said. "You get together with your contacts in Max's group and see if they would assist us."

"I'll do that right away. Assuming they're willing, how soon would you be ready to meet?"

"Let us meet in two hours. We'll come to the meeting ready to leave from there and attempt a rescue. If your friends are unwilling to help, you will give us the information you know, and we will attempt it ourselves."

~~~~

The men took off to make plans. I got my jewelry box down from the closet and knocked on Grandma's door.

"Hi, Grandma," I said when she answered.
~~~~

"Did you find your cousin?" she asked.

"Not yet. But I think I know where she is."

"That's good," Grandma said. "Hopefully, you can get her without too much fuss. She then looked at the box in my hands.

"Um, somebody broke into my apartment this morning. Would you be able to keep this until I can get my door fixed?"

Grandma gave me a look and shook her head. "Out of all the apartments in the building, they always seem to go after yours."

"I know," I said as I shrugged my shoulders. "It's crazy."

"I'll keep your box," she said. "I'll also call building maintenance and have them order you a new door. Although, I have no idea how much they'll charge you for something like that."

"Thanks, Grandma," I said as I started down the hallway. "I need to get Danielle. I'll see you at the wedding."

~~~~

I went down to my car and called Max. "Danielle was likely taken when she pulled into the apartment parking lot to visit Grandma. Her car is still there. Plus, someone broke into my apartment sometime last night or today, presumably to find me."

"It sounds like your assignment with Scottsdale General is starting to ramp up again."

"Yeah," I admitted. "I thought it was over, but you may be right."

"What do you need?"

"Would you be willing to help rescue Danielle? They're probably holding her in the same place they had me. I didn't make any commitments other than I'd bring up the idea with you. You'd be dealing directly with Sebastian. He's Danielle's second in command."

Instead of answering right away, he paused, as if considering. "Let
~~~~

me ask you something," Max said. "And think about it before you give me an answer. Do you think the kidnapping and the Black Death's worry over it is genuine?"

His question shook me a little. I was going to blurt out, "Of course, it's genuine." But I paused to think about it.

I mentally went over everything that had happened over the past couple of hours. I then reexamined everyone's actions and emotions.

"As far as I can tell, everything is just as it appears," I said. "I do believe someone was in the process of going through my apartment, looking for me, when Danielle pulled into the parking lot. They probably mistook her for me, and they took her. What are you getting at?"

"Don't take this the wrong way," he said. "But when I'm forced to quickly place myself in an awkward or dangerous situation, there's usually something behind it that isn't obvious."

"I see why you're questioning it. But I don't feel anything like that. I can sense they're floundering over this."

"If we don't offer assistance, how do you think they'll handle it?"

"From what I've seen, they have no idea how to rescue Danielle, other than to storm the building. They apparently have some experience in doing that, and it usually doesn't work out well for the hostage."

"It's easy for something to go wrong. When you're in a building, and everyone but the hostage has a gun, accidents often happen."

"Plus, I was the one who suggested you had someone in the group who might be able to assist. They hadn't even considered asking an outsider for help."

"You didn't mention Gabriella or me by name?"

"No. They still have no idea who in your group would be on the rescue team."

"Good, that gives me a measure of confidence. There's always the possibility they've done their homework and have discovered our past work. If that's the case, this operation would be tailor-made to draw both Gabriella and me in."

"Well, what do you think?" I asked. "Are you willing to risk it? If you succeed, it will strengthen the relationship between the two groups."

"I've been thinking about that aspect as well. Honestly, that's the real draw to this. And yes, I'm willing to take the risk. Plus, I know Gabriella is always ready for a little bit of fun."

"Great. I'll let Sebastian know you're willing to discuss it. Do you have a preference on where we meet?"

"Let's make it somewhere near where you think she's being held, and it needs to be neutral ground. I would imagine the people at the Black Death are asking the same questions about us. Tensions will be high, no matter how this goes."

"I have the perfect place," I said. "There's a vacant lot south of Curry Road, right against the Salt River. It's been for sale for as long as I can remember. I think the street is called East Gilbert Drive."

"How close is it to the target building?"

"A quarter of a mile as the crow flies, maybe a little less. But it's three or four streets over. There's no way they could know we were there unless they had someone driving around the neighborhood checking on random vacant lots."

"Okay," Max said. "Look up the address and let me have it. I'll need to make a few phone calls."

"How can I help?"

"I'll need a map of the building and the grounds. It will need to be as accurate and as complete as you can possibly remember. What I need in particular are the room layouts. Where the doors and windows are. Best routes in and out. Think you can put something like that together quickly?"

"It will be crude, but I can do it,"

"Very well," he said. "You start working on the map. Contact the Black Death and give them the location where we're meeting. We'll meet you at the lot in two hours."

~~~~

I went back to the office and pulled a big piece of paper from the bottom of the copying machine. I then sat in my cubicle and began to draw the layout of the building.

Fortunately, the business wasn't very large. In my short time there, I think I pretty much saw the entire thing. There were only half a dozen rooms in total, not counting what looked like a loading ramp and the large room where the women had been working.
~~~~

Chapter Fifteen

I drove out to the vacant lot and wasn't surprised to see that Max and Gabriella were already there. They were sitting in a black Cadillac SUV and appeared to be having a conversation.

An unmarked blue utility van was parked a short distance away. The sliding door was open, and Carson was quietly sitting on the edge. He was wearing a Navy SEALS baseball cap. He had on a black combat outfit, complete with body armor.

Looking into the van, I saw two other guys. I'd seen both of them before but didn't know their names.

Two black SUVs and a beat-up cargo van pulled up on the street, next to the vacant lot. *Panadería Rosetta Hernández* was painted on the side of the van, along with two giant cupcakes.

Max and Gabriella climbed out of their vehicle and looked at the newcomers. Like Carson, they were dressed for combat.

Sebastian and Roberto climbed out of their SUV. Both of them eyeing Max and Gabriella. Four men then got out of the second Black Death SUV and fanned out around the dirt lot.

I was relieved when no one seemed overly hostile or was openly carrying arms. It would raise tensions if everyone had a gun in their hands, plus it would look rather suspicious if a patrol car were to drive by.

I went over to Sebastian. “I’m glad you’re here. Come on over and let me make introductions.”

Both men followed me, but Roberto stopped about ten feet from Max. Gabriella had also drifted back to get a better view of the entire group. Sebastian continued until he was directly in front of Max.

“This is Max Bettencourt,” I said. “Max, this is Sebastian, second in command of the Black Death.”

Max walked forward and extended his hand. Sebastian shook it and his eyes opened wide. I could see him taking in the fact that Max was in full combat gear and was obviously going on the raid.

“You are directly participating in the effort to rescue Danielle?” Sebastian asked. He was clearly a little shocked.

“I’m going to lead the group in,” Max quietly said. His voice had a steely and commanding quality I’d never heard before.

Sebastian looked like he was still having a hard time believing what he had heard. “But you are head of your entire organization,” he said. “There has been so much bad blood between our groups. Why would you risk yourself to rescue Danielle?”

“We’ve just negotiated a truce between my group and yours,” Max said. “I don’t want to see anything happen to change that. Three of us have some experience in hostage rescue. I don’t want to sit by and have something unfortunate happen to her.”

“Very well,” Sebastian said as he slowly nodded his head. “No matter what happens today, I will let it be known you have personally put yourself in danger to help us.”

“Gabriella and Carson will be going in with me,” Max said, pointing out both people. “It would be best if we went in with two teams of two. It would also be good if one of your men was directly involved with the rescue.”

At hearing this, Roberto stepped forward. “My name is Roberto

López. I'll go in with you. Protecting Danielle is my responsibility. I should have been with her when she was taken. I'll be there when we rescue her."

Max looked at Sebastian for approval. The second in command of the Black Death nodded his head. "Yes, I want one of my men to be with you at all times. I know Roberto. He will not panic if things become tense."

"Roberto," Max said as he stepped forward to shake his hand. "It's good to have you with us. I'm going to pair you up with Carson. He has extensive training in combat and hostage rescue. Go to the blue van. He'll get some body armor on you."

As Roberto went to the van, Carson pulled out an oversized bullet-proof vest. He then helped strap the armor onto Roberto.

"We've suspected the group from Scottsdale General Hospital has somehow been interfering with the narcotics business," Sebastian said. "I've been hearing rumors about them ever since I arrived in Arizona, four years ago."

"From what we've learned," I said. "They've been operating for almost seven years."

"Yes, that matches with what Carlos told us," Sebastian said. "However, I don't think even he realized the scope of their operation."

"They've been good about flying under the radar," Max said. "We've also suspected narcotics were getting to the street from an independent source but had no idea who the supplier was."

"Carlos was in the process of mounting a campaign of aggression to take control of their operation. I believe he was planning a raid on their secret facility. But when Carlos died, the plans went with him. Until today, none of us knew the location of their operation."

No one said anything for a few moments. Carlos had been killed during a negotiation meeting several months earlier. Tony hadn't started the gunfire, but Carlos was dead because of it. Sebastian, Max,

Gabriella, and I had all been there.

"I've been keeping my superior, Tio Francisco, apprised of the situation." Sebastian's voice became quiet as he spoke to Max and me. "He's willing to let us handle the situation ourselves, for the time being. However, he's also sending Largo to come up and assist us."

Crap.

A cold shiver swept through me. I'd met Señor Largo a couple of months before when Danielle was having problems with the group. Although he and I seemed to work together as an effective team, Danielle said he was a man who was both violent and sadistic.

She'd gone on to describe Largo as the cartel's problem solver. He was someone who'd eliminate any threats to the organization, whatever it took, often through brutal methods. Danielle said whenever Señor Largo showed up, there'd likely be carnage.

I suppose, in a way, I'd been lucky to have him on my side. He ended up taking out a guy named Raul, who had been a severe pain in my ass for months. If he hadn't been watching over me, I likely would have been killed.

Sebastian seemed to know I understood the implications of Señor Largo coming to Scottsdale. Likely from the look of shock on my face.

"Who's Señor Largo?" Max asked.

"He's their version of Gabriella," I said.

Max nodded his head in understanding. He then looked at Sebastian. "When will he get here?"

"His plane lands in a little over two hours. Once he arrives, I must yield operational control to him. If we fail to rescue Danielle, he will be the one to decide what to do next."

"What do you think Señor Largo will do if we haven't rescued her by then?" Max asked.

"I've worked with him and know of his reputation," Sebastian said. "He'll gather twenty men, and we'll raid wherever he decides she's located. Even if Danielle comes out unharmed, we'll need to deal with the aftermath of a bloody massacre. This isn't a backwater in the jungles of Mexico. We'll have the FBI down on us faster than I can snap my fingers."

Max looked thoughtful for a moment. "We'll need to cross our fingers they're holding her in this building, then make sure the rescue goes smoothly."

"Amen to that," Sebastian said.

Max glanced at me. "Do you have the map?"

"I've got it right here," I said as I held up the rolled piece of paper.

"Very well," Max said. His voice was steady, but I could tell he was starting to operate at a different level.

We went to the side door of the blue van. From the way Roberto kept shifting and adjusting the straps, it was probably the first time he'd ever worn a bullet-proof vest.

Max took the map from me and spread it out on the van's floor while we gathered around.

"Would you describe the location?" Max asked me. "Give us as much detail as you can."

"The building is two streets over and halfway up the block. It's on the west side of the street. The parking lot is here," I said as I pointed.

"Entry points?" Max asked.

"The front door is most likely the only way in. Although, it might also be possible to get in through the loading dock," I said as I again pointed.

"We'll check it out, but we've already driven by the building and I think you're most likely right. We'll need to start this at the front door."

Max looked at me. "It might be best if you could help get us in. It looked like there was an intercom, perhaps even a camera on the door. Having a civilian asking to be let in will raise fewer suspicions. After that, I want you to leave the area.

Oh, crap.

I didn't think I'd be directly participating. But I should have known I'd somehow be involved. I simply nodded my head.

"Talk about the rooms," Max said. "What is the purpose of each one?"

"This is where they tortured me," I said, pointing to a room on the map. "Danielle will likely be in there if they're still interrogating her."

"Alright," Max said. "That room will be our primary target."

"After they were through asking me questions, they held me in a storage room, here." I again pointed. "This one will be easy to spot because the door has a sliding bolt on it."

"That makes the storage room our secondary target," Max said.

"What is this room?" Gabriella asked, pointing to the space next to the storage room."

"That's the office. If you get there, you're at the very back of the building. The office has a door on the back wall that leads out to the parking lot. It's locked but can be opened by pushing on the bar. When I was there, there wasn't an active alarm on it."

"And this room?" Max asked, pointing to the large area containing the loading dock.

"This is where they were opening cases, presumably narcotics, and repackaging the drugs for the street. Half a dozen women were working when I was there."

"This is good map," Gabriella said. "Very clear."

"How many bad guys do you think are there?" Max asked.

"I saw three, plus Lillian. There might have been one or two more working in the drug room."

"I understand," Max said. "Let's count on at least six. We need to assume they're all armed. Some may have automatic weapons."

"Yes," Sebastian said. "They'd need to be armed in case of a raid on their drug operation by the police or a rival gang."

At that, Roberto smiled. "Well, they aren't far off in worrying about a raid."

Max walked around to the back of the blue van and everyone followed. A wooden case, maybe three feet long and a foot high, sat on the floor.

Max opened it, and inside were several pump-action shotguns. They were unusual in that part of the stock, and the handle of the pump were colored orange.

"These guns fire a beanbag filled with bird-shot," Max said as he handed out the weapons. "Keep in mind, these have a limited range. To be effective, you need to be closer than fifty feet to your target. As long as you don't make a headshot, they shouldn't seriously injure anyone. However, a beanbag to the belly will definitely put someone out of action for fifteen or twenty minutes."

"How many rounds?" Roberto asked as he lifted the gun to get a feel for it.

"There are six in tube and one in chamber," Gabriella said as she handed everyone two extra shell-holders with five additional beanbag rounds in each. "Here are ten more, but if all goes well, they will not be needed."

"And if someone doesn't go down or reaches for a weapon?" Carson asked.

"Protect yourself at all times," Max said. "If you need to use your pistols, don't hesitate. But if no one is killed, the better off we'll all be. Keep in mind, this is a hostage rescue, not a vendetta."

No one said anything for a few moments. Max looked at Sebastian, who nodded his head.

"Listen up. Everyone gather around," Max called out. His other two men and the four soldiers from the Black Death came to the back of the van.

"Listen up," Max said. From the way he spoke, I knew he had gone into full military mode. I could see him back with his old unit, surrounded by a dozen uniformed men while barking out orders. It was a little frightening, but he was also completely awesome.

"We're going in as two teams," he continued. His voice was loud, clear, and had an edge of command to it. "Gabriella and I will go in first, closely followed by Carson and Roberto. We'll keep it tight until we start to meet resistance."

He looked around to see if there were any questions. When no one said anything, he continued.

"The rest of the men will form a perimeter around the building to prevent anyone from escaping. The main exits will be the front door, the loading dock, and from the back office. But there may be other exits we aren't currently aware of. Everyone will need to keep their eyes open."

Max, Gabriella, and Sebastian then spent another five minutes finalizing plans and working out contingencies. At last, everyone seemed satisfied.

"Sebastian?" Max asked, loudly enough for everyone to hear. "Is this plan acceptable? Is there anything you wish to change?"

Sebastian thought for a moment. "You seem to have this well thought out. I have no further changes."

"Alright," Max said. "Let's move out."

~~~~

The members of the Black Death climbed into their vehicles and took off. According to the plan, they would park on the street about a block on either side of the business. Then they would wait for the rescue party to go in.

Carson climbed into the driver's seat of the SUV with Max riding shotgun. I was seated behind Max, Roberto was in the middle, and Gabriella was behind Carson.

We had started up the street to the business, but Max had Carson pull our vehicle to the curb. A large black sedan, like a Mercedes or a BMW, was pulling out of the parking lot of the target location. They turned north and headed up the street toward Curry Road.

Max pulled out his phone and called Sebastian. "A black sedan just pulled out. Did you see it?"

"Yes," I faintly overheard Sebastian's voice from the phone. "I've ordered my men to discreetly follow. They will report where it goes."

"Very well," Max said to Sebastian. "I see everyone's in position. We're going in."

Max disconnected the phone and directed Carson to park alongside the building. Carson found a place that wouldn't be visible from the business's windows.

"Let's do this by the numbers," Max said. "Roberto, stay close to Carson and follow his lead. If we make good decisions, this should be simple and quick."

Everyone nodded their heads. "Alright," Max said. "Take your positions. Safety's off."

Max, Gabriella, Roberto, and Carson pressed themselves against the wall, out of view of the main entrance. I went up to the front door and tried the handle, but wasn't surprised when it was locked.

There was a buzzer and intercom next to the door. I pushed the
~~~~

button and held my breath.

About a minute later, there was some static, and the intercom came to life. "Yes?" a man's voice asked.

"Hi," I said. "I'm Rachel. I'm here to start working."

"You've got the wrong place," the voice crackled. "We have everyone we need today."

"No, I'm sure this is the right place," I said, trying my best to sound sincere. "I usually work up at Scottsdale General. They sent me down here for the afternoon."

There was a pause. "Hold on," the man said. His voice had a touch of annoyance. "I'll be right out."

A minute later, the door was cracked open by an unfamiliar guy in his early twenties. From the uninterested look on his face, he didn't seem to recognize me.

The man looked me up and down, then pushed the door open further. "I don't think you're needed here today," he said. "Come in, and we'll figure out what to do with you."

Without a word, Max and Gabriella slipped inside the door. I heard some muffled noises, then everything was quiet.

Max stuck his head out and motioned for Carson and Roberto to follow. He pointed to me and made a motion for me to take off.

Both vans pulled into the parking lot and men quickly poured out. Under Sebastian's direction, they rapidly surrounded the business.

From inside the building, I heard the sound of several shotgun blasts. They were quieter than I would have expected. Fortunately, I didn't hear the louder sounds of a pistol or rifle shot.

I quickly lost count of the number of shots fired within the business, but there must have been at least eight or ten. Everything became quiet as we nervously stood around the building.

Ten minutes slowly ticked by and I could tell Sebastian was debating sending in more men. Before he had a chance to act, his phone rang.

"She's not here," I heard Roberto say from the phone. "Send in some men with zip ties. We need to secure the people."

One of Max's men produced a bundle of plastic handcuffs. Sebastian directed two of his men and one of Max's into the building.

Once they were inside, it was another ten minutes before anything happened. Then, the back door from the offices opened, and the four raiders came out.

Gabriella and Max were leading a man between them. He was dressed in a white button-down shirt and a tie. His face had a nasty bruise along one side and his hands had been bound in front of him with steel police handcuffs. As with a lot of the people I see around Scottsdale, he looked familiar.

"Where's Danielle?" I asked once the group reached the blue van.

"She was here, but they moved her," Roberto said.

"They apparently moved her right before we arrived," Max said. She must have been in the black sedan we saw leaving the lot."

"Who is this?" Sebastian asked.

"I'm J. Barrett Knight," the man said. "I'm the CEO of Scottsdale General Hospital. Thanks for getting me out of there. If you can get these handcuffs off me, I can tell you exactly where they took the girl. My brother has her."

At a nod from Max, one of his men started digging through a toolbox in the van, presumably to look for a handcuff key.

While we were waiting, Max looked around at the group. "Is everyone alright?"

Gabriella, Roberto, and Carson looked back and forth at each other and nodded.

"What about the enemy?" Max asked.

"I shot three of my beanbags," Roberto said. "They were remarkably effective. Once they took a round to the belly, it seemed to completely incapacitate them."

"Gabby?" Max asked.

"I use six rounds. I double-tap everyone I come into contact with, just to make sure."

"Did anyone need to use live ammunition?"

Everyone shook their heads.

"Gabby?" Max asked. "What about you?"

"No, I no use live ammunition." At this, she looked a little downhearted, but then her grin turned mischievous. "I did use my knife on one of them."

Max raised an eyebrow. "And?"

"He will live. Even after taking two rounds to the belly, he looked like he might be going for gun, so I use knife to stop him."

"How bad?"

Gabriella smiled. "He will need some stitches." As she said this, her face flushed with excitement and she shivered in pleasure.

Wow.

"How many were in there?" I asked.

"There were six guards and five women working the narcotics room," Max said. "There were also three men who looked like common street pushers. I'm sure they come in and out all day. These three were just the unlucky ones who were there at the wrong time. There was also a woman who seemed to be the leader."

"That's Lillian Abbot," Barrett said. "She's my supply chain director. This is her operation."

"We have all of them cuffed," Max said. "They're in the narcotics room and two men are watching over them."

"Did you find a nasty-looking guy with long hair and a thin face?" I asked. "His name's Benjamin Todd. He's the jerk who took such pleasure in torturing me."

"Benny went with the woman," Barrett said. "Apparently, they found out she had some sort of gang connection. From what I overheard, they were going to pressure her into using her gang to make some sort of distribution deal."

"We need to get Danielle," Max said as he looked at Sebastian. "But I also want this narcotics operation closed down."

"I agree," Sebastian said. "They've been a problem for us for too long."

Everyone then looked at J. Barrett Knight. One of the men had just unlocked his handcuffs and he was rubbing his wrists. As the head of the hospital selling the drugs, I expected him to object or try to make some sort of deal.

"Oh, I agree," he said. "Shut it down. The whole thing has spiraled completely out of control. My brother's been using the narcotics operation to finance his lifestyle for years. Lillian pretty much runs the hospital now. I don't even care all that much what happens to me. I just want out. Shut it down."

"We have the ringleader, the guards, the street pushers, and the drugs, all in one place and ready to be taken away," Sebastian said. "However, we should release the women who were simply repackaging the narcotics."

"I agree," Max said. "They aren't who we need to be concerned about."

"Shall we call in an anonymous tip?" Sebastian asked.

"I don't know if we'd get a proper response to something like that," Max said as he looked at me. "We'll need something more direct. Do you or Gina have anyone you can call to get the right people over here without getting caught up in it?"

"I think I do," I said. "Let me go somewhere and make a call."

Chapter Sixteen

I climbed into the front seat of Max's SUV and closed the door. After taking a moment to compose myself, I made a call to Reno.

"Hey," I said when he answered. "Remember me?"

The phone went silent for a few seconds and I thought we might have gotten disconnected.

"Laura Black," he said. "I didn't think I'd ever hear from you again."

"Um, surprise!"

"What can I do for you today? You didn't call to ask me out again, did you?"

"Well, no."

"Oh, okay," he said, sounding a little disappointed. "So, why did you call me?"

"You said to call you if I ever needed something official."

"I'm listening."

"Are you still on the narcotics team?"

"No, I'm back on homicide. Knowing your history, I'm actually a little surprised our paths haven't crossed."

“Hey, it’s been months since I’ve found a dead body.”

“That’s good to know. You have something going on with narcotics?”

“I have information on a large narcotics ring that’s been operating out of Scottsdale General Hospital.”

“Really? We’ve suspected an organized drug distribution network has been going through the hospital for years. Still, no one has ever been able to prove anything. You think you’ve come up with something solid?”

“Yeah, it’s pretty reliable. Who should I contact?”

“I’d go with Lucinda Alvarez. She’s heading up the city’s narcotics task force. She was sitting at her desk ten minutes ago.”

“Perfect, could I get her number?”

“I’ll text it. Oh, I don’t know if you’ve heard. Chugger McIntyre made detective a couple of months ago. He’s Lucinda’s new partner.”

“Chugger made detective? I didn’t even know he was trying.”

“From what I hear, he did well on the tests. He’ll make a good detective.”

There was a pause when neither of us spoke.

“So, how have you been?” Reno asked.

“I’ve been good. Busy with work. It’s that time of the year again.”

“I remember about you and the Snowbirds.”

“Um, how have you been?” I asked.

“I’ve been good. There’re always murders to solve, even in Scottsdale.”

There was another pause. I guess I hadn’t thought this part through very well.

"Well, take care of yourself," I said. "It was good talking with you."

"Same here," he said. "I'll see you the next time you find a dead body."

Great.

The phone went silent as Reno disconnected, but it soon buzzed with his text. I called the number.

"Alvarez," the woman on the phone answered.

"Detective Alvarez, my name's Laura Black. I got your number from Jackson Reno."

"What can I do for you, ma'am?"

"I have a tip for you. The people who've been running the narcotics ring out of Scottsdale General Hospital are currently in handcuffs in their drug storage and processing warehouse. It's about two blocks south of Curry Road. I'll give you the address."

I gave her the details on the location and I could hear her taking notes.

"That address is technically in Tempe," the detective said. "But we often coordinate with them. Is there anything else you can tell me?"

"The ring leader is a woman calling herself Lillian Abbot. In reality, she's Ruth Skaggs. She's the current Director of Supply Chain at Scottsdale General. She's also wanted for parole violations from running a previous narcotics operation in Mississippi."

"Alright," detective Alvarez said in a non-committal cop voice. "Anything else?"

"The building is full of the drugs they've taken out of the hospital. Some of them are still in the original cases. A lot of them have already been repackaged to sell on the street. There are a few of the street-pushers being held there as well."

The phone went silent for a moment. "Ma'am, you aren't

associated with the DEA by any chance, are you?"

"No, I'm not with the government at all."

"Huh," she said. "This is the second tip I've received about Scottsdale General today. I'd like you to come to the station and make a statement."

"Um, I'd rather keep my name out of this, if I could. Ask your partner, Chugger, about me. I think he'll vouch for my character."

"Hold on for a second," she said. The phone then went silent for almost a minute.

"Alright, ma'am," she said when she came back on. "Chugger says we can trust you. We'll take it from here."

~~~~

I climbed out of the SUV and saw the women from the business coming out to the parking lot. Knowing they wouldn't be arrested made me feel a little better about the whole thing. They were only trying to feed their families.

Max walked over to me. "Well?" he asked.

"I expect the first patrol car to be here within five or ten minutes. There'll likely be a joint Tempe and Scottsdale narcotics task force here within the hour. They might even pull in the DEA."

"Thank you for doing that. I'll feel a lot better once this is shut down for good."

Max went to talk to Sebastian. After a brief discussion, they both started barking out orders.

Men climbed back into their vehicles, and everyone took off. Carson took the driver's position in our SUV with Gabriella riding shotgun and Max and me in the back.

"We're going to regroup at the vacant lot," Max said. "Sebastian is leaving two men to watch over things. They'll make sure no one
~~~~

escapes before the police arrive."

~~~~

Within a few minutes, our group had re-formed in the vacant lot. Everyone then gathered at the back of the Black Death bakery van.

J. Barrett Knight was also there. From the cuts on his wrists and the bruises on his face, I could see he'd been badly mistreated.

"What do you know about the woman?" Max asked Barrett. "Her name is Danielle."

"They brought her in earlier this morning for questioning. I've been locked in a storage room for the past two days, so I don't know anything for sure. Based on the screams I heard, Benny must have used his stun-gun on her three or four times. Lillian uses him as her enforcer, and he's a nasty piece of work."

"What happened to her then?" Sebastian asked.

"They brought her into the storage room with me. She was weak, but I talked with her, and she seemed to be okay. They took her out again just before you raided the building."

"Where did they take her?" Max asked.

"I overheard Lillian talking to Benny," Barrett said. "They've taken her to Oswald's house."

"Who's Oswald?" Max asked.

"He's my brother. He's also head of the Wolfe-Knight Family Foundation."

"Where is the house located?" Sebastian asked.

"It's on the northeast side of Camelback Mountain. On Yucca Road off of Cameldale Way."

As Barrett called out the address, I punched it into my phone.

"Damn," I said out loud.
~~~~

"What?" Max and Sebastian asked at the same time.

"Sorry," I said. "But it looks like Oswald Knight lives next door to Stig Stephens."

"What?" Roberto asked. "You mean Stig Stephens, the movie star?"

"Yes," Barrett said. "The estates there are so big we really never have a lot to do with the neighbors, but Stig Stephens does live next door to Oswald. I've been to his house a couple of times for charity fundraisers. It has a nice view of the city, especially from around the pool. I live half a dozen houses to the west of there."

"That matches what my men reported to me," Sebastian said to Max. "The black sedan pulled up to a gate at that address. A uniformed security man let the vehicle into the compound. After that, my men could go no further."

"Do you know where in the house they might be keeping Danielle?" Max asked.

"It could be anywhere," Barrett said. "But the house has a wine cellar with a couple of smaller rooms with thick wooden doors that lock from the outside. They could easily use one of those to keep someone prisoner."

"Could you draw a map of the house for us?" Max asked."

"I could give you the general layout. It wouldn't be exact."

"Give us what you can," Max said. He then looked at Sebastian. "We should get off the street. Do you have somewhere nearby we could go?"

"We run a company called Southwest Desert Transport," Sebastian said. "It's about half a mile east of here. We can use the offices there for Barrett to create his map and to plan out our next moves."

I looked at Max. Traveling into an enemy stronghold would be risky, but he didn't hesitate. "Alright," he said. "Lead the way."

"As soon as Barrett gets started on the map, I'll need to go to the airport to meet Largo," Sebastian said. "Once he arrives, he'll be in control from our side."

"What do you think?" Max asked. "Will he be willing to use our help?"

"Honestly, I don't know. I'll update him on what happened today and advise him to use your expertise. It'll then be up to him to make the decision to work with you or not."

~~~~

We climbed into our vehicles and drove to Southwest Desert. It was a small trucking company where I had first met Danielle. As I later found out, it was also a front for the Black Death and part of their drug import operation.

Along the way, Max called Johnny and updated him on the situation. He then called his admin, Cheryl, and asked if she could send over a satellite image of the address Barrett had given us.

We pulled into the parking lot and Max had a quick meeting with his men. He decided they would stay outside and maintain a low profile. At the same time, Gabriella, Carson, and I would go inside with Barrett, Roberto, and Sebastian to work out the new plan.

With Sebastian leading, the six of us walked into the offices. Coming back and seeing my desk from the time I'd briefly worked here was a rather odd feeling.

"Laura?" I heard a voice ask. "Laura Brown? What are you doing back here?"

I turned to see a woman named Phyllis looking at me. Next to her was another woman I knew named Irene.

They'd trained me in billing and scheduling while I'd been here, working on an undercover assignment for Lenny. I'd given them the name Laura Brown and was surprised they still remembered it.
~~~~

“Hi, ladies,” I said as I walked over to them. “How have you both been?”

Irene looked around the office and shrugged her shoulders. “We’re both still here. This place never changes.”

“I see you’re moving up in the world,” Phillis said as she eyed Sebastian. “We were sorry to see you go. Come on back if you’re ever looking for a job.”

“Thank you,” I said. “I’ll keep that in mind.”

We walked into the plant manager’s office and gathered around a conference table. Roberto found a large piece of paper and some pencils. Barrett went to work on the map of the house while Sebastian took off to pick up Señor Largo from the airport.

“I’ll come up with a general plan of the estate,” Barrett said. “But you’ll have to remember, I’ve never gone through Oswald’s house intending to make a map of it.”

“Do the best you can,” Max said.

As Barrett started on the outlines of the house, he told us what he was drawing. “Here’s the main living room. The bedrooms are in this wing. The kitchen is next to the game room. The entrance to the garages is back here. This is where Oswald has his office.”

Ten minutes later, he had the map more or less complete. Everyone asked questions on entry points, exit points, the number of security personnel, and their likely locations.

“What is this area?” Gabriella asked as she pointed to a short hallway between the living areas and the rest of the house.

“It has something to do with the home security system,” Barrett said. “I asked Oswald about it once. He said it was to keep the bad guys out.”

“Can we avoid it?” Max asked.

"Not really," Barrett said. "It's at the choke point between one side of the house and the other. You can look down on the hallway from a balcony on the second floor. If there's a man up there, he could fire down on you."

"We'll need to take out the security forces before we get there," Max said. "How many men are stationed in the compound?"

"There's usually one at the gate and two or three in the house. One of the guards walks the perimeter every fifteen minutes. Benny will also be there."

With the map complete, we only had to wait for Señor Largo to arrive. I used the time to ask Barrett the main question that had been bugging me. "With all of your family's money, why have they turned to crime?"

"That's not an easy question to answer," he said. "My family's run one of the top philanthropic foundations in Scottsdale for the last three decades. We have over two-dozen ongoing community programs, everything from battered women's shelters to camps for kids with special needs."

"That's a noble goal," I said. "But do you really need to finance it by selling drugs on the street?"

He shook his head and gave a short laugh. "It didn't start out that way. Dad started the foundation back in the eighties. It was solid with a large endowment to provide ongoing financing. Unfortunately, my dad died a dozen years ago and my brother has a lifestyle that burns through cash. Within about five years, the foundation was starting to run dry."

"How do you fit in with this?"

"We were minority owners of Scottsdale General and we were bound by contract to build a new wing at the main hospital campus. My brother made it part of the deal to have me installed as the President and CEO. He then hired Lillian to run a narcotics operation."

"You didn't set up the drug ring?"

"I didn't have a clue they were using the hospital to funnel drugs into the community until I'd been working there for over a year. I had to piece it together for myself. I then had a meeting with Lillian. When I confronted her with the facts, she confessed to what was going on."

"Why didn't you make her stop?"

"I tried. But she told me I needed to talk with my brother if I had a problem with it. When I confronted Oswald, he let me know the money from the drug ring was the only thing still holding up the family foundation."

"Wow," I said. "I've never heard of anything that crazy. But others at the hospital must have known. It's not like you can hide something like that for long."

"Oh sure, several people knew. But Lillian has blackmail material on everyone who matters. Well, it started out as simply gathering evidence. Over the past two or three years, having intimate relations with one of the girls has turned into a reward for them to keep their mouths shut."

"And if they don't keep quiet?"

"If it seems like someone's about to go to the police, they're killed and it's made to look like suicide."

"The curse of Scottsdale General? We read about it. The paper made it seem like it was common knowledge that people at Scottsdale General sometimes killed themselves for no reason."

"When Lillian had one of the doctors killed four or five years ago, she let it leak to the paper that it was all part of a suicide curse. Now, everyone in the Valley knows about it."

"It seems like a convenient excuse to use whenever someone dies."

"Yes, and the drug ring had been running smoothly for several years because of it. The doctors were too scared to do anything about it. Between blackmail and bribes, they'd been trained to look the other way."

"Did you say it *had* been running smoothly? As in past tense?"

"That's right. Last week, Lillian's operation started to fall apart."

"What happened?"

"Someone broke into the Palmer townhouse and began filming our operations there. She shut down the activities and was going to move it somewhere else. Benny managed to capture the woman who'd planted the cameras, but someone on the inside helped her escape."

I sighed. "That was me. But I didn't know about your drug ring. I was only trying to get a video of Doctor Palmer being unfaithful so his wife could divorce him."

"Seriously?" he started laughing. "Well, Lillian became convinced the entire operation had been compromised. She went nuts trying to learn who you were and who'd helped you escape."

"I escaped on my own. I hope too many people weren't hurt because of it."

"Well, she had Benny bash in the skull of the head of medical operations, Isaac Elmaghrabi. She then had Benny toss him off a bridge."

Oh my God.

Barrett must have seen the look on my face because he held up his hand to stop me from saying anything.

"It didn't have anything to do with you," he quickly said. "I think Lillian was only tying up some loose ends. She's suspected Isaac for several months. When she questioned him about who had helped you escape, things between them escalated rather quickly. Benny was brought in to question him using his stun-gun. You read about the results."

"I don't like the idea of someone being killed because of something I did, no matter how remote the connection."

"Lillian was also in the process of shutting down the narcotics distribution center and relocating it somewhere else." He let out a short laugh. "Although, it looks like she was a little too slow on that."

"Why were you being held there? It looks like they were treating you pretty roughly."

"Lillian was convinced the hospital was about to be raided and shut down by the police or the DEA. She was setting me up to be the fall guy."

"How was that going to work?"

"Benny had me write a note confessing that the entire narcotics operation had been my doing. Lillian has the note and was planning on putting it next to my body after I committed suicide. I'd only be one more victim of the curse of Scottsdale General. After things calmed down, Lillian would then be free to set up operations somewhere else."

"How could anyone believe something like that?"

"I overheard them talking in the hallway. I would be taken to my home and killed as soon as the police showed up at Scottsdale General. By raiding the distribution center, you and your friends saved my life. I do appreciate it."

"What happened to the blonde woman who was with the men at the townhouse? Is she alright?"

"You mean Aurora?"

"I don't know her name. Tall, thin, long bouncy blonde curls."

"Yeah, that's Aurora. She's fine. It's crazy, but we've ended up paying her almost as much as we do the doctors. Unfortunately, it looks like she's out of a job."

Through the open office window, we heard the sound of vehicles pulling into the parking lot. Max got up and Gabriella followed.

We looked out the window to see almost a dozen men get out of two black SUVs and the bakery van. In the center of the group, I recognized Señor Largo.

As I remembered from the only other time I'd worked with him, he was slightly older than a typical gangster, maybe in his early fifties. Although he was dressed in slacks and a golf shirt, he had the look of a gunslinger from the old west.

He was a tall man with a handlebar mustache, a lean weathered face, and piercing blue eyes. His dark blond hair was still cut in a short military style but had grown out a little since the last time I'd seen him.

Hanging by a strap over his shoulder was a brown leather pouch. Like Gabriella's, the bag looked big enough to carry a compact machine gun, along with several high-capacity magazines of ammunition.

Max looked at Largo and let out a long breath.

"Gabby?" Max asked.

"I see him," she said. "He looks to be ex-Fuerzas Especiales, probably FES."

Carson slowly shook his head. He groaned like a man who knew his job had gotten a little more complicated.

"He has a Mexican Special Forces tattoo on his forearm," Max explained to me. "It's their version of the Navy SEALS."

"From what I know about him, it makes sense," I said.

"This could go one of two ways," Max said. "I think we'll be okay, but everybody be ready."

Gabriella unzipped her black bag and began to stroke her Uzi with the tips of her fingers. I knew she probably had a couple of hand grenades in there as well. "We will be ready," she said.

"Barrett," Max said. "Go wait in the outer offices. We'll call you in if we have any questions."

Barrett quickly left the room. He obviously wanted no part of being close to so many people with guns.

"You'd better go too," Max quietly said to me.

"I'd like to stay with you."

"This might end badly," Max said as he shook his head. "You'll be in harm's way."

I held my arms up and made a point to look around the office. "We're at one of the main locations of the Black Death, surrounded by twenty men," I said with a small laugh. "If there's a shootout, I don't think I'll be any safer in the main office as opposed to in here."

Max nodded his head in acknowledgment. I went over to a chair in the corner of the office and sat. Carson took a similar position in the far corner.

Chapter Seventeen

Less than a minute later, Sebastian entered the room, followed by two grim-looking men. Roberto came in next, followed by Señor Largo.

Largo stood near the doorway and surveyed the room. He only briefly glanced at me before spending several seconds looking over Max and Gabriella, his eyes lingering on their body armor. Largo then studied Carson, who was also dressed for combat.

After a few moments, Largo seemed satisfied that he knew who everyone in the room was and what their roles were. He made a small gesture with his hand, and the two goons left and closed the door.

Gabriella seemed to be in a trance, her eyes never leaving Largo and her hand never coming off her Uzi. Her breathing had quickened, and her face had started to flush with a pink glow. You could feel the tension in the room as if it were something alive.

"Sebastian has told me of your efforts to rescue Danielle," Señor Largo said. He spoke slowly with a thick Spanish accent. Each of his words seemed to carry meaning. "He says we owe you a debt and we can trust your motives. However, I do not know you, nor do I trust you. I do not know why you seem willing to place yourself in danger to help a rival."

"We just made peace between our groups…" Max started to say.

Largo waved his hand as if acknowledging the statement. "Yes, peace is a good thing, of course. However, it is in your interest to have our group fall into chaos, is it not? You could then more easily take over what you were not able to obtain through the assassination of Carlos or in the negotiations."

"Today, we're only here to rescue Danielle," Max said. His voice again had the tone of command. "Over the past few months, I've come to know and respect her. But beyond that, I don't want another struggle for power within your group. The last time led to death and loss of profit for both sides. I believe it's in the mutual interest of our groups to work together on this."

Largo glanced at me, still sitting in the corner. "What is Laura Black doing here? What is her role?"

I saw Max stiffen, but I held up my hand to stop him from saying anything. "I'm only here to help Danielle," I said.

Largo thought for a moment and nodded his head. "Yes, you recently performed a service to Danielle and our entire group. You could have backed away from the danger then, but you did not. You are a brave woman, and I believe your motives toward Danielle are true."

"We're all worried about her," I said. "Max and his group have military training in hostage rescue and he's willing to help. We've all worked hard to establish peace between the two groups. You might as well use the resources you have available."

Largo stared into space and weighed the situation, obviously forming what had to be a difficult decision. I could see him going over the pros and cons in his mind.

Carson appeared to be relaxed, but he was paying close attention. He was wearing a pistol on his hip, and I noticed the strap had been unfastened.

Out of the corner of my eye, I saw Gabriella's hand tighten on her

Uzi, her face turning crimson. Her mouth had dropped open, and she was starting to breathe faster.

"Very well," Señor Largo said. "I see the wisdom in what you propose. However, let this be understood. I will be the one who leads the rescue team in."

"Agreed," Max said.

I let out a breath I didn't know I'd been holding. Carson relaxed, and Gabriella's empty hand slowly came out of her bag. From the way her bottom lip poked out, she looked disappointed.

"I propose two teams of two enter the house," Max continued. "You and Carson lead us in." As he said this, he pointed to the big man in the corner. "I'll go in with Gabriella. We'll each leave a couple of men on the perimeter to warn us if anyone new comes in."

"Agreed," Largo said. "Do you have a map of the house and grounds?"

"Yes, and we have the man who drew it. It's his brother's house. We can fill you in on the background story as we go along."

Barrett was asked in, and everyone again went over the map. Largo asked many of the same questions as Max and Gabriella had. The four raiders then huddled around the map to sort out some of the details.

"What are you going to do now?" I asked Barrett.

"I'm going to turn myself in. By now, the police will have raided the drug warehouse and arrested Lillian. They'll probably show up at the hospital sometime tomorrow, the day after, at the latest. I know I'll be next on their radar."

"If you need an attorney who likes to take on hard criminal cases, give my boss, Leonard Shapiro, a call. Have him go in with you. Call this number, and Sophie will set you up." I then handed him one of Lenny's cards from the office.

"I've heard of Leonard," he said as he looked at the card. "He's the one who got Muffy Sternwood's boy out of trouble about a year ago. I was first going to see if any of the foundation's lawyers were qualified to handle something like this. But if not, I'll give him a call."

~~~~

We left the building and gathered around the blue van in the truck company parking lot.

Largo strapped on the body armor Roberto had been wearing. He seemed more comfortable with the bullet-proof vest than Roberto had.

Max unrolled a satellite picture of the outside of the house. It had apparently been brought over while we'd been inside. He laid it flat on the floor of the van while Largo, Carson, and Gabriella gathered around.

"Trying to take out the guard through the gate will likely only raise the alarm," Max said. "We brought along a small tactical ladder. I propose we hop the wall and enter the compound here."

He pointed to a portion of the outer wall. It was around the corner and out of direct view of the gate. "We can then swing back around and take out the guard from behind."

"That is smart," Largo said. "From there, the obvious path into the house is through the main entrance. However, going in through the front door may be a problem. Any defensive measures they have will be strongest there. I would enter in through this door to the side." He pointed to a point on the map near a six-car garage.

"I was thinking that as well," Max said. "Let's head out."

~~~~

We drove in a small caravan of two black SUVs and the blue van. Once we got to Cameldale Way, we pulled over in a small dirt lot that seemed to be for use by maintenance vehicles. Max then directed one of the SUVs to park about a hundred yards further up the road to watch for anything unusual.

Using the blue van to block the view of what we were doing from the street, everyone got out. Gabriella handed out the beanbag shotguns and two extra shell holders to the raiders.

Señor Largo seemed pleased when he felt the weight of his gun. "I can see the benefit of this," he said. "However, I will not hesitate to use my pistol if the situation calls for it."

"Neither will we," Max said. "But for the sake of both groups, I don't want anyone killed or seriously injured if it can be avoided. That will only complicate things for everyone."

"Agreed," Largo said.

It might have been my imagination, but as with Gabriella, he seemed disappointed that he wasn't going to use live ammunition on anyone.

Carson used the strap on the shotgun to sling it across his back. Max slid out a small black extension ladder from the back of the van and handed it to him.

"Is everyone ready?" Max asked.

There was a murmur of acknowledgment from the three other raiders.

"Let's do this," Max said. "We'll go in, get Danielle, and get out as quickly as possible. Protect yourselves at all times. Any last questions?"

No one had any. Max then looked to Largo, who nodded his head.

Carson silently placed the ladder against the white-stucco wall and quickly scampered over the top. Largo, Max, and Gabriella rapidly followed.

A rope had been tied to the ladder. Once everyone was inside the compound, they silently pulled it over the wall.

It was like a magic trick. One second there was a ladder leaning against the ten-foot-high wall. The next second it was gone. From start to finish, the entire event lasted less than a minute.

Sebastian and Roberto joined me at the SUV. From the looks on their faces, I could tell they were as worried about Danielle as I was.

As Sebastian had reported, a uniformed guard was stationed inside the main gate from the road. We could dimly see him from where we were parked.

We briefly saw a blur of movement. Again, it was like magic. The guard patrolling behind the gate disappeared.

The three of us sat in the SUV on the side of the road and waited. The two men were in the front, and I was alone in the back.

The blue van with two of Max's men was directly behind us. The second SUV was still positioned a hundred yards up the street.

Everyone settled in to wait.

~~~~

Minute, after minute ticked by. Through our open windows, we thought we might have heard a couple of dull thuds of the beanbag shotguns going off, but we couldn't be sure.

At five minutes, Max checked in to say they had entered the house and were looking for Danielle. We expected a follow-up call, but there was nothing.

The three of us were getting frustrated, sitting in the SUV and not being able to do anything. Sebastian checked in with the men in the other vehicles every five minutes or so, but everything was quiet.

~~~~

When fifteen minutes had slowly ticked by, we all started to get nervous. During the planning, Max said they would likely be in and out in twenty minutes, thirty minutes tops.

I had seen Largo having a private discussion with Sebastian before the raid. I didn't know how long he'd been instructed to wait before calling in a general attack from the Black Death, but I suspected we were getting close.

At thirty minutes, Sebastian reached for his phone. As he did, the front gate opened, and a black sedan came racing out. It turned down Cameldale Way and rapidly accelerated. Within about ten seconds, the gate closed again.

Sebastian got out and motioned for the men in the SUV to follow the sedan. The big vehicle took off to learn where the sedan ended up.

"Damn," Sebastian said after the street again became quiet.

"Let's think this through," I said. "We don't know who was in the car. But I'm thinking it could hold five men, six tops. That means either Danielle or at least some of the team is still inside."

"I agree," he said. "I should call this in. We have men on standby."

"From what I understand, you haven't had any luck in the past whenever you send in a big raiding party. From what I hear, they simply shoot anything that moves."

"That's true," he confessed. "But we can't wait for our people to simply come out on their own."

"I know," I said. "We need to go in and get them."

I saw the look he gave me.

"Hey," I said, trying to sound braver than I felt. "This should be simple. According to Barrett, there are only three or four guards in the compound. Max already took out the one at the front gate. And, I bet one of them was driving the car. Worst case, there should only be one or maybe two still in the house."

"Don't forget about Benny," Roberto said. "He could still be in there. That guy sounds completely insane."

"Well, hopefully, he left in the car."

"Okay," Sebastian said after he thought about it for a moment. "It makes sense for us to go in and try to rescue them. But how are we going to enter the compound? There's a ten-foot-high wall around the estate, and the ladder's on the other side."

"I think I know a way in," I said. "Um, I suggest that one of you follow me in. The other one should stay out here to coordinate with the rest of the team."

At a motion from Sebastian, Roberto went to the back of the van and grabbed the last beanbag shotgun. He smiled as he held it up. "I have a pistol, but this should be more useful."

"Good," I said. "We'll definitely need the gun. But we can't walk around in this neighborhood looking like bandits."

I dug through the back of the SUV and came up with an old sweatshirt.

"Use this to wrap it up," I said as I handed it to him.

"I'll give you fifteen minutes," Sebastian said as he looked at his watch. "But if I don't hear from you by then, I'm calling in a general raid."

~~~~

Roberto and I walked up the street and eventually spotted the gate to Stig Stevens' estate.

"This is where the actor lives?" Roberto asked as we walked up to the entrance. "I agree with your thinking. There's likely a common wall between the two properties. But how do you propose we get over the gate? It looks higher than the last one."

I lifted the cover off a keypad, which was embedded in a post next to the road.

"Well," I said as I started pushing buttons. "Assuming Stig never got around to changing the gate code, it's eleven, fifteen, ninety-two."

As soon as I entered the last digit, there was the whirring of a motor
~~~~

and the gate smoothly swung open.

I started to walk up the drive and turned to see Roberto still standing at the gate.

“Wait a minute,” he said, clearly confused and slightly suspicious. “How did you know the code to Stig Stephens’ front gate?”

“It’s a long story,” I said. “Hurry up. Let’s cut through to the end of the property. If I remember correctly, we should be able to hop over the wall in the back without any problems.”

~~~~

We skirted along the wall as we walked toward the vast bulk of Camelback Mountain. The landscaping at Stig’s estate was lush, beautiful, and well maintained. The property reminded me of one of Tony’s resorts.

After walking past two hundred yards of palm trees and tropical foliage, we had made it past the central part of the house. We were getting to the point where I could see the back of the property, where Camelback Mountain jutted up.

A voice called out to us. “Hey, you two. Stop.” The voice was coming from somewhere above us, and it sounded familiar.

I looked up to see Jerry Phifer, Stig’s long-time business manager, standing on a balcony on the house’s second floor. He had a drink in one hand and a cigarette in the other.

He wore an open terrycloth robe despite the cool December temperatures, which revealed a pair of red swim trunks and two boney white legs. His hair had grown longer and was even more unkempt than usual.

“Hey, Jerry,” I called out. “It’s me, Laura Black.”

“Laura? What are you doing out there?”

“I’m working on an assignment. We heard there might be some
~~~~

trouble next door."

"Yeah," he said. "I think you're right. It sounded like someone was shooting over there a few minutes ago. I've been trying to look over the wall, but I can't tell what's going on."

"A friend of mine might be in the house. We're going over to check it out."

"Sure thing," Jerry said. "But if you're going to jump the wall, go all the way to the back. It's only about four feet high where it butts up against Camelback."

"Thanks, Jerry," I called back.

"You do know that's Oswald Knight's house, right? He has security guards. You want me to call the police or anything?"

"No, I think we'll be okay."

Jerry shrugged his shoulders then seemed to have an idea. "Hey, Stig's having a New Year's Eve party on Saturday night. I know he'd love to see you again. I think Christine will be here as well. Why don't you come over? It'll start up around nine or so. If the gate's closed, I see you still remember how to get in."

"Thanks," I shouted back. "Unfortunately, I'm going to a wedding on New Year's Eve. But, sure, feel free to invite me the next time Stig has a party. It would be great to see him again."

"Alright then," he said. "I'll see you around. Good luck over there." He lifted his drink in a salute, flicked the cigarette butt into the yard, then turned and went back inside.

~~~~

Roberto and I climbed towards the back of the estate until we came to the nearly vertical rock wall that was Camelback Mountain. As Jerry had said, the wall dividing the two properties at this point was no more than four or five feet high.
~~~~

"You stay here," Roberto said. "There's only one shotgun. I have a pistol I could give to you, but it's basically useless for what we're doing, except as a last resort."

"I'm not letting you go in alone. Keep your pistol. With all of the guns in there, I'm sure I'll be able to pick up something helpful along the way."

"Okay," he said as he shook his head. I wasn't sure if he seemed glad for the company or not. "But please be careful. I don't want Max or the black-haired woman with the crazy eyes coming after me if this doesn't go smoothly."

"Don't worry," I said. "They're both used to me doing stupid things."

Roberto unwrapped the shotgun and handed me the sweatshirt. I didn't want to leave it on the ground, so I tied it around my waist.

He hopped the wall then let me know the coast was clear. When we'd both made it over, we looked down the hill to the massive house.

"Everyone went in at a point close to the front gate," Roberto said. "Should we follow their footsteps or go in through the back?"

"I'd say the back way. If there're some bad guys still in the house, they won't expect it. At least, I hope not."

~~~~

Roberto called Sebastian to let him know we'd made it over the wall and were about to enter the house.

Unlike Stig's professionally maintained estate, Oswald Knight's landscaping mainly consisted of dirt and rocks with a few dry and stunted bushes. From the dead trees and bits of trash that had accumulated over the years, I could see that the Knight family's fortune had indeed dwindled.

We made it to what looked like the bedroom wing of the house. We tried the first sliding glass door we came to, but it was locked.
~~~~

Not wanting to make a lot of noise by breaking it, we went to the next door along the perimeter. This one opened smoothly.

Roberto went in first, shotgun at the ready. I quietly slipped in behind him.

The bedroom we entered was lived in and was nicely furnished but very messy. Dirty clothes, food wrappers, and empty beer bottles were in several piles scattered around the room. The effect was to give the place the aroma of a locker room next to a trash dumpster.

We stopped and listened, but the house was completely quiet. I think I would've felt better about it if there'd been some noise in the distance.

We left the bedroom and went down a long hallway. Although it was beautiful with polished marble floors and white Greek columns, I was struck by the lack of furniture or any sort of artwork on the walls. It didn't look like any sort of mansion I'd ever been in before.

We went around a corner and saw a uniformed guard on the floor. His back was against a stone balcony railing.

He was alive, but his face looked like someone had kicked it a couple of times. It was puffy and red, with one eye swollen completely shut. He held a revolver in his limp hand and seemed to be waiting for something or someone.

When the guard saw us, it seemed to focus his attention. With surprising speed, the guard lifted the revolver, his one remaining eye on Roberto.

Roberto swung the shotgun up, and they both fired off a shot. I heard a grunt of pain next to me. Roberto had fallen to the floor and was clutching the upper part of his leg.

The beanbag glanced off the guard's arm, but he didn't seem to notice he'd been hit. He slowly lifted the revolver and pointed it at Roberto, trying to finish him off. I could see the gun sway in the guard's hands as he tried to regain his focus.

Roberto quickly regained his senses and managed to swing the shotgun around. He racked in another shell, sighted the gun, and fired.

This time, the beanbag hit the guard squarely in the chest. He let out a grunt, and his eye rolled up in his head. The guard's revolver clattered to the marble floor as he toppled over.

From what I could tell, the bullet had put a crease through the outside of Roberto's leg. He was grimacing in pain and had started to bleed. I untied the sweatshirt and gave it to him to hold against the wound.

I thought he'd be okay once we got him to a doctor. Still, Roberto would be out of commission for the rest of this fight. I helped him move against a wall where he could have some protection.

"I'm going to see if I can find Max and Danielle," I said. "I don't think the guard will give you any trouble, but I'm going to disarm him anyway."

"Okay," Roberto said through gritted teeth. He racked the shotgun, the spent shell clattering to the floor. "You take this. I'll still have my pistol."

As I walked toward the balcony, I noticed the area had a strong medicinal smell. The guard had passed out and was completely limp.

A pair of handcuffs were in his belt, and I used them to secure his hands behind his back. I then picked up his revolver and tossed it into one of the rooms, further down the hall.

The medicine smell was even more pungent as I looked over the balcony railing. Max, Gabriella, Carson, and Largo were sprawled out on the polished marble floor of a short rectangular room.

I recognized it from the map Barrett had drawn. He said the hallway was part of the house's security system.

I had a brief moment of panic as I saw their unmoving bodies. But as I looked closer, I could see they were all breathing.

I knew I needed to go down and make sure they were alright, but I didn't know if any other bad guys were still in the house. I carefully made my way around the balcony and found a sweeping marble staircase.

Shotgun in front of me, I crept down to the first floor and found the door to the room where everyone was passed out. It was locked from the outside, but it was easy enough to open.

As I swung the door wide, the medicine smell rolled over me. Although I desperately wanted to rush in to check on everyone, I stepped back to let the room air out.

After waiting for almost a full minute, the smell had mostly gone away. I went in to make sure everyone was alright.

Gabriella and Carson were moaning and weakly moving their limbs. Señor Largo was still out, but he seemed to be breathing without difficulty.

Max had started to come out of it and was trying to sit up. But he was still disoriented and kept blinking his eyes.

"I'm here," I said as I sat next to him. "They hit you with some sort of knockout gas. You should be better in a few minutes."

"I think Danielle's still in the wine cellar," Max mumbled as he swung his arm around to steady himself. "We need to get her out."

"I'll do it," I said. "Roberto's upstairs. He took a bullet to the leg, but I think he'll be okay. Sebastian's going to call in a general raid in a few minutes. We need to get everyone out of here as soon as we can."

I left the hallway and walked toward where Barrett had indicated the kitchen and dining room would be. Once there, I looked around for an entrance to the basement. It wasn't hard to spot.

In a short hallway next to the kitchen was a heavy wooden door. It was beautifully painted with *Wine Cellar* in scrolling gold letters. The words were surrounded by lushly painted grapevines. Below these were several half-full glasses, grapes, and bottles of red wine.

I took a deep breath, opened the door, and went in.

Chapter Eighteen

I found myself on a landing at the top of a dimly lit stairway. I could see that it curved down to the basement.

As silently as I could, I tiptoed down the stairs. I still held the beanbag shotgun and the weight of it in my hands felt reassuring.

When I reached the bottom of the stairs, most of the cellar was in darkness. A single dim bulb hung down from a cord in the ceiling in the center of the room, providing the only illumination.

The air had a slightly sour and musty smell. Some bottles of wine must have started to go bad, or maybe some had leaked onto the floor.

I looked around for a light switch, but nothing was obvious. I could make out a dozen huge wine racks. Some were against the walls, some stretched across the basement.

Barrett said there were rooms down here that could be used as a prison cell. I needed to search through all of them. If Danielle wasn't here, then it was likely she'd been in the car we'd seen speeding away from the estate.

I didn't see any doors near the bottom of the stairs. I reasoned the dungeon rooms must be on the far side of the cellar. I took a few cautious steps in the direction that seemed the most likely to find them.

With a whizzing sound, something flew past my head, brushing against my hair. It smashed into the stone wall behind me and loudly shattered.

What the hell?

It only took a moment to realize someone had thrown a bottle of wine at me. Even as I came to this understanding, another bottle flew out of the darkness, hitting me in the leg.

Fortunately, the bottle glanced off my thigh rather than landing directly on my kneecap. Still, the pain was intense, and the muscle immediately cramped.

Whoever had thrown the bottle must have hit the cord holding the light. The bulb was now swinging widely, causing the shadows to jump and swirl around me.

I ducked behind a well-built but half-empty wine rack, grabbed at my leg, and looked around for the person throwing the bottles. I knew whoever it was, they'd be using the shadows to hide.

It took me a moment to spot my assailant against a far wall. I could only see an outline of the man in the dimly lit cellar, but I knew who it was.

Benny stepped out of the shadows and flung another bottle at me with a smooth overhand motion. The bottle hit the wine rack I was hiding behind and shattered.

I was splashed head to toe with wine. From the way it smelled, my mind automatically registered it was either a cabernet or a merlot.

Benny grabbed another bottle of wine from the rack next to him and lifted his arm to throw it. I poked the shotgun through an opening in the wine rack, sighted the best I could in the moving shadows of the swinging light, and fired.

In the enclosed space of the wine cellar, the blast from the shotgun was deafening. The beanbag hit him solidly in the stomach. He dropped the wine bottle, and it shattered on the stone floor.

He doubled over in pain and let out a shout of fury. But instead of going down, being shot only seemed to enrage him.

Benny slowly stood and glared at me. He was breathing hard and had a wild animal look in his eyes.

"You'll pay for that," he growled at me. "I'm going to make you suffer."

The grin on his thin face had turned nasty as he began to stumble toward me. I could tell he had murder on his mind. He pulled out the pink stun-gun from his pocket and flicked it on.

I racked the shotgun. The spent shell casing clinked on the floor. The echoes bouncing off the stone walls seemed to magnify the sound. As calmly as I could, I took aim.

Benny was making no efforts to evade being shot. He was stalking towards me with blind hatred and rage in his eyes. The grin on his face had grown wide with lustful anticipation.

The bright spark of the stun-gun loudly crackled and snapped in the enclosed space. It lit up Benny's face from below with an eerie flickering glow.

I squeezed the trigger and felt the shotgun kick. The beanbag blasted out with a thunderous boom. It hit Benny in the center of his chest, directly above his heart.

This time it seemed to do the trick. Benny's eyes rolled up in his head as he staggered backward and crashed into a wall. As he collapsed and curled up in the fetal position, his pink stun-gun clattered to the stone floor.

With a sense of relief, I walked over and picked up the device. It was heavier than I expected, and the handle was hot.

I needed to find Danielle and get her out of here as soon as possible. There was no telling who else was in the house and what sorts of mischief they would treat us to.

I felt my way through the cellar until I started to get my night vision. Across the room, I saw the outline of two heavy wooden doors. The first one was open, revealing a small dark space beyond.

The second door was closed. A thick sliding bolt had been set into place, firmly locking it.

I felt another surge of relief upon seeing the locked door. My fear had been that the rooms down here would all be empty.

Something grabbed my ankle, nearly pulling me off balance. As I flung out my arms, I dropped the shotgun. I distantly heard it clatter to the floor.

I looked down in horror to see Benny. He had crawled over and was trying to pull me down. I struggled to get out of his grasp, but he held me with an almost supernatural strength.

Benny grinned up at me, further tightening his grip on my ankle. He was yanking and twisting his hand, doing his best to knock me over.

With his other hand, Benny was pawing at the shotgun. He'd gotten a couple of fingers on the end of the barrel and was slowly dragging it towards him.

Judging by the furious look on his face, I knew if I hit the floor, he'd do his best to kill me. Using his bare hands, if nothing else.

Benny got a firm grip on the shotgun and managed to pick it up by the barrel. He was trying to get to the trigger while also keeping hold of my ankle.

I pulled again to tug my foot out of his grasp, but his hand was like a band of iron. I tried again and again, but it was no use.

I looked down, and Benny was now grinning with triumph. He had managed to slide his hand to the trigger. As if watching in slow motion, he brought the shotgun up and pointed it at my chest.

His hand shook with the force of trying to pull the trigger. While waiting for the blast, I remembered I hadn't yet ejected the spent shell or loaded a fresh one.

Benny must have also realized this. He let go of my ankle, and his hand flew to the pump. He slid it back, and I saw the spent casing tumble out of the shotgun.

I did the only thing I could think of. I squeezed the trigger of the stun-gun and watched as the bright white spark crackled across the electrodes.

Benny's eyes went wide as he saw what was about to happen. I then brought the sparking stun-gun down to his upturned face.

"No!" he yelled out. But as the stun-gun made contact, he let out a wild gurgling scream, and his body went into violent convulsions.

I know I probably held the electrodes against his face longer than was recommended. Still, the last thing I wanted was for him to get up and attack me again.

Eventually, the stun-gun stopped working. I shook it to see if I could get a few more seconds of sparks out of it, but it was dead.

Huh? I must have drained the batteries.

I looked down at Benny, who had curled into a fetal position. He was whimpering, and his body was twitching. I had to wonder if this is what I looked like after Benny had used the stun-gun on me.

I saw a switch on the wall and turned it on. Bright light flooded the room, and it no longer looked as ominous as it had.

I quickly grabbed the shotgun and walked to the locked door. "Danielle," I called out. "Are you in there?"

"Laura?" I heard her weakly call out. "I'm here. I'm locked in the room."

"Don't be afraid," I said as I slid open the bolt and opened the door.

"I'm here for you."

~~~~

I helped Danielle out of her cell. Her eyes were blinking in the bright lights of the wine cellar.

She had several bruises on her arms and legs, her hair was a hot mess, and her makeup was smeared over her face. Thankfully, I didn't see any serious injuries and her eyes were bright. Her hands were tied behind her, and I didn't have a knife.

I put my arm around her as we slowly walked up the stairs. When we emerged into the kitchen, two worried-looking men rushed over to help. One of them brought out a knife and carefully cut the ropes.

Since she seemed to know them, I could only assume Sebastian had called in the rest of his team. I left Danielle with the men and went to find Max. I quickly made it back to the hallway where I'd left him.

By now, everyone had more or less come out of their drug-induced sleep. All of them were moving, and they all had their eyes open.

Gabriella and Carson were trying to sit up. Largo wasn't very active yet but didn't seem too far behind.

I went over to Max and sat next to him. He seemed to be almost back to normal. "Hey, how are you feeling?"

"Like crap," he said.

"But you still look good," I said as I held his hand.

"Do I take it you and Roberto came in after us?"

"I was worried. You were a lot later than you said you'd be. We didn't think it would be helpful to call in a Black Death raiding party."

"That's probably good thinking. Did you find Danielle?"

"Yes. She was roughed up a little, but she's safe. What happened to you?"
~~~~

Max glanced at Largo with an annoyed look on his face. "As soon as Largo led us into this room, we realized it was a trap. Somebody tossed a gas grenade down from the balcony. I grabbed it and tried to toss it back over the railing. Unfortunately, I'd already breathed some of it in, and my throw was weak. The canister only clattered back to the floor."

"We found a guard upstairs who was in bad shape. What happened to him?"

"As I was starting to fade, I saw somebody look over the balcony. He had a gun in his hands, and he pointed it at me. He probably had orders to kill all of us. Both Gabriella and Señor Largo shot him in the face with a beanbag. I saw him fall backward as I passed out.

Ouch!

"He won't be shooting anyone for a while," I said. "What should we do next?"

Max closed his eyes and let out a deep breath. "We need to leave before the police organize and raid the compound, but you'll have to give us a minute. The effects from the gas are fading but aren't gone yet."

"You rest," I said. "I'll go check on Danielle. I'll be back in a few minutes. Then we can all leave."

I found Danielle standing next to a small table in the kitchen, where she was downing a glass of pinot noir. Seeing the half-full bottle on the table, it appeared this was already her second one.

I could tell she was angry from the look in her eyes, yet she smiled as I came over. I took it as a good sign.

"I needed that," Danielle said as she set the glass on the table and let out a long sigh of contentment. "I was getting thirsty down in the basement."

"Are you alright?" I asked.

"Honestly? I'm so mad I could bark like a dog. I'd gone over to see Grandma Peckham this morning, and they ambushed me. I guess you'd pissed them off about something, and they thought I was you."

"I figured that. I'm sorry you got pulled into one of my problems."

"That jerk with the pink stun-gun used it on me three times while he interrogated me. I kept trying to tell him they had the wrong girl, but all that did was piss him off. He kept insisting I was you and asked why I was trying to fake a Mexican accent."

"The man with the stun-gun is named Benjamin Todd. I've learned his friends call him Benny."

"Well, Benny laughed as he shocked me," Danielle said. "I could tell he was really enjoying himself. The more I cried out in pain, the wider he grinned."

"He did exactly the same thing with me," I said. "The guy has some serious problems."

"A woman came in as Benny was shoving the stun-gun into my stomach for the third time. She seemed to be the brains of the operation."

"Her name's Lillian Abbot. She works as the Director of Supply Chain over at Scottsdale General. They brought her in to run an operation selling the hospital's narcotics on the street. From what I can tell, she's been doing it for six or seven years."

"Yes, that makes sense. I've been slowly putting it together for myself. I think that explains why the city always seems to be flooded with cheap pills. But I think they'll find their supply lines have been permanently cut."

"What happened when Lillian came in?"

"She looked at me for several minutes and undid my hair. At the time, it was still in a bun. At first, she told Benny I wasn't the person they wanted and to get rid of me. Benny really liked that idea. From the leering smirk on his face, I could guess at some of the things he wanted to do to me before he finished me off."

"Lillian gave the same orders for me. According to one of the guards, Benny likes to stun his women once or twice before he assaults them. That way, they don't struggle as much."

"I can see him doing that. Benny was under orders to kill me and to dump the body."

"They've set up some sort of mass grave out in the desert somewhere," I said. "I have to wonder how many people Lillian has ordered to be killed."

"Before Benny got a chance to do anything, Lillian had one of the street pushers come over and look at me. He seemed to recognize me but said I was high-up in a Phoenix street gang called the Marauders."

"What did Lillian do once she thought you were a leader in a gang?"

"Her mood completely changed. She apologized for Benny shocking me and said our two groups would come to a business arrangement. She thought Oswald Knight could convince me to use my gang to distribute their drugs."

"And if you didn't agree?" I asked.

"If I didn't go along with their plan, she said they'd kill me and wipe out my entire gang."

"That's a great place to start the negotiations," I said with a laugh.

"Benny got upset when he found out he wouldn't be able to torture, abuse, and kill me. He kept describing how intense the pain would be when he stunned me in the sensitive parts of my body. He then stunned me again in the car on the way up here. He did it simply for the fun of it."

"What happened when you got here?"

"Oswald made a half-hearted attempt to recruit me. I did my best to string him along so he would release me."

"I take it that didn't work."

"It would have, but when he found out the drug warehouse had been raided, he decided to pack everything up and move out. Oswald told Benny to put me down in the wine cellar and the cops could find me later."

"That couldn't have been good news."

"Not at all," she said with a sad laugh. "Benny dragged me down to the cell in the basement. I think he wanted to shock me another couple of times and maybe even quickly abuse me before everyone left. From the look on his nasty face, I could tell whatever he was thinking about doing had him completely turned on."

"As I said, the guy has problems,"

"Fortunately, he'd only begun to tease me with his stun-gun when the shooting upstairs started."

"What did Benny do then?"

Danielle started to laugh. "He hid like a rat. It was completely pathetic."

"That sounds like Benny," I said.

"He wasn't armed with anything other than his pink stun-gun. From the shotgun blasts we were hearing from upstairs, he knew he was pretty much helpless and in serious trouble."

"The shotguns you were hearing were from our rescue party. Señor Largo's here, and he's working together with Max."

Danielle shook her head and sighed. "My father sent Largo to Arizona? I know he'll be disappointed in me. I didn't stop myself from being captured."

"There's no way you could've known. They were after me, not you."

"Still, it doesn't surprise me that they ended up working together. Both Largo and Max are intelligent men. Hopefully, Largo was able to keep his temper in check."

"He's acted rather reasonably so far," I said. "What happened at the end when Benny locked you in the room?"

"At first, I think he was planning on using me as a hostage or a human shield. But when we didn't hear anything for about twenty minutes, Benny thought they'd gone away. He locked me in the room and took off. That was when you came down the stairs. Fortunately, without a gun, all he could do was throw wine bottles at you."

"Hey," I heard a voice from across the room. "Are you two ready to leave?"

Max was standing at the door to the kitchen. Señor Largo was next to him. Neither one looked to be in great shape.

"Dani," Largo said in a fatherly tone. "We must leave before the police arrive."

"Yes," Danielle said, a tone of command in her voice. "Get everyone out, right away."

Danielle's men had gone through the house and removed any sign we'd been there. It wasn't likely the police would care when they raided the place, but you can never be too careful.

We went out front to several waiting SUVs and vans. Men were hurriedly loading equipment into the vehicles.

I was standing next to Danielle when two men dragged Benny out of the house. As usual, he didn't look happy.

His hands were cuffed behind him, and he had a black gag stuffed in his mouth. The side of his face was red from where I had stunned him.

Even though he had recently taken several thousand volts to the face, he was still able to weakly struggle and kick out. As they ushered him to the bakery van, he noticed Danielle and me standing against one of the SUVs.

His face twisted in anger, and he shouted out a long stream of profanity. Even with the gag, it was pretty easy to hear what he wanted to do to us. None of it was complimentary.

The men finally stuffed him into the back of the van and swung the doors closed. We could still hear him cursing at us through the walls of the vehicle. It was almost like the words were coming out of the cupcakes.

"What are you going to do with him?" I asked.

Danielle gave me a small twisted smile. I'd never seen her look like that before, and honestly, it gave me the chills.

"Benny's going to be our guest. From the sounds I heard in the basement, I take it you have his stun-gun. Would you mind if I borrowed it for a few days?"

I pulled it out of my pocket and gave it to her. "You can have it, but I'm afraid it's dead. I drained it when I used it on Benny's face."

"Thanks for letting me know," Danielle said. "I'll send someone out for a box of fresh batteries. I wouldn't want Benny to miss out on any of the fun."

Danielle looked down at the stun-gun and twisted her hand to get a good look at it from several angles. She shook her head and gave out a grunt of laughter when she saw the smiling cartoon kitty on the side of the device.

"What's going to happen to him?" I asked, nodding my head toward the van.

"Well, now that I have Benny's pretty pink stun-gun, the one he likes to use on women so much, I think I'll hang him up someplace nice and secluded. I need to pay him back for what he did to me. I'll then make sure everyone in the core group takes a turn at giving him a few volts."

"What happens when you're done with him? Will you turn him over to the authorities?"

Danielle shook her head. "Laura, I wouldn't worry about Benny. After three or four days, no one will ever see him again. I hope that doesn't bother you."

"Um, no, sure. I understand."

Danielle shrugged. "Benny's an animal and must be treated as such."

The groups finished packing and had started to climb into the vehicles to take off. I could see Danielle was beginning to fade. It had been a long day for her.

"Thank you for coming to rescue me," she said. "I know I haven't always treated you like I should, but you've always been there for me. I won't ever forget that."

"It's no problem. I know you'd do the same for me. Although, I'm hoping neither of us has to rescue the other one, for at least a little while."

She let out a small laugh. "Here's to hoping. See you at the wedding."

She climbed into the front of the lead SUV, and everyone took off.

Max dropped me off to get my car. He offered to let me stay at his place, but I needed to go home and make sure my apartment door was secure for the night.

On the way home, I called Sophie. "Hey," I said when she answered. "You aren't going to believe the day I've had today."

"Don't tell me," she said with a laugh. "Was it shitty?"

"Shitty doesn't even begin to describe it. I'll tell you and Gina all about it later, but I wanted to give you a head's up. There's a chance

J. Barrett Knight might call the office looking for Lenny to represent him in his role in the hospital narcotics operation."

"Seriously? That would make Lenny forget about Elle. He could milk a butt-load of money from something like that. He wouldn't have any excuses for not redecorating the office."

"I know, but it might not happen. Don't tell him ahead of time."

"Are you kidding? If Lenny finds out he had a million-dollar payday slip through his fingers, he'll be worse than ever. But don't worry. I'll keep his schedule light for the first part of next week, just in case."

~~~~

I made it back home and looked at the door. It was still shut, but both the door and the frame would need to be replaced. I rolled my eyes at how expensive that would be.

When I went in, I searched the apartment, but no one was there. I also didn't see any signs that anyone else had been there during the day.

I shoved the couch against the door and went to sleep.
~~~~

Chapter Nineteen

I woke up the following day to the sound of women's voices coming through the bedroom wall. It took me a second to remember that today was New Year's Eve. Grandma would be getting married tonight.

As I listened to the conversations, I could tell it was the happy and good-natured talking of three or four women, including Grandma herself. I supposed she'd have people coming and going all day.

Marlowe was asleep in the bed with me. He doesn't take to strangers and must have escaped Grandma's as soon as the first of her visitors arrived.

~ ~ ~ ~

After I crawled out of bed and got myself going, I called Kristy to get an update. When she answered, she sounded tired.

"How are you doing?" I asked.

"It's been a rough couple of days. Apparently, Andrew's known about Julie's feelings towards him for quite some time. I don't think they were having an actual affair. It was more like some sort of low-level office flirtation."

"That has to be hard to learn about."

"Yes, but I'm glad everything's out in the open. We can start to deal with it. At least the problems will stop."

"What did you learn about the wedding tonight?"

"I called Maggie at the Barrington and told her what happened. She said she'd gotten a voicemail but suspected some mischief. She was going to call me before she fully canceled the venue."

"That's great news."

"I also got ahold of the florist, the photographer, the videographer, and the DJ."

"And?"

"Well, the DJ was upset. He'd already made plans to go to a New Year's Eve party, but everyone will show up. The florist also wasn't happy, but since I'd already paid ahead of time, they couldn't refuse. I also explained to everyone what had happened and that the problems will stop."

~~~~

An hour before I was due to head over to the wedding, I pulled on a mid-length maraschino-colored dress. I didn't often get a chance to wear it, but I liked this one. Since it had a sweetheart neckline and spaghetti straps, it would really show off the diamond Tony had given me.

I walked next door to Grandma's to retrieve my jewelry box. The door was open, and the place was a hive of activity. People I didn't know were busily making phone calls and attending to last-minute details.

I saw a woman in the kitchen with a drink in her hand. I immediately recognized her as Megan, one of Grandma's granddaughters.

"Hi, Megan," I said as I walked up to her. "I recognize you from the pictures. I'm Laura, Grandma's next-door neighbor."
~~~~

Recognition flooded her face. "Of course. Grandma's told me all about you. You're the private eye who's been helping to make sure everything's going okay with the wedding planner."

"That's right. I'm happy to report everything's going to be perfect for tonight."

Megan blew out a sigh of relief. "I'm thrilled to hear that. After hearing about all of the problems, I was starting to get worried. I'm glad you were able to take care of things."

Grandma came up to us. "Laura," she beamed. "You look gorgeous."

"Thank you," I said. "I'm heading over to the Barrington to help Kristy with the last-minute arrangements. I wanted to let you know I talked with her this morning. It looks like everything will go smoothly tonight."

"Thank you for your help. I know I often ask favors from you, but I do appreciate everything you do for me."

My face flushed with heat, and it probably came close to matching my dress. "It's no problem," I said. "I was happy to do it."

I grabbed the jewelry box from Grandma and went back to my place. I put on the pendant and looked at it in the mirror.

The rainbow sparkles that flashed from the diamond were breathtaking. As I hoped it would, it looked stunning with the dress. It also brought up memories of my first adventure with Max and Tony.

When I looked down at the box, I realized I couldn't leave it in the apartment with the broken door. I decided to go all out and put on Jackie's diamond and ruby tennis bracelet, along with Elizabeth's ruby ring.

I next slipped on the earnings Max had given me at Christmas. As I suspected, they matched the other pieces perfectly.

I usually don't wear all of my jewelry at once, especially if someone was looking for me. But today, I felt relatively confident. Plus, I knew with Max and Danielle at the wedding, we wouldn't be robbed. Something might blow up, but nothing would be stolen.

~~~~

I made it to the Barrington a few minutes before five. The wedding wasn't going to be until seven, but I wanted to be there to help with anything that might happen at the last minute. I'd promised Grandma her wedding would be perfect, and I was willing to do whatever it took to make it happen.

Once I got there, I quickly found Kristy. She was walking through the chapel, holding her tablet.

"Well?" I asked.

"Everything looks great," she said with a wide smile. "I think tonight will go well. Thank you for your help. It was well worth the money to know the problems will stop."

"I'm glad we could find out who was sabotaging you."

Kristy's face fell a little. "Yes, it really sucks about Andrew and Julie. But I'll worry about that next week. Tonight is all about having a flawless wedding."

I nodded my head in understanding.

"By the way," Kristy said. "I love your dress. It's the first time I've seen you dressed up…."

Her voice trailed off, and I saw her eyes dart between my pendant, the earrings, the bracelet, and the ring. She was about to say something but held it back with a slightly confused look.

I followed Kristy around for another twenty minutes, and she'd been right. Everything looked perfect.

~~~~

While the wedding party was gathered in the chapel for pictures, the girls started to drift in. Gina was first to arrive, holding hands with Jet. She was in a sapphire dress and was wearing the diamond earrings Elizabeth had given her.

It was the first time I'd seen Jet dressed in anything other than casual clothes, and he looked incredibly handsome. I felt a tweak of jealousy but quickly shook it off. I was glad Gina had finally found someone who could keep up with her.

Sophie arrived next with Milo trailing behind her. She was wearing a green dress with Raquel Welch's diamond and emerald necklace.

Milo had on a brown suit that was a bit tight on him. From the way he fidgeted as he walked, I could tell he was only waiting for an excuse to take the tie and jacket off.

"You're looking like one of the cougars with all that hardware on," Sophie said as she eyed my jewelry.

Gina laughed and shook her head. "I figured you would have sold some of that by now."

"The only thing I've sold is the gold nugget from Mindy. Maybe I'll sell the rest someday, but everything has a memory behind it."

Sophie started laughing, and I turned to see Danielle and Roberto slowly walking towards us. He was limping slightly but looked good. She'd used make-up to cover the bruises she'd gotten the day before.

But what had gotten Sophie's attention was Danielle's dress. She had on a red spaghetti strap that looked remarkably like mine.

"Oh my god," Gina laughed. "You two really do look like twins tonight."

As Danielle stood next to me, Sophie pulled out her phone and had us pose while she took pictures.

"I should have remembered you'd wear a red dress to match your jewelry," Danielle said as she laughed and shook her head.

“You look great,” Gina said to Danielle. “It’s good to see you. We’ll all have to go out again sometime soon.”

“I know,” Danielle said. “It’s my fault. I’ve been busy with work. I’ve gotten some new responsibilities, and I never seem to have any free time.”

“That’s amazing,” I heard Max say as he came up to us. “You two really do look remarkably similar.”

Max was dressed in a black suit, a white shirt, and a black bow tie. He looked utterly delicious. My heart sped up as he stood next to me and gave me a hug.

Damn, he’s gorgeous.

Kristy stuck her head out of the chapel and opened the doors. We all ended up in a pew on the bride’s side. With a bit of subtle maneuvering, we got Max on one end and Danielle on the other. I knew they both like to be on the outside, and there was no use tempting fate by having them sit next to each other.

Something seemed wrong, and I realized Roberto wasn’t acting as Danielle’s bodyguard. I swiveled my head around to the back.

In one corner stood Señor Largo. His leather satchel hung over his shoulder as he slowly scanned the crowd.

In the other corner stood Gabriella. Her black bag was also dangling against her side as she watched over the chapel.

I know I should have felt terrified at the thought of the two of them together like this. Still, after the events of the previous day, I knew I was probably safer in this room than anywhere else I could be.

~~~~

The ceremony between Grandma and Bob was beautiful, and we all dabbed our eyes the entire time. Fortunately, there were no problems, and everything went smoothly.
~~~~

We then drifted into the reception hall and found our table. Earlier in the evening, I had switched around the place cards to make sure Max and Danielle weren't sitting next to each other.

I kept looking for problems, but everything off went without a hitch. The appetizers and dinner were served, and the drinks flowed from the bar. The music was pleasant, and everyone was having a great time.

After we finished dinner, I found myself at the dessert table with Gina. "Sophie was telling me Andrew's admin had a creepy crush on him," she said. "And she's the one who'd messed up everything?"

"Yup, she was very efficient at doing it. She almost succeeded in ruining Kristy's business."

Gina got a melancholy look on her face and shook her head. "You know, this puts Kristy and her husband in a no-win situation."

"What do you mean?"

"Think about it. Things can't stay the way they are. Andrew either has to fire his admin or divorce his wife."

"Well, sure. I assume he'll fire Julie. It seems like a no-brainer."

"I wouldn't make that assumption. Think about our office. Sure, it's Lenny's name on the door, but Sophie's the one who actually runs the place. If this admin's been with Andrew for over ten years, she's the one who's keeping the business going on a day-to-day basis."

"Do you think he would divorce his wife so his business wouldn't suffer?"

"I guess it depends. Is Julie older or younger than Andrew?"

"She's younger, by maybe ten years."

"And is she pretty?"

"Yeah, she's okay."

"There you go," Gina said. "Even if Andrew divorces his wife, he has a ready replacement."

"Wow, do you really think it could work out that way?"

"We've both seen stranger things."

"Well, if they do get divorced, at least we could send some more business to Lenny. I didn't use up the original retainer Kristy gave us, and you know how he hates giving refunds."

~~~~

After dessert, I walked over to where Señor Largo was standing. He had staked out one of the back corners of the ballroom. Gabriella had the other. They were both continuously scanning the crowd for any unforeseen trouble.

"Señor Largo," I said. "It was good working with you again. I'm glad you were here for the rescue."

"It is my job," he said with a shrug. "It's a shame we were so quickly put out of action, but the final results were good. It was fortunate you were there to help us out again."

"Danielle's a friend of mine. She would have done the same for me."

"Still, this is the second time you have performed such a service for our group."

Maybe that'll make up for the time I tipped off the police to your shipment of heroin?

"Hopefully, this is the last time you'll need to come up to Arizona to work on a problem. I heard on the news that the police raided the safehouse where Lillian and Oswald Knight had been hiding."

"Yes, our men followed the black sedan to the new location in Queen Creek. We then called in an anonymous tip to the police. They were very eager to get their hands on both of them."
~~~~

"Um, should I ask? How's Benny doing?"

Señor Largo's smile was twisted. It reminded me a lot of Danielle's, and I shivered in fear.

"I'm afraid Benny is not doing very well. Danielle ordered everyone in the core group to use the pink stun-gun on him. Unfortunately, at this point, it doesn't take very many shocks before he passes out from the pain."

"Really, I would've assumed he was a tough guy. Um, how many shocks before he passes out?"

"Sometimes it takes four or five, sometimes only one. It depends on where you apply the electrodes. Some areas of his body seem to be especially sensitive to pain."

Ouch.

I know I should have felt more empathy for what Benny was going through, but I couldn't. He had laughed with joy when he'd used his stun-gun on both Danielle and me.

I also knew he'd planned on shocking me several more times before committing even worse atrocities. If you balanced everything out, removing him from society was probably a good thing.

I then walked over to the corner where Gabriella was standing guard.

"Hi," I said. "I'm glad you're here. I didn't expect to see you tonight."

"Max say he not need me, but Tony and Johnny both insist. They remember what happened at last wedding."

"Hopefully, this one won't be as exciting. Can I get you a coffee or a dessert?"

"No. You are kind, but I never eat while on duty. Max gave me the report you were able to find on Viktor. The information seems solid.

I do not know how you were able to obtain such government intelligence, but thank you for helping me."

"It's no problem. Sophie was the one who ran the database requests. We're both worried about you and want to help."

"The report is good. Even if information is out of date, it lets me know where he has been seen and where his base of operations is. It will be enough to start."

"When do you think you'll need to head out there?"

"Soon. I need to finish planning, but then I will go."

"Thank you for helping to rescue Danielle. I know it put your life in danger."

Gabriella shook her head and let out a snort of disgust. "The only one who put my life in danger was Largo. He lead us into trap. It is mistake to have someone else in command when Max and me are better. From what Max say, you were the one who rescued us."

"All I did was help Roberto with the guard and let some fresh air into the room where everyone was passed out. But I'm glad I was there to do that much."

~~~~

The after-dinner activities were starting up. Everyone in our group watched and clapped from the table.

One of the moms walked around the room holding a baby that Kristy had placed a "Baby New Year" sash on. She was adorable, and everyone was taking pictures.

Bob's older brother had on a "Father Time" robe and was holding a plastic scythe. He was happily playing it up as he took pictures with some of the younger women.

Sophie asked Milo to get her a drink, and as if by telepathy, all the men at the table got up and walked to the bar.
~~~~

"So, what do you think?" Sophie asked the three of us when the men had left. "Are any of you ever going to do this again?"

"What?" I asked. "You mean getting married?" That was a good question and one I wasn't going to answer unless I had a few more drinks in me.

"I don't know," Gina said. "I'm just getting used to the idea of dating somebody. Getting married again seems like a pretty big step."

"I wouldn't have a problem getting married again," Danielle said. "As long as he doesn't mind that I have a rather active career."

"I don't know if I ever will," Sophie said. "I might be able to live with a guy, assuming he likes to cook and do housework. But I get the feeling whoever I'm with would want to have kids. I don't think I'll ever be ready for that."

Gina and I looked at each other.

"I don't think I'm cut out for children," Gina said. "If I ever do anything like that, I'd probably adopt someone a little older."

"I'd love to have children," Danielle said as a broad smile lit up her face. "An entire house full. I couldn't think of anything nicer than that."

Sophie looked at me. "Well?" she asked.

"Don't look at me," I said. "I'm not ready to have children."

But even as I said this, I felt a slight tug at the back of my mind. Realizing this was a shock. I stopped taking the sip of champagne, even as the glass was pressed against my lips.

Oh, damn.

"Are you okay?" Gina asked.

I came out of it and finished my sip.

"That was weird," Sophie said. "You sort of froze for a second."

“I’m fine,” I said. “I’m hoping they get to the cake soon.”

~~~~

By midnight, some of the crowd had already taken off, but most had stayed to ring in the new year. The DJ led the group in a countdown, and everyone shouted out, “Happy New Year!”

Party poppers had been freely handed out, and the room was quickly awash in streamers and confetti. Max and I were still on the darkened dance floor, the slowly rotating disco ball providing most of the illumination.

He bent down to give me a wonderful new year’s kiss. As he did, I felt it tingle all the way down to my toes.

“How long do you want to stay?” he asked.

“I’m ready now. The wedding went perfectly, and I think Kristy can handle it from here.”

“Do you want to come back to my place?” he asked.

I shook my head. “I’ll need to stay at the apartment for the next few days. The building super ordered a new door, but it will take a couple of days before he can install it. Besides, with Grandma being gone, Marlowe will want some extra attention.”

“What about you?” Max asked. “Will you need extra attention for the next few days?”

“Definitely,” I said. “Although, whoever’s paying attention to me may need to spend the night. Know of any volunteers?”

“I might be willing to help you out,” he said as he gathered me into his arms for another passionate kiss.

Yes!
~~~~

About the Author

Halfway through a successful career in technical writing, marketing, and sales, along with having four beautiful children, author B A Trimmer veered into fiction. Combining a love of the desert derived from many years of living in Arizona with an appreciation of the modern romantic detective story, the Laura Black Scottsdale Series was born.

Comments and questions are always welcome.

E-mail the author at LauraBlackScottsdale@gmail.com

Follow at www.facebook.com/ScottsdaleSeries

Twitter: @BATrimmerAuthor

Made in the USA
Monee, IL
30 May 2021

69853521R00184